It could be nothing, Jack told himself, but the hairs on the back of his neck told him otherwise. He kept one eye on the cab. Glanced again at the Lincoln behind them. The bicycle messenger beside them.

Tony and Morris were still chatting back and forth, oblivious to anything out of the ordinary.

Then the taxi in front of them abruptly stopped. It didn't swerve toward the curb for a fare, just hit the brakes in the middle of the street. Tony instantly hit his own brakes, lurching them all forward.

"Bloody hell!" Morris cursed again as his hot coffee spilled.

That's when Jack saw it—the skinny messenger dumped his bicycle and rushed their vehicle, hand reaching into his canvas shoulder bag.

"Down on the floor *now*!" Jack pulled the Glock from his holster, popped the door, kicking it open, right into the assassin. The man flew backward and stumbled against the curb.

Jack dived, crouching, from the minivan as the front windshield shattered, showering Tony with safety glass. Two holes drilled through Jack's empty seat. Then the rear window exploded inward.

Crouching low, Bauer leveled the Glock at the man on the ground. "Don't move!" he commanded.

The man on the sidew[...] canvas bag, freeing the .4[...] him in the face.

DECLASSIFIED

COLLATERAL DAMAGE

MARC CERASINI

Based on the hit FOX series created by Joel Surnow & Robert Cochran

HarperEntertainment
An Imprint of HarperCollinsPublishers

This is a work of fiction. Names, characters, places, and incidents are products of the author's imagination or are used fictitiously and are not to be construed as real. Any resemblance to actual events, locales, organizations, or persons, living or dead, is entirely coincidental.

HARPERENTERTAINMENT
An Imprint of HarperCollins*Publishers*
10 East 53rd Street
New York, New York 10022-5299

ISBN: 978-0-06-143118-0

HarperCollins®, ▰®, and HarperEntertainment™ are registered trademarks of HarperCollins Publishers.

First HarperEntertainment paperback printing: March 2008

Printed in the United States of America

Visit HarperEntertainment on the World Wide Web at
www.harpercollins.com

10 9 8 7 6 5 4 3 2 1

To Will Hinton, a most patient editor.

And to Agent John P. O'Neill, the FBI's top expert on Al Qaeda and Osama Bin Laden, and lead investigator of the *USS Cole* and African Embassy bombings. O'Neill left the Bureau in frustration because he believed the U.S. government did not take the threat of terrorism seriously enough. In August 2001, Mr. O'Neill became the security chief of the World Trade Center. On September 11, 2001, he was last seen walking in the general direction of Tower Two, minutes before it collapsed. His body was found a week later.

After the 1993 World Trade Center attack, a division of the Central Intelligence Agency established a domestic unit tasked with protecting America from the threat of terrorism. Headquartered in Washington, D.C., the Counter Terrorist Unit established field offices in several American cities. From its inception, CTU faced hostility and skepticism from other Federal law enforcement agencies. Despite bureaucratic resistance, within a few years CTU had become a major force in the war against terror. After the events of 9/11, a number of early CTU missions were declassified. The following is one of them.

Wars may be fought with weapons, but they are won by men. It is the spirit of the men who follow and of the man who leads that gains the victory.
GENERAL GEORGE S. PATTON

DECLASSIFIED

COLLATERAL DAMAGE

PROLOGUE

"Hello, Jack."

A shadow fell across Jack Bauer's desk. He looked up from the report he'd been reading, into the eyes of District Director George Mason.

Jack stood, rubbed his chin. "Good to see you, George."

Mason's thin lips tightened. "I'll bet."

"How are things in Tacoma?"

Mason set his briefcase on the floor. "Oh, you know, Jack. It's about as far from *real* Washington as you can get. Makes a guy feel lost, out of touch. *Banished*, if you know what I mean. And all because of the 'Company' he keeps."

Jack arched an eyebrow. "So you're lonely, George?"

Mason smirked. "I still have friends. Oh, and by the

way—Teddy Hanlin sends his regards. And so does his partner, *Seth Campbell*."

Campbell wasn't actually working *with* Mason any more. The corrupt CTU agent had been caught taking bribes. He was now serving a ten-year sentence in a Federal penitentiary. Jack was the one who'd put him there.

Mason's mention of him now was a clear tell. He wanted Jack to know exactly why he'd barged into Jack's office late on a Friday afternoon: *payback*.

Jack hid any reaction to Campbell's name, simply closed the report on his desk with a sharp sweep of his hand.

Mason's crafty eyes darted to the desk, then back to Jack. "You've been reading the weekly operational review, I see."

"You don't miss a trick, do you, George?"

"Then you know CTU's New York division will be activated in three days."

Jack nodded. "It only took six years."

"Things move slower on the East Coast," Mason said. "The situation there is . . . political."

"Right. The Agency's political. This is news?"

"I mean it's more so there than here. Brice Holman has been running investigations out of the Agency's regional office for the last three years. Now he's finally getting his own Manhattan-based CTU Operations Center and a full staff. But there are apparently some jurisdictional disputes, turf wars. A lot more toes get stepped on. But I don't have to explain about toes getting stepped on, do I? Not to you?"

Mason slid Jack's overflowing in box aside and settled on the edge of his desk. "I've got a job for you, Jack.

Washington—the *real* Washington—ordered me to dispatch an operational consultant with solid managerial experience to oversee activation of the East Coast Division—"

"Hold on, George. That kind of assignment is way above my pay grade. I thought Bill Buchanan out of Seattle was handling this."

"He was, until a pair of his agents defused a bomb at the base of the Space Needle this morning."

Jack blinked. "That wasn't in today's threat report—"

Mason chuckled. "You won't hear about it on the evening news, either. No sense in causing panic."

Bauer's features darkened. "You mean no need to alert the public to the danger of terrorism, so that when the day comes that we *can't* prevent an attack, the citizens won't be prepared to deal with it?"

"Yeah, Jack. That, too." Mason laughed. "God, relax, Bauer. The bomb was planted by some eco-green fringe group protesting logging or something. They've already been caught."

"Good." Jack folded his arms. "Then Buchanan can go to New York."

Mason shook his head. "Unfortunately, with a procedural review of the situation, coupled with the drafting of an after action report, Bill is stuck in Seattle for the next few weeks. That means you'll take Manhattan." Mason smiled.

Jack's phone rang. He ignored it.

"Don't worry, Jack. I won't send you alone. I can spare Almeida. I'd like to give you Jamey Farrell, too, but since Milo Pressman transferred to Langley, we'll need her here.

You can take O'Brian instead. You two worked well in Las Vegas, and you'll need a guy like Morris because any major glitches will most likely be technical—"

"Listen, George—"

Mason silenced Bauer with a raised palm. "This should be an easy assignment. You'll show Brice Holman the ropes in New York, help him organize his staff and set up protocols to interact with the other divisions and agencies—"

"Why me?"

"I want you to liaise with the other authorities in the region," Mason purred, ticking them off with his fingers. "I'm talking about the New York City Police Department, the Office of Emergency Management, the DEA, the local branches of the Secret Service, the Federal Bureau of Investigation. Smooth over any problems and—"

"*Smooth over* problems?" Jack cut in. "I'm the last person you should be sending for that. The last time I had contact with the New York branch of the FBI, I exposed one of their agents as a traitor and *neutralized* him."

"Which is why you're the perfect man for this job." Mason tightened the knot on his tie. "It shows the other guys we mean business."

Mason picked up his briefcase and set it on Bauer's desk. "The codes, protocols, and operational drives are here. Agent Holman and his staff are expecting you to arrive first thing Tuesday morning. Enjoy your weekend with Tracy and your son—"

"It's *Teri*. And I have a *daughter*."

"Like I care. You're going to New York, Bauer. Your flight leaves Monday."

1 2 3 4 5 6 7 8 9
10 11 12 13 14 15 16 17
18 19 20 21 22 23 24

....

THE FOLLOWING TAKES PLACE
BETWEEN THE HOURS OF
7:00 A.M. AND 8:00 A.M.
EASTERN DAYLIGHT TIME

....

7:00:02 A.M. EDT
New York, New York

Jack Bauer glanced at the World Trade Center, rising above the rooftops of Lower Manhattan. The weather was clear this Tuesday morning, the June sunlight gleaming against the two identical skyscrapers of glass and steel.

In the driver's seat to his left, CTU Agent Tony Almeida turned the Dodge minivan onto Hudson's slow parade of traffic. The taxis, buses, SUVs, and luxury sedans were all heading downtown, toward Tribeca, the Financial District, or the Jersey delivery system known as the Holland Tunnel.

As their minivan slowed to a crawl, Jack continued to stare at the twin towers. Back in '93, the bombing of those buildings—by a blind Muslim cleric and his insane flock—had been the impetus for creating CTU.

Ironic, thought Jack. *One of the last major urban areas to get its own CTU Operations Center is the very city that was attacked by terrorists. Doubly ironic because no one wants it. Not the FBI, not the DEA, not even the local authorities . . .*

Just one month ago, the senior Senator from New York had argued that the presence of CTU was redundant in a city where even the NYPD had its own overseas operatives countering terror threats.

Sure, at its inception, CTU had been granted special powers by Congress, among them the ability to conduct counterespionage and counterterrorist operations on U.S. soil, against U.S. citizens if necessary—a mandate the CIA had never before been given. But Jack knew it would take months, maybe even years, before CTU's New York operations would be effective. He didn't know what his superiors expected him to accomplish by sending him here—

"Bloody hell!" Morris O'Brian blurted from the backseat.

Tony had slammed on the minivan's brakes, and Morris's steaming hot Starbucks had sloshed over his hand. "Seven o'clock in the bloody morning, and traffic is already snarled. This town is worse than L.A."

Jack peered through his passenger-side window. Workers were already crowding the sidewalks. A young Hispanic bicycle messenger, wearing a red "Tri-State Delivery" Windbreaker, a canvas bag slung over his shoulder, pedaled along the curb beside them. The messenger could have sped up, Jack noticed, but he didn't. Just kept pace with them for some reason.

"Look at these people. It's a beautiful, sunny day, and not a convertible in sight," Morris went on. "What's the matter with them? Are they vampires?"

Tony smirked into his rearview. "Maybe they're afraid of pigeon droppings."

The cab that had swerved in front of them to score a fare now raced away. Traffic flowed faster and another taxi slipped in front of them.

Jack lifted his chin, pointed. "The building's three blocks ahead, on the right."

Tony nodded and continued in the right lane.

CTU's New York offices occupied the top three floors of a ten-story office building. Jack unhappily surveyed the scene. Unlike CTU Los Angeles, which was located in a remote, industrial section of the city, the Manhattan offices were on a teeming city street, surrounded by bustling businesses.

The United States Customs Service was practically across the street. On the next block, a curved modern office building housed an international advertising agency. Behind CTU, a massive UPS complex sprawled across two blocks. Beyond that, the West Side Highway and the Hudson River both flowed with traffic.

There were people piled upon people passing through this area on any given day, and Jack knew that any one of them could pose a threat. With their headquarters so vulnerable, CTU New York was going to have to spend energy just covering its own back.

A horn blared behind them. In the rearview, Jack noticed a black Lincoln Continental cutting off another car in order to slip in right behind them. Traffic was flowing faster in the other lanes, but he stayed behind them instead, hugging their bumper. The driver wore a Lakers cap pulled low. His eyes were invisible behind mirrored sunglasses.

Jack frowned at the Lakers cap, glanced out the side window again, at the messenger on the bicycle. The young Hispanic male was still keeping pace with them, occasionally glancing over.

Jack looked ahead. The yellow cab in front of them drove right by an attractive businesswoman, trying frantically to wave it down. The cabbie ignored the fare. *Why?* His ON DUTY light was illuminated. And there was no one riding in the back of his taxi—at least that Jack could see.

It could be nothing, Jack told himself, but the hairs on the back of his neck told him otherwise. He kept one eye on the cab. Glanced again at the Lincoln behind them. The bicycle messenger beside them.

Tony and Morris were still chatting back and forth, oblivious to anything out of the ordinary.

Then the taxi in front of them abruptly stopped. It didn't swerve toward the curb for a fare, just hit the brakes in the middle of the street. Tony instantly hit his own brakes, lurching them all forward.

"Bloody hell!" Morris cursed again as his hot coffee spilled.

That's when Jack saw it—the skinny messenger dumped his bicycle and rushed their vehicle, hand reaching into his canvas shoulder bag.

"Down on the floor *now*!" Jack pulled the Glock from his holster, popped the door, kicking it open, right into the assassin. The man flew backward and stumbled against the curb.

Jack dived, crouching, from the minivan as the front windshield shattered, showering Tony with safety glass. Two holes drilled through Jack's empty seat. Then the rear window exploded inward.

Crouching low, Bauer leveled the Glock at the man on the ground. "Don't move!" he commanded.

The man on the sidewalk pulled his hand out of the canvas bag, freeing the .45. He rolled to aim—Jack shot him in the face.

Another pop, and a bullet whizzed by Jack's ear.

He spun and glimpsed the shooter, crouching in the backseat of the cab that was blocking them. The big, bald white guy grimaced, showing gold front teeth.

Jack leveled his weapon, fired. The cab's back window shattered, but the squealing tires were already rolling onto the sidewalk. The vehicle sped away, scattering confused and screaming pedestrians before lurching back onto the street, in front of a parked city bus.

An engine gunned behind him, and Jack turned to find the Lincoln driver trying the same move as the taxi.

"Stop the car now!" Jack shouted.

The Lincoln tore off the passenger door as it sped around the Dodge. The maneuver gave Jack a clear shot at the driver. He took it. The gun bucked in Jack's hand. The window spiderwebbed, and the driver's shoulder exploded in a haze of blood, muscle, and bone.

The driver was thrown forward, head striking the steering wheel. The Lincoln careened into a magazine kiosk and came to a halt.

Jack was beside the vehicle in seconds, Glock clutched in both hands. He checked the backseat, but no one else was in the car.

The driver's sunglasses and Lakers cap were gone now, and Jack recognized the man. He yanked the door open, dragged him out of the car, and slammed him down on the sidewalk.

"Who told you I was in New York?" Jack demanded, shaking the man by the lapels of his jacket. "Talk, De Salvo. Who tipped you off? Who set me up?"

The man's eyes were glazed with pain. He tried to laugh, coughed blood instead. "Go to hell, Bauer, you lousy son of a . . ."

His head lolled. Jack knelt over him and checked for a pulse, found none. He quickly searched the dead man, came up with a wallet and tucked it into his own pocket.

Tony rushed over, holding his weapon. He stared at the dead man. "Who is he?"

"*Was*. Angelo De Salvo. His two older brothers masterminded the Hotel Los Angeles robbery."

Tony whistled. "No wonder he wanted you dead."

Sirens warbled, drowning out the street noise as three NYPD squad cars converged on the scene. Jack and Tony holstered their weapons and displayed their IDs. While the police circled them, both CTU agents glanced down the street, at the building that housed the Unit's New York headquarters. The place was still as a grave.

"I don't get it," Tony quietly said to Jack. "A firefight a block away, and no response from CTU?"

Jack frowned at his destination. "Looks like it's time to light a fire under these people."

7:48:17 A.M. EDT
CTU Headquarters, NYC

Jack Bauer leveled a cold gaze on the New York agent who met him at the elevator. She wore a pinstriped suit with a questionably short skirt and stacked heels. Her black hair was caught in a long, smooth ponytail. She had an olive complexion and large, dark, slightly almond-shaped eyes, with features that suggested Middle Eastern heritage. She introduced herself as Layla Abernathy.

"I need to meet with Director Brice Holman." Bauer's voice was less than friendly. "Now."

"Oh yes. Of course!" Agent Abernathy appeared momentarily flustered, her gaze darting from Jack to Tony to Morris. But her composure returned inside of five seconds, and she matched Jack's hard stare. "Brice should be here any minute. I called his cell several times. I'm sure he'll check in soon—"

"That's not good enough," Jack cut in. "I left specific instructions that all CTU personnel were to be present when I arrived this morning." He took a step closer. "*Where* is Brice Holman?"

Layla Abernathy frowned. "I think he's in New Jersey."

Jack exchanged a glance with Tony, then asked Agent Abernathy, "What's he doing in New Jersey?"

"I don't know," Layla replied. "That is, I'm not sure. I'm not even supposed to know about—"

"What's his exact location? Be specific."

Abernathy took an uneasy breath. "Have you ever heard of a place called Kurmastan?"

7:50:31 A.M. EDT
Hunterdon County, New Jersey

Stretched out on his belly in a field of tall grass, Special Agent Brice Holman, newly appointed Director of CTU's New York Operations Center, gazed down at the tiny hamlet of Kurmastan.

Dubbed "Meccaville" by the farmers and horse breeders who lived around it, Kurmastan was primarily populated by men who'd converted to Islam in state and Federal penitentiaries, along with members of their families who'd also converted.

Ignoring the sun beating down on his head, the forty-five-year-old agent checked his watch, rubbed the sweat from his eyes, and went back to peering through a pair of digitally enhanced micro-binoculars.

Before coming to this rural field, Holman had reviewed almost two years of satellite surveillance on this small religious settlement. But those pictures failed to capture the dilapidated seediness of the place.

A dozen clapboard houses sat within the dusty compound, along with seventeen rusty mobile homes, all of them centered around a communal dining hall made of cinder block. A dirty boulevard ran through the center of town. One end was dominated by Kurmastan's only visible source of income—a factory that turned recycled pulp into cardboard boxes.

The other end held a house of worship, by far the most luxurious structure in the place: prefabricated steel with a resin facade sculpted to look like a Middle Eastern mosque, complete with a metal-framed minaret.

The mosque was no surprise to Holman because the settlement had been founded by Ali Rahman al Sallifi, an Islamic cleric with ties to radical elements in Pakistan and Egypt—and it had been on CTU's watch list since the agency was established.

Unfortunately, most of the "watching" of Kurmastan had been done by satellite. Things had changed about a month earlier, when Brice Holman's own boss, the Northeast District Director, ordered any active investigation of this compound to cease. The unit had limited resources, Holman was told, and they were needed elsewhere.

Holman privately disagreed. Just before he'd been ordered to stop investigating Kurmastan, a well-connected activist group had begun loudly leveling "profiling" charges on Executive Branch agencies, and Holman suspected the decision to give Kurmastan a wide berth was at least partly political.

Deciding to have a look for himself, Holman had driven out to the compound, watching it for an entire weekend.

During that time, he encountered an FBI agent who'd also been watching the place, and had received a similar command from his own boss in Washington.

It wasn't unusual for FBI surveillance units to trip over CTU in the field. Agents occasionally even shared information, sidestepping the current "wall" between agencies.

When Holman met Jason Emmerick of the FBI, that's exactly what had happened. The two agents silently agreed to disregard the law prohibiting them from swapping intel. All by themselves, they connected the dots on "Meccaville," and a frightening picture began to emerge.

Both men had observed military-style exercises, including weapons training and obstacle courses. There was suspicion of stockpiled armaments and chatter between residents of the compound and parties in Pakistan and Afghanistan.

Holman and Emmerick came up with a plan to continue watching the "Meccaville" compound, in violation of their superiors' directives. And surveillance chatter soon suggested something was about to go down. Something big. Unfortunately, the agents were still lacking hard evidence to prove it.

Today, with luck, they would finally get that evidence.

According to recent chatter inside the compound, a "package" from Canada was expected to arrive at Newark Airport. Holman and Emmerick believed the arrival of this "package" was the key to setting off whatever powder keg the men inside this compound had primed.

An hour earlier, two African-American males had left this compound to "pick up the package." One of the men was bald; the other wore his hair in long cornrow braids. Both were in their early thirties, clad in blue suits.

Holman recognized the bald man as a former gang-banger from Jersey City. His name was Montel Tanner, or at least it used to be. Holman didn't know what Tanner called himself now that he'd found religion. The other man, with the cornrows, Holman hadn't seen before.

Each of these men had slipped behind the wheel of a brand-new black Hummer and took off. Jason Emmerick and his partner took off, too, tailing the two Hummers.

Holman was so certain something major was about to happen, he'd finally briefed his own CTU Deputy Director, Judith Foy, on their rogue operation. Now Judy was on board, too, and due to hook up with Emmerick and his partner at the airport to aid in the surveillance.

Meanwhile, Holman had positioned himself on a hill above the compound. He'd been staked out here since the wee hours of the morning. As a breeze rippled the grass, stirring his black tangle of hair, he lowered his micro-binoculars and shook his canteen.

Empty.

Thirsty and hot, Holman was about to return to his vehicle for a refill when a flash of sunlight off chrome caught his eye. He zoomed his binoculars in on the factory. The loading bay doors stood open, and a semi rolled out.

In itself, this wasn't unusual. At four that morning, a truck had departed the factory, full of flattened cardboard boxes. One had left at five as well, also packed with paper. *Adhan* came next—the call to prayer—sung from the mosque's metal-frame minaret by a young African-American man in denims and a Yankees T-shirt.

The truck leaving now looked like the others Holman had seen: a Mac sleeper cab hauling a steel trailer, the logo for Dreizehn Trucking painted on its side. But when Holman glimpsed the interior of the cargo bay, he didn't see flat stacks of cardboard boxes. Instead, Holman saw bunks. Six of them lined the walls. He spied movement. There were men inside that trailer; he counted at least eight. One had an AK–47 resting across his knees.

Before Holman could get a picture, an arm inside the truck slammed closed the steel doors. The truck continued rumbling toward the compound's gate, sped through and toward the rural route beyond.

Holman cursed, rising quickly, and left his hiding place, creeping through the tall grass, back to his van.

That's when he heard a woman scream.

7:55:46 A.M. EDT
Kurmastan, New Jersey

Yesterday evening. That's when they'd grabbed Janice Baker. Around six-thirty P.M., they'd put a hood over her head before dragging her away. She had a clue where she was because the men hadn't taken her far, and they'd traveled by foot.

It sounded like her abductors had carried her into their compound, then down a flight of stairs. There they'd tied her up, ignoring her muffled demands to release her, to turn her over to the sheriff for trespassing.

Gasping for breath under the thick material, Janice had struggled against the ropes that bound her to the hard chair. Finally, she'd heard a door slam and was left alone. The place was damp and quiet. Like a grave. When the forty-year-old stay-at-home mother had first smelled the scent of freshly turned earth, she'd gasped, her panic rising.

Did they lock me in a cellar? Or toss me into a hole? Are they planning to bury me alive?

With effort, she'd tamped down her fear. *Why put me in a hole?* she'd wondered. *Why not just call the sheriff and have me arrested?*

Janice had been cross-country jogging for years along the same rural trails, long before Kurmastan existed. The men of the town had complained several times to her about trespassing. The first time they caught her, she hadn't even realized she'd strayed onto private property. They cursed her out, but let her go.

The second, third, and fourth times were just like today—she'd chosen to disregard the NO TRESPASSING signs and jog where she pleased. Men of the town saw her, yelled from a distance, cursed at her, but she ignored them. If they caught her, what could they do? Call the sheriff? Fine her fifty dollars tops?

When she'd been spotted the evening before, however, she was stunned by what had happened next. Soon after a few men yelled at her, two of them had set a trap. They'd jumped out of the brush and dragged her to the ground.

They didn't find her easy prey. Janice had managed to kick one man in the groin. He was a big African American who looked like a football player, but her blow slowed him down. She'd also managed to rake her fingernails across the other man's face, right before he'd put the hood over her head.

They'd left her tied up for hours and hours. She'd lost track of time, hadn't slept much, and now she was hungry and thirsty. When she heard a door open, she felt a mixture of terror and relief.

"Who's there," she demanded. She tried, and failed, to sound fearless. "I demand you let me go!"

Janice heard footsteps, felt strong hands fumbling with the knot around her neck. Someone was untying the hood. *Good. Maybe they've finally called the sheriff. Maybe now they're going to let me go!*

The hood was ripped off her head. Still tied to the chair, Janice was dazzled by harsh light from a naked light bulb that dangled from the ceiling. The room had earthen walls shored up with untreated logs—a root cellar? There was a small vent near the ceiling—bright sunlight slipped through. She squinted, realizing it was morning. They'd held her here all night!

The stranger who'd torn off her veil remained behind her, out of sight. A minute went by, then another. But the man didn't say a word. He didn't untie her, either.

"What are you doing?" Janice asked.

There was silence for another minute. Then came a quiet murmuring in another language. It was crazy, but Janice thought the man was praying.

"I demand you release me!" she cried. "This is kidnapping! Don't you realize that? Let me go this instant!"

Without a word, the man stepped around the chair to

stand in front of her. Janice Baker's eyes went wide when she saw the machete in his hand.

Once again Janice Baker screamed.

7:58:46 A.M. EDT
Just outside Kurmastan
Hunterdon County, New Jersey

At the sound of the bloodcurdling scream, Holman had tensed and begun snaking on his belly, moving as close to the compound as he dared. Using his binoculars, he continued to scan the area for any sign of violence. Any sign of the woman who'd screamed.

But he saw nothing out of the ordinary. A few male residents were talking casually outside the mosque. Two females strolled out of the cinder-block dining hall, chatting with each other as if nothing was wrong.

He listened for more screams, but now heard nothing more than the birds chirping in the trees.

Holman knew he hadn't imagined that scream, and he knew how dangerous some of the men in Kurmastan could be—many of them were lifelong criminals with rap sheets as long as a bureaucrat's career.

Part of him wanted to charge through the front gate, find out what had happened. But that would compromise the investigation. They'd probably call the local sheriff and accuse him of trespassing. Holman couldn't even begin to consider explaining his rogue operation to a local official.

Seething, he carefully moved away from the compound

again, backtracking to his van. He retrieved water and an energy bar, and then returned to the hill to continue his surveillance of the compound. At noon, he was scheduled to leave the area and hook up with Emmerick at a nearby motel, where they'd compare notes and plan their next move.

Holman needed to brief Emmerick about that tractor trailer he'd seen with armed men in bunks inside. And Emmerick needed to brief him about that "package" from Canada.

Until then, Holman would continue to keep his eyes open for any sign of that woman, whose terrified cry kept playing through his head.

1 2 3 4 5 6 7 8 9
10 11 12 13 14 15 16 17
18 19 20 21 22 23 24

• •

**THE FOLLOWING TAKES PLACE
BETWEEN THE HOURS OF
8:00 A.M. AND 9:00 A.M.
EASTERN DAYLIGHT TIME**

• •

8:05:48 A.M. EDT
CTU Headquarters, NYC

"This is wrong, Agent Bauer," Layla Abernathy declared. "You have no authority to do this. I'm sure Director Holman will be here any minute. Why can't you just wait to hear his explanation?"

Jack Bauer's features darkened. "You've called the Director. Repeatedly. And so have I. Brice Holman either can't respond, or refuses to—"

"Yes, but—"

"And you've tried to locate the Director using the GPS chip in his phone, correct?" Jack interrupted.

Layla frowned. "Apparently Holman deactivated it."

Jack clenched his fists, trying like hell to maintain his composure. "The Director and his deputy are *unreachable*, your guards downstairs say your exterior cameras are *offline*, and someone tried to assassinate me and my team on the street outside. You do see a *problem* here, don't you, Agent Abernathy?"

They were standing at the computer console on Brice Holman's desk, inside the Director's corner office. Jack had powered up the man's computer, only to find it double password protected. He now intended to break into his system.

Jack punched the intercom. "O'Brian, report to Director Holman's office."

Jack faintly heard his own voice amplified inside the massive threat room. He stood up straight and faced Agent Abernathy. "You mentioned a place," he said.

Layla nodded. "Kurmastan. It's a seventy-five-acre compound in New Jersey populated by an Islamic religious group—most of them prison converts. Ali Rahman al Sallifi runs it. He's a radical cleric who sought political asylum in America after he was expelled from Egypt."

Jack blanched. "Our government granted asylum to this guy?"

"The Imam received political support from several powerful individuals. The Saudi Arabian Ambassador made a personal appeal to the President—probably because he didn't want al Sallifi and his followers stirring up unrest in his own country."

Jack briefly closed his eyes. He liked to believe elected

officials had the best interests of its country's citizens at heart. But when a Federal agent had to ask himself what side his own President was on, it was a bad day.

"By far the Imam's biggest sponsor is New Jersey Congresswoman Hailey Williams," Layla continued. "She's a close advisor to the President. Anyway, six years ago, the Imam established a community called Kurmastan, then renamed his flock the Warriors of God."

"*Warriors* of God." Jack folded his arms. "So now it's a paramilitary organization?"

Layla nodded. "A core group of Middle Easterners live inside the compound with the Imam, but most of the people in Kurmastan are former prison inmates converted by the cleric's followers. Some of the clerics minister to the prisons in New York and New Jersey. Others are inmates themselves."

"And these activities are permitted?"

"Under the banner of religious freedom, the Warriors of God openly recruits new members through various social service organizations, including the prison system," Layla replied, yanking a file from the drawer.

"Why hasn't CTU launched a full-scale investigation?"

Layla raised a dark eyebrow. "The District Director of the Northeast Region *nixed* it."

Jack processed that bit of information, and he had to admit, he wasn't all that surprised. The District Director for the Northeast was Nathan Ulysses Wheelock.

Wheelock hadn't worked his way up through the Agency, served in the military, or done fieldwork of any kind. The man was a political appointee of the current Administration; and his wife—before she'd retired to write legal thrillers—had been a civil rights attorney with a client list that included high-profile anti-defamation organizations.

Jack faced Layla Abernathy. With Brice Holman and his Deputy Director, Judith Foy, out of the office, Abernathy was the ranking agent in New York. He wanted to get a handle on her.

"You're Iranian, aren't you, Agent Abernathy?" Jack asked pointedly. "Did I recall that correctly from your file?"

Layla glanced away, obviously uncomfortable. "I was born in Iran, but I left with my mother before I was two years old. I don't remember anything—"

"But you speak Farsi?"

She nodded. "My stepfather saw to that. At one time, he was the U.S. Associate Ambassador to Iran. Back in the seventies, he knew the Shah—"

"Your father was Richard Abernathy."

"My *step*father. He married my mother after my real father was executed by the thugs in charge of Iran. With the help of Canadian friends, my mother came to America. And just for the record, I'm also fluent in French, Spanish, Italian, and German."

Jack fell silent a moment, regarding her again. "So why are you posted *here*? With your security clearance and linguistic skills, you should be on the fast track at Langley, or in a job at the DOD, maybe even the White House."

"I'm not interested in listening to Iranian intelligence chatter from thousands of miles away or analyzing the speeches of its current ayatollahs. I made that very clear on threat of resignation, frankly. I want to do fieldwork, Agent Bauer. And my language skills are just as valuable here in New York, where hundreds of languages are spoken—"

The door opened and Morris O'Brian entered. "You called, boss?"

"What's the status on security?" Jack asked.

An hour ago, Bauer had hit the roof when the guards downstairs had told him the exterior cameras weren't working, which was why they'd never noticed the firefight on the street. Jack had dispatched Morris to fix the problem.

"I've got the system up and running now," Morris replied. "It was just a little glitch, really. I left Almeida behind to establish a network that integrates the cameras in the lobby, the parking garage, and the roof with Security Station One."

"How long will that take?"

"I could do it in fifteen minutes. Tony should be done in an hour or so. Once the network is established, we can watch everything on the monitors."

Jack leaned close to Morris. "How about that other matter?"

O'Brian fished the bloodstained wallet out of his jacket, handed it back to Jack. "It's a fake ID," Morris said. "Angelo De Salvo was living under the alias Angel Salinas, in an apartment in the Bowery. He worked for Fredo Mangella, an international restaurateur who owns four-star dining spots in Paris, Madrid, London, Rome, and here in New York. Mangella has an office above Volaré, his eatery on Mulberry Street."

Bauer nodded. "Good work. Now I have another job for you. This one's urgent. I want you to crack the security on Director Holman's computer."

Morris's eyes went from Jack Bauer to Layla Abernathy and back again. Then he dropped into the Director's chair. "This might take a little time," he warned.

"Just do it," Jack replied. He faced Abernathy. "You have something to show me?"

Layla nodded. "These files contain security briefs— summaries of just about everything we've got on Kurmastan, up until the District Director shut down the investigation."

Jack accepted the thick file, leafed through it. Inside, he found photographs and reams of surveillance reports— two years' worth.

"Let's find a conference room to review this," he said.

8:31:58 A.M. EDT
Parking garage
CTU Headquarters, NYC

A pair of utility workers blithely strode down the ramp, into the restricted parking garage ten floors beneath the CTU offices.

In the lead, a slight African-American man, in a blue Con Edison uniform under an oversized yellow vest, carried two large steel toolboxes. Under black-rimmed, bottle-thick glasses too large for his narrow face, the man's dark brown eyes appeared wide and alert.

The other man was tall and blond, with a flat face, ghost-blue eyes, and Slavic features. His neck seemed too thick for his uniform, and the sleeves were rolled up around his burly arms. He carried a circle of electric cable over one shoulder, a hazard vest slung over the other. This one was in the middle of a story.

". . . so I told the bitch I couldn't pay her rent this month because I lost two large at OTB . . ."

The smaller man snorted. "Serves you right, putting your cash down on the ponies. What did your woman say to that?"

Both security guards stepped out of the glass-enclosed hutch and approached the utility workers.

"She said if I want the honey, I gotta feed the bear," the blond man replied. "Can you believe that? And you know what I said?"

"Excuse me, gentlemen," a CTU guard interrupted. "You're not supposed to be down here—"

The blond man dropped his hazard vest, leveled the hidden 9mm USP Tactical at the guards. The silencer took care of the noise, muffling the gunshots in the low-ceilinged garage.

The first bullet caught the guard in the throat. The second blew the back of the head off the other man.

"So what did you say?" asked the slight black man, pushing up his thick glasses.

"I told the bitch that I'd rather go bear hunting," the big blond replied, lowering his weapon.

The black man set down his boxes, moved into the bulletproof hutch, and jumped behind the computer console.

The big blond dragged the corpses out of sight behind a parked car.

Footsteps sounded, and the blond man paused, drawing his weapon again. He immediately relaxed when he saw the man in the CTU uniform striding quickly down the ramp.

"Have the cameras been deactivated?" the newcomer asked.

The black man stuck his head out of the hutch. "I don't think they were functional. But if they were, they aren't now."

The newcomer in the CTU security uniform moved toward the blond. The blond man took the badge and name tag off one of the murdered guards and handed it to the newcomer.

"Come on," the black man said, retrieving his steel boxes. "The access shaft to the roof is over here."

The newcomer in the CTU uniform took over the security booth. He watched through the Plexiglas while his partners used electric screwdrivers to open a steel hatch in the wall. The blond man waited while his smaller partner crawled inside.

A moment later, the smaller man stuck his head out. "The cameras might not be working, but everything else is."

"Can we get to the roof?" the blond man demanded.

"The ladder goes to the top, but there are security systems and laser eyes on every floor. I'll have to disable them one at a time, all the way to the roof."

The blond man sneered. "Then you better get started."

"It's a bitch, man," his partner griped. "We could be

here all morning. It's gonna take us forever just to get to the roof."

The blond glanced at his oversized watch. "You don't have forever. The job *has* to be done in the next two hours. I suggest you get started."

Both men climbed through the hatch, and the blond pulled it shut behind them, leaving the screws in a pile on the concrete floor.

8:50:03 A.M. EDT
Central Ward
Newark, New Jersey

"Foy, you still on them?"

"I got 'em," replied Judith Foy, Deputy Director of CTU New York. Behind the wheel of her silver Lexus, she'd been tailing the shiny black Hummer since it exited the airport's short-term parking garage.

On the other end of the comm was FBI Special Agent Jason Emmerick. He and his partner were now tailing the second Hummer. Each vehicle carried a part of a "package" that had arrived that morning on a flight from Montreal. The "package" had turned out to be two Middle Eastern men.

"I know the man I'm tailing," Emmerick informed her. "He's an Afghani, goes by the name Hawk. I've got no ID on the man you're tailing. Contact us when your mark arrives at his destination."

"Roger." Judy continued following her black Hummer

to a blighted area of downtown Newark. In University Heights, the vehicle circled a sprawling Federal housing project—a breeding ground for the type of crime that had made the name Newark synonymous with urban violence since the 1967 riots.

Despite her experience, Agent Foy felt uncomfortable cruising these mean streets. A thirty-eight-year-old Caucasian woman behind the wheel of a Lexus was not a common sight in the Central Ward, where police cars were scarce, graffiti and gang markings everywhere. Even with the car's tinted windows, young men in gang colors, hanging out on every other block, watched her car with predatory eyes. Judith Foy recalled a DEA assessment that came across her desk last year which claimed this section of Newark was the crack cocaine capital of the Northeast.

Foy was a Jersey girl, too, though she hailed from affluent Bricktown on the state's southern shore. That safe, cozy little community was nothing like this blasted strip of urban blight.

She'd gone into the CIA right after graduate school. Her first assignment with the Agency had been in the Middle East. After eight years, she'd come back to the United States. Then the Agency had sent her to New York, to work with Brice Holman.

For the past three years, while red tape was being cut to allocate a fully staffed threat center, she and Brice had been the CIA's *entire* counterterrorist operation in New York.

She'd come to know and trust Brice. He had twenty years with the Agency, ten in the field. He had good instincts, and he'd always had her back. So when he came to her with this rogue operation, she didn't hesitate to back him. If Holman thought something bad was going down today, then it was. Violation of protocol was a small price to pay for stopping what could be another WTC bombing.

As Agent Foy rounded a corner, deftly avoiding a bunch of kids playing in the middle of the street, she saw the Hummer speed up as it raced down the block. She applied the gas, too, and easily kept them in sight.

"Yeah, I'm following you, genius," she muttered. "What are you going to do about it?"

The Hummer left the projects, moved into an area of decrepit warehouses and shuttered businesses. The vehicle was about half a block ahead of her when it swerved around a lumbering garbage truck, into a narrow alley.

Agent Foy sped up, but by the time she reached the alleyway, the Hummer had vanished. The narrow street occupied a space between two tall brick buildings that had once housed factories or warehouses. The industry was long gone, and the crumbling buildings were abandoned.

With a resigned sigh, she steered the Lexus into the cramped alley. The road surface was ancient cobblestone, and her tires rumbled so loudly, she feared for her suspension. Finally, she reached the opposite end of the alley and emerged onto a street lined with crumbling apartment buildings.

She spotted the Hummer at the end of that block, waiting at a stop sign for another garbage truck to rumble by. "Got you," she whispered triumphantly.

Agent Foy stepped on the gas and pulled onto the street,

intent on catching up to the Hummer. Her concentration was shattered when she heard a squeal of tires burning pavement. Her head jerked to the right, just in time to see the rusty grille of a GM pickup barreling down on her.

She pushed the gas to the floor, but it was already too late. The truck flew out of the hidden driveway, slammed into the passenger side of her Lexus. Foy threw up her arms just as the air bag deployed, smashing her backward in the seat. Shards of safety glass rained down on her, then the hood popped and she heard the angry hiss of steam.

The truck continued forward, slamming her car against the telephone pole. Wheels spun, pressing the Lexus until the frame bent, then snapped. Finally, the truck's front tire popped and its engine stalled. Smoke began to pour from under the hood. After the deafening crash, the quiet was eerie.

Over the hiss of steam from the truck's ruptured radiator, Agent Foy heard a door open, feet striking the pavement. Next came the sound of another vehicle approaching and skidding to a halt.

She peered through a gap in the wreckage. The black Hummer was back. The driver of the GM pickup that had hit her—a teenager wearing a hooded sweatshirt with the number 13 emblazoned on the back—dived into the Hummer through an open window. Then the Hummer sped away, the teen's legs still dangling out the window.

Agent Foy tried to move. With one arm pinned by the air bag, she unbuckled her seatbelt with her free hand. Most of the pressure on her abdomen vanished, but when she took a deep breath, bruised ribs ground together, and she cried out in a rattling gasp.

Every move a Herculean labor, she reached into her torn blazer for her cell phone. Hands slick with blood, she managed to press the speed dial button.

CTU Director Brice Holman's cell rang three times, before she was connected to his voice mail. From somewhere on the street she heard cries, then a face appeared at the window. The man wore a red 'do-rag over a retro Afro, a pair of gray city sanitation overalls.

"Jesus, lady, you okay?"

"I'm pinned," she replied weakly.

"Don't try to move. An ambulance is on the way."

She tried to reply, but waves of nausea and dizziness suddenly overwhelmed her. Desperate to report to someone, Agent Foy placed a second call, this one to CTU Headquarters in Manhattan.

8:55:57 A.M. EDT
Bilson Avenue, Central Ward
Newark, New Jersey

Paramedic Darnell Peasley saw the accident scene as soon as he swung his ambulance around the corner. "*Damn*," he said. "It's a bad one."

A silver Lexus was wrapped around a telephone pole; a faded red pickup truck had smashed into it. Smoke poured from under both hoods.

Darnell noticed a sanitation truck had stopped at the scene. Two workers were waving at him. A third was poking his head through the Lexus's window.

"The cops are here," said Darnell's partner, Luis. He

pointed through the windshield as Darnell parked his ambulance next to the sanitation truck.

Darnell was relieved to see the patrol car rolling toward them. Sometimes he and Luis had to wait for the police to arrive at scenes like this, which meant they remained inside their locked ambulance until the cops finally did show. On streets like Bilson Avenue, a paramedic took his life into his hands if he did anything else.

Two cops emerged from their car, and a police van was just arriving as Darnell popped his door and ran forward, clutching his medical kit.

"She's pinned!" called the sanitation worker, standing next to the Lexus.

"What about the truck driver?" Darnell asked.

"Punk ran away," one of the other sanitation workers cried. "Hopped into a black Hummer with tinted windows and took off."

"You got a license number for that?" the older cop demanded, showing attitude.

"I got the first couple of numbers," replied the black sanitation worker, mopping sweat off his forehead with his 'do-rag. He avoided eye contact with the white cop, directed his comments at Darnell and Luis.

The older cop and his partner immediately hauled him to their van for a statement. Darnell moved to climb into the twisted car. A third policeman tried to help.

"Anything I can do?" the cop asked.

The officer was young and white and earnest.

"I'll call when I need you," Darnell replied. "Now get out of the way and let me get this done before the Fire Department gets here and takes over."

The policeman quickly gave Darnell space.

That line always works, the paramedic mused. *Cops and firemen got no love for each other.*

He pulled a pair of disposable gloves out of his kit and slipped the white latex over his brown hands. Then he touched his fingers to the woman's throat.

The pulse was strong, but she was unconscious and probably in shock. He pushed the red hair away from her forehead and saw the bloody gouge where the rearview mirror had caught her. He slapped a pressure pad on the wound to stop the bleeding.

"How she doin'?" Luis called.

"Probably a concussion," Darnell replied.

He thought for a second that he'd heard a tiny voice—the car's radio? Darnell inspected the Lexus interior, spied the woman's purse on the dashboard, the bloody cell phone in her hand. He gently slipped the device from her limp fingers and dropped the phone into the bag he'd retrieved. In the purse, Darnell spotted a digital camera.

"Yo! Luis!" he called, tossing the purse to his partner. "Take her stuff so it can go with her."

1 2 **3** 4 5 6 7 8 9
10 11 12 13 14 15 16 17
18 19 20 21 22 23 24

• •

THE FOLLOWING TAKES PLACE
BETWEEN THE HOURS OF
9:00 A.M. AND 10:00 A.M.
EASTERN DAYLIGHT TIME

• •

9:02:11 A.M. EDT
Secure Conference Room
CTU Headquarters, NYC

Jack Bauer checked his watch and tossed the file onto the
conference table.

"I've heard enough about Kurmastan," he said sharply.
"You still haven't told me why Director Holman and Deputy
Director Foy are missing. Or why Holman's computer is
locked so tight not even Morris O'Brian can break through."

The woman lowered her eyes. "I really don't know—"

"You're lying," Jack said evenly. "You're hiding something—maybe something your bosses did or are doing."

Layla's dark eyes stared at the floor.

"You can't protect them, Agent Abernathy," Jack said quietly. "If you try, you'll only go down, too."

The woman glanced away, tightly folded her arms. Then she met Jack's gaze.

"Well," she began, "I think maybe I'm the reason there are so many security protocols on Brice Holman's computer."

Jack drummed his fingers on the tabletop. "Go on."

"Six weeks ago, I was assigned to help open this office, but I found Holman's activities to be overly guarded."

"What do you mean? Be specific."

"He'd disappear without explanation—and then *with* explanations that began to sound suspect. So two weeks ago, I got curious and cracked his files. I couldn't break the copy protection program or download anything, but I got a pretty good look. Brice believes a terror attack originating from Kurmastan is imminent. Whatever he's doing, he's doing it to protect the country."

"Why didn't he issue an alert?" Jack asked. "Talk to Langley?"

"I told you before, Agent Bauer. Holman was ordered to halt all surveillance on Kurmastan. And because I violated his computer, I'm afraid I may be the reason Brice doesn't trust the staff assigned to him now."

"He figured out you broke into his system?"

Layla nodded. "The next time I tried to gain access, he'd erected all kinds of new security barriers. I think my actions made him paranoid."

The conference room's intercom buzzed. "I'd better take this," she said.

"Put it on speaker," Jack commanded. He noticed her eyes flash with annoyance, but she did what Jack asked.

"Abernathy here."

"This is Peter Randall in Communications. I just received a strange call from Deputy Director Foy's cell."

Layla leaned forward. "Where is—"

"This is Special Agent Jack Bauer from CTU Los Angeles," Jack interrupted. "*What* did the Deputy Director say?"

"That's what's strange, sir," replied Pete Randall over the speakerphone. "Agent Foy didn't say anything. There was silence, followed by the sound of a siren. Finally, I heard voices, then the line went dead."

Jack and Layla exchanged looks.

"Did you trace the signal?" Jack asked.

"That's standard procedure," the comm tech replied. "But the call was so short we can't triangulate."

"I'll be right down," Jack replied, ending the call. Then he snatched the receiver and dialed Brice Holman's office. On the eighth ring, O'Brian picked up.

"What do you bloody want?" O'Brian barked. "Can't you see I'm busy?"

"It's Bauer."

"Oh. Hello, boss," Morris said smoothly.

"I need you at the comm station. Now."

Morris groaned. "Can't Almeida handle it? I've got my hands full with the locks on the Director's computer. This Holman person is nearly as devious as you are. Needless to say, I haven't quite cracked it—though I'm *close*."

"It can wait," Jack replied. "I need you to trace a cell

phone signal. The call didn't last long so there might not be much of a trail."

Morris snorted. "Child's play compared to this, Jack-o. I'll be there on the double."

Agent Abernathy led Jack down a flight of steel steps, onto the floor of the Operations Center. There were no offices, only workstations inside cubicles. When they arrived at the communications station, Morris was already there. He stood beside a lanky, thirty-something technician with a receding hairline and nervously blinking eyes partially obscured behind small, round glasses.

Jack extended his hand. "Peter Randall? I'm Jack Bauer. Have you retrieved the memory cache of Deputy Director Foy's call?"

Randall nodded. "I have, sir, but the call lasted less than two minutes, so triangulation will be difficult, even if we can isolate her digital trace inside the phone company's transmitters."

"You have signature protocols, correct?" Morris asked.

"Of course. Each member of this unit has intelli-signatures unique to them embedded in their cell phones."

Jack knew the answer to the next question, but asked anyway. "Have you tried to locate Foy using the GPS chip in her cell?"

The comm tech frowned. "She deactivated it, sir. I can't imagine why."

"I can." Jack glanced at Layla. "She didn't want CTU to know where she was."

"I think I've got something," said Morris.

Jack peered over his shoulder, at the high-definition

monitor. Morris tapped a few keys and a map of New Jersey appeared, the telecommunications grid superimposed over it.

"Deputy Director Foy's call came through a forwarding station in this little town here." Morris tapped the screen. "Pissant. Pissant, New Jersey."

Peter Randall cleared his throat. "That's *Passaic*, O'Brian. Passaic, New Jersey. It's an American Indian word."

Morris squinted theatrically. "I must be going goggle-eyed. I *swear* it says *Pissant*."

"Get on with it, Morris," Jack said tightly.

"Anyway, from the forwarding station in *Passaic*, I traced the signal back to communications grid A–NE 8804. That's right here—" Morris tapped the screen again.

"Newark," Jack whispered. He faced Layla.

"Retrieve the patient admission records from all the hospitals around Newark, see if anyone fitting Agent Foy's description has been treated in the past hour. Contact the Newark Police Department and the city morgue, too . . ."

"On it," Layla said, punching keys.

Jack laid a hand on Morris's shoulder. "I'm leaving for an hour, to check on that other matter," he said quietly. "The one that *delayed* us this morning."

"Bugger," Morris murmured. "Don't you want backup?"

Jack shook his head. "Not from *this* office. You and Tony hold down the fort until I get back. I'll be in touch if I run into problems."

Morris frowned. "Careful, Jack. I understand New York can be a very rough town."

"Agent Almeida? I have the system schematics that you requested."

Tony nodded, his gaze fixed on the monitor. "Yeah, thanks," he muttered. "Put them on the desk."

"Agent Almeida?"

It took a moment for the voice to penetrate his concentration. Finally, Tony looked up, to find a young woman with dark, curly hair and wide, oval eyes standing over him. She offered Tony a nervous smile.

"I just wanted to say . . . if you need anything . . . anything at all, I'll be in the next cubicle." She pointed to her workstation with a thumb over her shoulder. "My name's Delgado, Rachel Delgado. Like I said, call me. If you need me."

The woman wore black slacks and platform shoes. Her tight, white blouse had a low neckline, showing more than ample cleavage. Tony shifted uncomfortably in his chair. "Ah . . . thanks."

As she walked away, Tony watched her swaying hips— until Rachel Delgado glanced over her shoulder and caught him peeking.

Tony quickly shifted his gaze—then the computer beeped, and it was back to work. He grabbed the schematics that Ms. Delgado had brought him and looked them over. In a few minutes, he'd isolated the problem, which turned out to be a glitch with the physical system and not a software issue.

Tony stood, hung his jacket over the back of the desk chair, along with his shoulder holster and the Glock inside it. Then he rolled up his sleeves and used a screwdriver from the console kit to open the access panel behind the computer.

The guts of the system revealed, Tony began to physically reroute the entire network through a different set of servers by reconnecting several dozen ports to ultrahigh bandwidth links.

9:49:55 A.M. EDT
Mulberry Street

After a short cab ride, Jack Bauer exited the taxi on the corner of Canal and Mulberry. At the teeming intersection, he considered his next move.

It was clear to Jack that someone at CTU New York had tipped off De Salvo and his crew. They knew about Jack's arrival in the city, and enough of his schedule to set up an ambush in the middle of Hudson Street in broad daylight.

Or did the leak originate somewhere else, out of the Tacoma office, perhaps? Jack decided to have a long talk with George Mason after this was over.

Angelo De Salvo had harbored a deep grudge against Jack—for good reason. Jack had led the siege in L.A. that had ended with the deaths of De Salvo's father and two brothers.

Angelo hadn't been with his family during that takedown, but he was a career criminal with a long rap sheet.

He was also a hunted man, and according to O'Brian's research, De Salvo's alias—Angel Salinas—never had more than nine hundred dollars in his bank account. So there was no way he could have paid for the services of professional hit men.

So *who* had helped him mount this morning's ambush?

De Salvo was dead now, but whoever had helped him was still very much alive. Jack intended to find the source of the payoff money. He would start with the dead man's employer, Fredo Mangella.

Jack walked down Mulberry Street, the main drag of New York's shrunken Little Italy. The street was narrow but clean and colorful, with century-old brick buildings of six and eight stories, housing Italian restaurants, cafés, and gourmet pastry shops at street level. There were iron streetlamps and sidewalk tables with Campari umbrellas, but few tourists were around at this hour of the morning.

Most of the pedestrians were Asian, heading toward the streets around Mulberry, which belonged to Chinatown, a large area of Lower Manhattan that had grown even larger over the years with the influx of Asian immigrants, reducing Little Italy to no more than a few blocks.

Morris had provided an exact address for Mangella's chic new eatery, but Jack found the place difficult to miss. Volaré sat halfway down Mulberry, inside an old building that obviously had been gutted and reconstructed with a two-story-high facade of glass framed by gleaming chrome.

The restaurant wasn't open, but Jack spotted a tall man entering through the front door. He wore sunglasses and a dark suit, had a pallid complexion, and wore his white-blond hair long, just past his shoulders.

Jack watched the place a few more minutes from across the street. Then he moved to enter the restaurant.

Volaré's interior was large and airy, with a ceiling high enough for an authentic Italian racing plane from the 1930s to be suspended above the perfectly placed tables. On the ground floor, double doors to the kitchen were set in a shiny chrome wall beside an Art Deco chrome-plated bar. Jack spied an upper balcony with silver rails and a spiral staircase that flowed down to the main dining area. There were no tables on the balcony, only a single door at the end of it.

For a moment no one appeared. Then a smiling woman exited the kitchen. "How can I help you?" she asked.

Elegant and waiflike, the thirty-something woman spoke with an unidentifiable European accent.

Jack forced a smile. "My name's Jack Bello, of Gardenia Cheese in Vermont. I was wondering if I could speak with Mr. Mangella about sampling our excellent product?"

For the briefest second the woman glanced at the door on the balcony. "I'm afraid Mr. Mangella is quite busy. Perhaps—"

"I'm only in town for the day, and I just need a moment of his time," Jack insisted.

The woman's smile faded, but she relented. "I'll see what I can do. Wait here, Mr. Bello."

She turned on her heels and walked through the kitchen doors. Jack immediately moved through the dining room and ascended the spiral staircase. He crossed the narrow balcony and paused at the door. Carefully he tried the knob, but it was locked. Then Jack pressed his ear against the door. He heard voices inside.

"The changeover has been made," a man said. "I'm catching a noon flight to Milan, out of JFK."

Jack strained to hear the other speaker's reply, but the second voice was so soft and raspy, he couldn't make out the words.

"Don't worry," the first man said. "I'll stay in Europe indefinitely. My assets here will lose their value after this, so I don't anticipate returning—"

A harsh cry rose from the dining room. "Hey, what the hell are you doing up there?"

Jack looked down and saw the bald man with gold teeth, the one in the cab who'd tried to murder him this morning. The urge to shoot him was strong, but Jack had to play it smart. He was here for information, not revenge. So he tamped down his rage.

But the cold play was blown anyway. Gold Teeth recognized Jack, too.

"Dominick! Petey! We've got trouble," he cried, reaching for the police special tucked in his belt.

Jack quickly turned and slammed his shoulder against the locked door. It broke inward, and he stumbled across the threshold into a tiny office with a cherrywood desk and Tiffany lamps.

Jack scanned the room for an escape route. There were no windows, only another door on an adjacent wall. Standing by that door was the pale man with the white-blond hair and the dark suit—the man Jack had spotted entering the restaurant a few minutes ago. His sunglasses were gone now; his strangely pinkish eyes blinked in surprise.

Behind an open laptop, an extremely portly man struggled to his feet, face flushed with outrage. "Who the hell are you?" he demanded.

Jack shifted his gaze to Fredo Mangella behind the desk. "My name is Jack Bauer. I'm an agent in the Counter Terrorist Unit. I need to speak with you—"

Jack heard clanging footsteps, as several men surged up the spiral staircase. He leveled his Glock at Mangella.

"Call your men off," he demanded. "I'm not here to arrest you. I just want to ask you some questions."

Fredo Mangella remained silent, considering Jack's words. There was slight movement, a drawer opening. Then a weapon appeared in the fat man's hand.

Jack shot Fredo Mangella twice in the chest. As the restaurateur dropped back into his chair, the standing white-haired man pulled a .45 and aimed it at Jack.

Before he could fire, the door next to him opened, striking the Albino's arm. His .45's barrel dropped as the woman who'd greeted Jack appeared. She stepped forward, preventing Jack from getting a clean shot, then screamed when she saw the guns, screamed louder when she saw Mangella's corpse flopped in the chair.

Jack heard the shouting voices of Mangella's men. He slammed the broken door shut with a spinning kick, then pressed his back against the wall next to it.

"Don't move," he cried, trying again to draw a bead on the Albino.

But Jack couldn't shoot. The pale man had curled his

long arm around the woman's throat and was using her as a shield.

"Pull the trigger and she dies," he rasped, his .45 back up. "Throw your weapon onto the desk and step away from the door or you'll die, and *then* she dies."

Looking into the Albino's ghostly eyes, Jack knew the man wasn't bluffing. He tossed his Glock on the desk beside the laptop and raised his hands.

1 2 3 **4** 5 6 7 8 9
10 11 12 13 14 15 16 17
18 19 20 21 22 23 24

. . . .

THE FOLLOWING TAKES PLACE
BETWEEN THE HOURS OF
10:00 A.M. AND 11:00 A.M.
EASTERN DAYLIGHT TIME

. . . .

10:00:06 A.M. EDT
Rural Route 12
Hunterdon County, New Jersey

"Hang back, Leight, I don't want them making us."

For ninety minutes now, FBI Agent Jason Emmerick
had been driving across the Jersey countryside, his twenty-
six-year-old partner, Douglas Leight, at the wheel of their
white Saturn.

"We've been following this Hummer since it left the
airport," complained Leight after they hit another bone-
jarring bump. "If they didn't make us, they're blind."

They were off the highway now, surrounded by trees

and plowed fields, wooden fences and cows. The rural road was narrow and dusty and in disrepair.

"It may not matter, either way," Emmerick said. An African American in his late forties with a lean, strong build, Emmerick was clad in pressed khakis and an Izod shirt, a navy-blue blazer over it. He reached into the blazer, his hand brushing the butt of his weapon as he pulled out a pack of Juicy Fruit. "Now that their precious package has arrived from Montreal, I don't think these guys will be changing plans."

"Well, they must *know* we're tailing them," said Leight, his sandy eyebrows knitting beneath his light brown crew cut. "And I think they're leading us on a wild-goose chase."

"They may know we're tailing them, but they've got a destination. This is the way to Kurmastan," Emmerick replied, shaking out a stick of gum and unwrapping it. "And if this Hummer isn't going there, it may take us to someplace new, which means it's someplace we should know about."

"Yeah," Leight grunted. "Like the Slurpee counter at the 7-Eleven."

"Okay, so they stopped at a convenience store," Emmerick snapped the stale stick of gum and popped it into his mouth. "Get over it. Everybody's got to take a piss sooner or later. Even terrorists."

Leight gripped the steering wheel. "I just wish I'd had the chance to grab a hot dog. I haven't eaten since last night. Good food, too—Val's a great cook. You should take me up on my invite, come on over for dinner some night."

"You two are getting married next month, aren't you?"

"Right, but it's the honeymoon I'm looking forward too." Leight grinned. "You're invited. Remember?"

"To the honeymoon?"

Leight smirked. "You wish. You got the invitation, didn't you?"

"I don't know. I'll check with Bettina. She's got her hands full lately. Our au pair went back to Ireland, and now she's trying to take care of the twins and her keep her freelance business going. And, by the way, for future reference, the 'terrible twos' aren't a myth. Want some gum?" Emmerick held out the pack.

Leight took a stick. "So this guy we're tailing. You said his name's Amadani. But you didn't know it was him we were waiting for, right?"

"Right."

"Yet you recognized him?"

Emmerick nodded. The second he saw Amadani at baggage claim—five-eleven male, late forties, gray hair, scar on his left cheek—he'd ID'd him.

"You mentioned an alias, too," said Leight.

"Yeah," said Emmerick. "Amadani's an Afghani who fought the Soviets as a boy. That's where he got his nickname—'the Hawk.' A few years back, he was convicted for selling a million dollars' worth of black market cigarettes with phony tax stamps out of a warehouse in Wayne, New Jersey. He hooked up with our boys in Kurmastan during his prison term. After he was paroled, he skipped the country. Since then, he's turned up in Madrid, Hamburg, London. And every time he appears, a terror attack follows inside of a week."

Leight's eyebrows rose. "And you know all that how?"

"Because I busted him, just like half the other punks in Kurmastan. You've only been my partner for what, eight months? I had a whole life before I took on your sorry rookie ass."

Leight cracked the window, spit out his gum. "Forgot," he said. "I don't like Juicy Fruit." He glanced at Emmerick. "Those guys in Kurmastan, they really bother you, don't they?"

"Sure," said Emmerick. "You're talking about a whole town full of felons, guys I spent the past twenty years trying to lock up. Now they're free again and up to no damned good." He shook his head. "It's pushing the same rock up the same hill all over again."

Leight snorted. "Don't get your underwear bunched, Sisyphus. We'll lock them up again, maybe forever this time."

Emmerick peered through the dust-flecked window. "Watch. He's turning again."

"Great. This road looks worse than the last one."

"Lay back, but don't lose him."

"I'll try, but it's too bad the packages separated into two Hummers. It would have been better if Foy could have come with us. We could have traded off. It would have been harder for them to make us."

Emmerick didn't reply. Back at the airport, he hadn't been able to ID the man who'd been traveling with the Hawk, and that bothered him. Fortunately CTU Agent Judith Foy was there to tail the unknown man, while he and Leight had stayed with the Hawk.

Up ahead, the black Hummer made its turn and suddenly sped up, trailing a cloud of dust. Doug Leight hit the gas, swerved the Saturn onto a narrow road.

Emmerick held on. The road was so pitted, it rattled the fillings in his mouth. He looked ahead; the Hummer crested a low hill between two rows of trees, and vanished from sight.

"Hurry. Don't lose him."

The Saturn crested the hill a moment later—and Emmerick saw the Hummer. The huge vehicle had come to a dead stop. It sat in the middle of the road, just over the rise.

"Holy shit!" Doug Leight cried, slamming on the brakes.

The Saturn skidded to a halt, not six inches from the Hummer's rear bumper. The billowing cloud of dust that trailed the Saturn rolled over it. When it settled, Emmerick saw a large, brown van had pulled up behind them. He glanced at the trees bordering the road on both sides—no escape there.

"We're boxed in," he said, reaching for his weapon. Before he could pull it free, the Saturn's windows blew inward.

A hail of automatic weapons fire ripped through the vehicle's thin aluminum skin. Gaping holes appeared in the doors, the roof. Headlights shattered in a shower of sparks. The hood flew open, and bullets pinged off the engine block.

In the front seat, the two FBI agents were struck dozens of times by the flying bullets, their bodies convulsing as they died. The invisible attackers continued to fire, bursting tires and blowing off a hubcap.

Finally, the volley ceased. In the sudden silence, three men in camouflage fatigues carrying AK–47s emerged from the trees and approached the shattered car.

An engine gunned, and the Hummer that carried the Hawk sped away. The brown van slammed into the Saturn's rear bumper and pushed the smoking car down the hill, through a wooden fence, and into a muddy pond.

Wild ducks scattered. The car hissed when it hit the water, steam billowing up from under the hood. It gurgled and bubbled in the muck, then finally slipped beneath the pond's brackish green surface.

10:03:37 A.M. EDT
Volaré, Little Italy

The man with the gold teeth and two others burst through the office door. One man wore a waiter's uniform and clutched an Uzi. The other wore kitchen whites and gripped a meat cleaver. They stopped dead when they saw Fredo Mangella slumped in the leather chair.

The Albino released the woman. Sobbing, she stumbled to the desk and dropped to her knees beside the corpse.

"This bastard killed your boss," the Albino rasped.

Jack didn't say a word. Instead, he focused his attention on the Glock, and the laptop beside it.

"Son of a bitch," Gold Teeth snarled, cuffing Jack across the face with the butt of the police special. Jack stumbled, but didn't go down. The urge to strike back was strong, but Jack resisted it, biding his time.

"Petey, go downstairs and lock the front door," Gold Teeth said, eyeing Bauer. "Me and Dom will take care of this bastard."

The man with the meat cleaver left, and Jack eyeballed Gold Teeth. "I saw you in the cab. You tried to kill me today. Why? Who paid you?" Jack demanded.

"Time for me to go," said the Albino, scooping up Jack's Glock. "I have an appointment elsewhere."

"Hey, wait a minute, Whitey," Gold Teeth said. "You've got some explaining to do."

"My business was with your boss," the Albino said. "I don't deal with underlings."

The waiter with the Uzi frowned, eyes on the Albino as he headed for the door. Gold Teeth grabbed the man's arm—

And Jack lashed out. With his left, Jack backhanded the Uzi out of the waiter's grip. Then he stepped in with a right hook, crushing the man's throat. The waiter bounced off the wall and went down, gagging and gasping for breath.

Jack snatched the laptop off the desk and bolted for the door.

"Stop him," the Albino cried.

Gold Teeth blocked his path, but Jack didn't stop. Crouched low, he slammed into the man. Together, they went through the door and over the restaurant's balcony railing.

Jack was on top when they hit a table, smashing it. Crystal shattered, china broke, silverware flew. Jack flipped over, and lost his grip on the laptop. It slid across the hard-wood floor.

Gold Teeth did a somersault, too, and landed beside him. Jack knew the man was hurting, but Gold Teeth didn't give up. He lunged as Jack scrambled across the debris-strewn floor, fumbling for the computer.

The kitchen doors parted and Petey returned, armed with his meat cleaver.

Jack gripped the laptop with both hands and brought it down on the back of Gold Teeth's head. The man grunted and went limp. Jack looked up to see Petey charging.

Then the Albino started shooting and the dining room exploded in a shower of shattering glass as the massive front windows came down in a deadly hail. Jack rolled under a table as razor shards rained down around him. Petey was struck, a two-foot icicle of glass piercing the top of his skull.

The Albino shifted fire, peppering the ceiling. The racing plane lurched on the wires, then one wing dipped. Jack knew he was doomed unless he moved.

Tucking the laptop under his arm, he dived through the broken window. The suspended antique airplane came down a split-second later, smashing the tables and sending broken chairs and shattered china rolling onto the sidewalk.

Ears ringing from the noise, Jack stumbled to his feet, tightened his grip on the laptop, and took off. He wanted to go back for the Albino, but he was unarmed now, and he suspected the computer and its contents were more important.

As sirens wailed in the distance, Jack hailed a cab. On the ride back to CTU, his cell phone went off. Jack checked the number, took the call.

"Hi, honey," Teri Bauer chirped.

"Hi, sweetheart." Jack closed his eyes. The adrenaline was still pumping; he struggled to control his tone, make everything sound all right. "It's nice to hear your voice."

Teri laughed. "It's only been a day, but it's nice to know you're missing me already."

"I am."

"Listen, Jack, I know it's early, but I wanted to call anyway. I didn't wake you, did I?"

"I'm up," Jack replied. "It's actually not that early here."

"Oh, of course, that's right. The time difference. Well, Kim wanted me to ask a favor. She wants a Coldplay poster from the MTV store. Apparently it's in Times Square. That's where they do their live TRL shows—at least that's what Kim told me. You'll do that, won't you?"

"Yeah. Sure." Jack glanced at the passing traffic, exhaled at the idea of something so normal, so easy. Buying a poster to make his daughter happy. He smiled. "Anything I can get for you?"

"No, honey. Just bring yourself home in one piece. Okay? Stay safe."

"I'll try," said Jack. "Things here . . . they're a little . . . disorganized. But I won't forget Kim's poster."

"Great," said Teri. "I have to get going, but how's New York otherwise? Did you go to any nice restaurants yet?"

"Actually," said Jack, "I just came from one."

When he finished rerouting the security links, Tony Almeida closed the panel and rebooted the system. While he waited through the startup procedures, Tony popped the top buttons of his black cotton shirt to cool off. Then he began the laborious process of enabling all the new network connections he'd just established, one link at a time. Alarms. Motion sensors. Elevator overrides; all had to be restarted. While he worked, Tony unconsciously rubbed the ragged scar across his chest.

The "program enabled" icon appeared, and soon Tony had real-time images on all twelve security monitors. He observed the parking garage, the lobby, the elevator shaft, the roof, the fire escape through an array of cameras.

"Mr. Almeida?"

Rachel Delgado was there, a Styrofoam cup of coffee in each hand. Tony's shirt still gaped, and the woman's eyes widened when she saw Tony's scar.

"My god," she cried. "Did that just happen?"

Tony flushed, closed his shirt. "No," he muttered, buttoning quickly. "It, uh . . . happened a couple months ago. Down in Mexico."

Rachel looked away. "Sorry, I didn't mean to pry. You were working behind the console, and it looked like an electrical burn, so I thought . . ."

"It is an electrical burn," Tony replied.

Rachel suddenly remembered the containers in her

hand. "I brought you some coffee," she said. "I didn't know if you liked it black or with cream, so I brought one of each."

"Thanks," Tony said, accepting the black. "Sit down. Join me."

"Okay," Rachel said, glancing at the workstation. "Wow, you have everything running again."

"Almost everything."

"Is that Con Ed guy on the roof helping you?" Rachel asked.

Tony's eyes were on the monitor. He'd seen the man in a blue utility worker's uniform, too, just before the guy had moved out of camera range.

Tony punched up the digital control panel for the roof camera. Using his mouse to move the lens from side to side, Tony scanned the black tarred roof. Soon he spotted the man again—he *was* wearing a Con Edison uniform.

"He looks busy," Rachel observed.

The man's back was turned. He was crouched at the base of one of CTU's microwave towers, tinkering with something impossible to see.

Tony frowned. He'd established the network connection to the motion detectors on the roof two minutes ago. Why hadn't those detectors gone off, sounded an alarm that someone was on the roof? He checked the circuit and got a "network connection lost" message.

Adrenaline pumping, Tony checked the alarm system and received the same warning. Someone had sabotaged the system as fast as he'd gotten it running.

"What's the matter?" Rachel asked. "You look upset."

Tony jerked his head at the monitor. "The Con Edison guy on the roof. He's an intruder."

Rachel rose abruptly, spilling her coffee on the concrete floor. "Oh my god. What do we do?"

Tony reached for the phone.

10:51:23 A.M. EDT
CTU Headquarters, NYC

Jack Bauer had just returned with the laptop under his arm. He went directly to Brice Holman's office, where Morris was still trying to crack the security on the Director's computer.

"Almost there, Jack-o," he promised.

Jack's cell warbled. He dropped the laptop on the desk, reached for the phone in his pocket.

"Bauer here."

"It's Tony. We've got an intruder on the roof."

Jack's gut turned to ice. "You're sure?"

"He's dressed like a utility worker," Tony replied. "But he didn't get up there by accident. I think he climbed up the maintenance hatch, deactivating the security systems as he went along. I'm down here establishing new links; he's up there cutting them."

"Do you know his precise location right now?"

"He's at the base of the microwave tower on the southwest corner of the roof. I can see him because I still have visuals."

"The intruder didn't disable the cameras?"

"He couldn't, Jack," Tony explained. "They're digital Wi-Fi and operate independently, with their own power source. The cameras have no wires to cut, no power source to disconnect. He probably doesn't have a clue he's being watched."

"Listen Tony," Jack said. "Don't mention the intruder to anyone, and don't set off any alarms. I don't want to spook this guy. I want him alive, for interrogation."

"Roger, Jack."

"Keep this line open, we'll talk when I get to the roof."

"Okay."

Jack closed the phone.

"What intruder?" Morris asked.

"Never mind," said Jack. "Give me your weapon."

Morris slipped the Glock out of its holster. "Take it. I hate the damned things. I'm only packing heat because it's regulation in the field." Morris looked around the office. "If you want to call this the *field*."

"Stay here and keep doing what you're doing," Jack said, checking the weapon. "And when you're done with that computer, get started on the laptop."

Jack slipped out of Director Holman's office, Glock in hand.

"Oh, that's fine," Morris grumbled. "Guns flashing, intruders all over the place, and no one tells *me* a bloody thing . . ."

Jack moved quietly and quickly along the balcony of the Operations Center, careful to keep the Glock low. He found the door to the staircase, and used the universal code key Layla Abernathy had given him to enter the restricted area.

The stairwell was well lit, and stank of fresh paint and industrial-strength cleaning fluid. Jack took the steps two at a time, his heels echoing hollowly in the cavernous space. He led with the Glock, clutched in both hands.

Jack paused at each landing, wary of ambush. So far, however, the stairwell remained deserted.

Finally, he reached the door to the roof. Jack flattened himself against the wall and slowly turned the knob, pushing the door open a few inches. Warm air and bright sunlight flooded through the crack, filling the stairwell. From below, Jack could hear street sounds. With one hand, he drew his cell phone out of his pocket.

"Tony," he whispered.

"I'm here."

"Where is the intruder now?"

"He's still at the microwave tower, but he's not crouching anymore. I think he's packing up to leave."

"Roger," Jack whispered. "Stand by."

He put Tony on hold and used his CTU phone's GPS as a compass, determining that the southwest corner of the roof was through the door and to the right. Then Jack tucked the cell into his pocket and slipped through the door, stepping cautiously onto the roof. The rubber insulation felt spongy under his feet, but Jack was grateful the material muffled the sound of his footsteps.

He moved to the right, until he saw the steel microwave tower, its multiple dishes framed by the gleaming World Trade Center towers in the distance. He crept to a massive air-conditioning system, and ducked behind an aluminum vent.

From his position, Jack had a good view of the micro-

wave tower, right down to its concrete base. But there was
no sign of the intruder.

"Damn," Jack grunted.

He flattened himself against the air conditioner, snatched
up his phone again. "Talk to me, Tony—"

"He's moving, Jack. He's headed to an access hatch on
the northwest corner."

Fixated on his target, Jack closed the phone, raised his
head over the edge of the air-conditioning unit. Looking to
the northwest, he spotted a slight African-American man
with black-framed glasses, wearing a blue uniform, walking toward an outhouse-sized structure projecting from
the flat roof. The man carried two metal toolboxes in his
hand, a bundle of wire over his narrow shoulders.

Jack took off at a run, circling power units and a sky-
light to reach a point where he could intercept the intruder.
Then, lifting his Glock, Jack stepped into view.

"Halt," he cried. "You are in a restricted area. Drop the
boxes and get down on the ground *now.*"

The man's eyes were wide behind his thick glasses. He
immediately dropped the boxes—then he took off, sprint-
ing to the fire escape twenty yards away.

"Stop or I *will* shoot," Jack warned, stepping forward.

The man sped up. Jack dropped to one knee and aimed.
At the last second he lowered his Glock, firing at the man's
moving legs.

But just as Jack pulled the trigger, the man stumbled.
Instead of hitting his knee, the 9mm bullet caught him
squarely in the back of the head. The man went limp, his
shattered lenses tumbled over the edge of the building

as his corpse hit the roof with a muffled thump, his head inches from the ledge of the fire escape.

Bauer cursed.

Glock pointed at his victim, he cautiously approached. Jack didn't need to check the man's pulse to know he was dead. The back of his head was blown out, blood and brain matter splattered on the roof. Jack holstered his weapon, bent down, went through the man's pockets, but found nothing—not even a wallet.

Still crouched, he turned the dead man onto his back. On the man's forearm, Jack noticed a tattoo of a stylized number 13. He searched the front pockets of the man's uniform, frowned when he came up empty again.

Then he remembered the steel boxes. Jack rose and turned, his back to the fire escape. He took one step, and a bright flash exploded in his head. He never saw the blow coming. His legs buckled and he crashed to his knees.

Despite the sharp stab of agony that rattled his skull, Jack fought to stay conscious, until a vicious kick to the side of his head sent him sprawling.

A blond man in the Con Edison uniform stepped off the fire escape, rubbing his fist. He glanced at his dead partner, then drew his weapon. The silencer was still attached to the muzzle, and he placed it against Jack's bloodied temple.

Moaning, Jack coughed. "If you kill me, you'll never get off this roof alive."

The blond man chuckled, pushed the silencer until it gouged Jack's flesh.

"Shut up and die," he said.

1 2 3 4 **5** 6 7 8 9
10 11 12 13 14 15 16 17
18 19 20 21 22 23 24

. . . .

**THE FOLLOWING TAKES PLACE
BETWEEN THE HOURS OF
11:00 A.M. AND 12:00 P.M.
EASTERN DAYLIGHT TIME**

. . . .

11:00:16 A.M. EDT
CTU Headquarters, NYC

On the ground, the silencer digging into his temple, Jack
had no time to make a move before the final gunshot. When
it came, Jack felt no pain. Instead, the pressure against his
skull simply fell away.

Jack instantly realized he hadn't been shot. The blond
man lurched backward, onto the fire escape, one limp
hand brushing at the quickly spreading red stain on his
blue shirt.

As Jack pulled his weapon, a second bullet caught the
blond man in the throat. The blond dropped his gun, and

his body pitched against the metal railing. Limply, without a sound, he fell headfirst into the street below.

Glancing around, Jack saw Tony Almeida, Glock still in hand. Tony walked over, helped Jack to his feet.

"Jack, are you—"

"I'm fine," Jack said hoarsely.

Tony stepped back, holstered his weapon.

Jack closed his eyes, took a breath. With every move, he was battered by waves of dizziness. Ignoring the pain, he opened his eyes, reholstered his own Glock.

Tony stepped to the fire escape and peered over the railing. "Sorry, Jack. I know you wanted one of them alive."

"Forget it," Jack rasped. "Let's find out what they were up to."

It took them less than a minute to find the bomb. It was planted at the base of the microwave communications array—a digital clock connected to a two-pound bundle of C–4.

Jack crouched low, fighting a wave of nausea. "I can defuse this," he said.

Tony pulled him away. "You're in no condition to do this. Let me handle it."

Before Jack could protest, the cell phone went off in his pocket. He answered, "Bauer."

"It's me, Jack-o," Morris said. "Where have you run off to?"

"I've been . . . busy," Jack said.

"I have news," Morris continued. "Both good and bad."

"Okay," Jack said while he watched Tony use a gravity knife to sever the wire that led from the explosive charge to the timer. Tony then opened the back of the clock and removed a small battery. Immediately, the numbers stopped flashing and the digital face went dark.

Jack quietly exhaled.

"Are you there, Jack?" Morris demanded. "It's not polite to ignore a man who's called you."

"I'm here," Jack replied wearily. "What have you got for me? The good news."

"I've broken through Brice Holman's security firewall," Morris declared with a hint of pride. "The contents of the Director's computer are yours to peruse."

"Good work, Morris. What's the downside?"

The memory's been wiped clean. Holman's cache is empty. And get this . . . According to the computer log, the memory was wiped this morning at six twenty-one A.M."

"Then there's a mole in CTU New York. Maybe more than one. We checked the entry logs. We know Brice Holman was never here today. That means somebody else deleted those files." Jack paused, rubbed his aching temple. "How about the laptop I brought you?"

"I'm afraid all Fredo Mangella was doing was converting currency. Dollars into euros. Millions of them. It was all on the up-and-up." Morris frowned. "Might be a dead end, Jack."

"No," Jack insisted. "It's important, but I don't know why. Not yet. We're still missing a piece of the puzzle."

"I'll keep looking, but all I see are recipes and payroll records. You won't believe what an executive chef earns!"

"Listen, Morris. One more thing. Tony Almeida has a device for you to check out."

Morris sighed. "Now what would that be, boss? A computer? Another laptop?"

"A bomb," Jack replied.

11:28:05 A.M. EDT
CTU Headquarters, NYC

After swallowing two cups of black coffee and three Advils, Jack felt considerably better. Tony had gone back to finishing his work on the security system, and Morris had taken the explosive device to the blast-proof room for further examination.

Now Jack was sitting behind Brice Holman's desk, waking his computer out of hibernation. The firewalls were down and Holman's computer cache was empty, as Morris had said.

Jack moved to the nonsecured files Holman kept, and ran a search using keywords *FBI*, *DEA*, and *ATF*. At first dozens of interagency alerts came up—practically all of them were Most Wanted List updates, Amber Alerts, or government releases. Jack filtered them out.

Then he found the draft of an e-mail to Judith Foy. Holman had never finished or sent the message, but the e-mail mentioned "our friends at the FBI" and "Jello and Rollo," obviously code names.

Jack punched the intercom and summoned Layla Abernathy.

"I want you to contact Andrew McConnell," he told her the moment she walked in.

"The Director of the local FBI office?"

"That's right. I want you to ask him if any of his agents are involved in an investigation of the Warriors of God, Imam Ali Rahman al Sallifi, or the compound at Kurmastan."

Layla nodded. "Anything else?"

"Don't be upset if you don't get any answers. Just report back to me. I want to know what McConnell says, word for word. His tone, his attitude, his inflection."

"If you want all that, why can't you talk to him yourself?" she asked.

"You'll see," was Jack's only reply.

11:33:16 A.M. EDT
CTU Headquarters, NYC

Layla left Holman's office with a stiff stride. She could understand Jack Bauer's being unhappy with the present situation, but she didn't like being kept in the dark. Brice had kept her that way for weeks, and she'd had enough of it.

She didn't care for Bauer's manner, either. He was obviously a gung-ho, Type A, goal-oriented alpha male. The kind of guy who'd roll over anything or anyone who got in his way.

Layla had made some discreet inquiries about the man and wasn't surprised to discover that Bauer had a reputation for being a loose cannon. Strangely, however, not one of Layla's contacts had characterized him as political. Apparently, for Jack Bauer, career advancement wasn't a high priority.

That impressed Layla, along with the man's reputation for being one hell of a field agent. He was also tight with Richard Walsh at Langley, which Layla knew would pretty much absolve him of most Agency sins.

On her way down the hall, Layla accidentally bumped into one of Jack's cronies. She froze when she saw the explosive in his hand.

"Oh my god," she whispered.

"No worry, luv," Morris O'Brian said with a smile. "It's inactive. I could crack it against the wall and absolutely nothing will happen."

Layla shook her head. "Well, do me a favor. And *don't*, okay?"

Morris grinned and punched the bricks of C–4 with his fist. "See? Perfectly harmless."

Giving Morris a wide berth, Layla headed back to her desk. "My god," she murmured. "These L.A. guys are *all* loose cannons . . ."

11:34:55 A.M. EDT
CTU Headquarters, NYC

Morris opened the door to Brice Holman's office without knocking, bounced the bomb onto the desk in front of Jack.

"What have you learned?" Jack asked.

"At first, nothing," Morris said with a shrug. "Only that

the C–4 was manufactured in Hungary, and that it didn't take a rocket scientist to build this thing. The bomb is right out of the anarchist playbook. Except for one little thing."

"Okay." Jack swung around in his seat. "Explain."

Morris sat down across from Jack. "Simple timer, two bricks of military-grade C–4, right?"

Jack nodded.

"Wrong," Morris declared. "Watch this."

Morris took one of the pasty, gray-white bricks of plastic explosives in his hand and broke it in half. He opened the two sections like a pomegranate, and displayed the insides to Jack.

"Is that a rock?" Jack asked.

"A pebble, actually," Morris replied. "From a New Jersey beach no doubt. The other brick has one tucked inside of it, too."

Jack rubbed his chin. "That doesn't make any sense. Stones make lousy shrapnel. Nails are better. And with half the C–4 gone from each brick—"

"More than half," Morris replied. "The explosive potential of this device is fairly weak. In fact, this thing couldn't do much more than bring down the microwave tower where you found it. That would put CTU New York out of action for a day or two, no longer."

"That makes no sense," Jack replied. "Why take all that trouble to sabotage the communications array? With a bigger bomb, the same two men could have destroyed this entire complex."

"It's obvious they didn't want to do that. They wanted CTU operational. It's the communications and satellite system they wanted disabled—"

The intercom buzzed, interrupting them.

Jack answered. "Yes?"

"It's Tony. We just received a security alert from Langley. We're to increase the threat level at headquarters to Code Red immediately. Specifically, we're to pay particular attention to our communications infrastructure."

Jack and Morris exchanged glances.

"Anything else?" Jack asked.

"Well, I put in a back-channel call to Jamey Farrell in L.A. She told me there've been three attacks on CTU satellite facilities—in Boston, New Haven, and Pittsburgh. These attacks were successful. The comm systems are down at all three units—"

Morris cursed.

"That's not all," Tony continued. "I just checked the City of New York's emergency response system and found out that the Fire Department was summoned to FBI Headquarters fifteen minutes ago. Apparently there's been a 'fire' on their roof."

Morris met Jack's gaze. "What do you want to bet someone took out the Agency's satellite capabilities?"

Why satellites? Jack wondered. *What is it the enemy doesn't want us to see? Are we even looking for the thing they're so eager to hide?*

A sharp knock sounded at the door.

"Come in," Jack called.

Layla Abernathy entered. "You were right, Special Agent Bauer. I spoke with Mr. McConnell personally and he blew me off."

"What did he say, *precisely*?" Jack demanded.

She glanced at her notepad. "I'll quote him: 'The Fed-

eral Bureau of Investigation cannot comment on an ongoing investigation.' End quote. Then Director McConnell
added a personal aside."

"Go on."

"The Director said that Frank Hensley was a personal
friend of his, and that he would rather burn in hell before
he shared information with Special Agent Jack Bauer of
CTU." Layla Abernathy raised an eyebrow.

"So much for cooperation among the agencies," Morris
muttered.

Jack frowned and glanced away from Agent Abernathy's
curious gaze. *I knew Operation Hell Gate would come
back to bite me on this assignment.* "McConnell stated
that Kurmastan and its citizens were part of an 'ongoing
investigation.' Is that correct?"

Layla nodded.

"Was that before or after you used my name?" Jack
asked.

Layla frowned. "After, sir."

"He's lying," Jack declared. "The FBI's investigation is
as dead as CTU's. McConnell is just trying to throw us
off by feeding us misinformation—or he already suspects
some of his agents are involved with Brice Holman's rogue
operation and he wants to cover their asses."

Morris shook his head. "With the satellite system down
on the East Coast and the FBI keeping us at arm's length,
we're effectively on our own."

Jack rubbed the back of his neck. "What else is new?"

The intercom buzzed again. Jack answered, putting it
on speaker.

"Special Agent Bauer? This is Rachel Delgado, Security. I wanted to let you know that I've located Deputy Director Judith Foy. She's been injured in the line of duty. A traffic accident, according to the police. Right now, she's a patient in Newark General Hospital."

Jack watched Layla. She remained composed, but her expression had fallen. She was obviously upset.

"Thank you Ms. Delgado," said Jack, disconnecting. He met Layla's gaze. "I'm dispatching Special Agent Almeida to Newark," he told her. "I want Tony to interrogate Deputy Director Foy as soon as possible."

Layla nodded. "I want to go with him."

"No," said Jack. Then he softened his voice. "I'm sorry, Agent Abernathy. I need you here. But I'd like you to send another agent. Someone you trust. Someone who knows New Jersey."

11:46:29 A.M. EDT
District Congressional Office
Flemington, New Jersey

"Congresswoman Williams? Are you ready for your eleven forty-five?"

"Yes, Melinda," Hailey Williams replied over the intercom. "Send him in."

The slender, African-American Congresswoman adjusted the gray blazer of her tailored, pinstriped suit. As her office door swung wide, she rose from behind her desk to greet the man striding into the room.

Hailey frowned, expecting a black man named Montel Tanner. Montel was the usual liaison between herself and Ali Rahman al Sallifi. In fact, it had been Montel who'd called her the day before, promising another lucrative donation to her upcoming campaign in exchange for a small favor.

Hailey had been only too happy to agree to the meeting. Her campaign coffers were alarmingly low these days, her expenses increasingly high, and she knew al Sallifi was a man who could be counted on for financial support.

Hailey had helped al Sallifi in the past, and she was more than willing to do so again. Yes, one reason was the money. Hailey was no stranger to hardball politics—and she was certainly no saint when it came to running her campaigns. But she did honestly believe in al Sallifi's work with prisoners.

Sure, Hailey appeared to be living a charmed life now: married to a prominent public defender, a graduate of Howard University, two graduate degrees from Princeton. But she was far from a child of privilege.

Hailey was the third daughter to a single mother, whose father had died at the hands of guards in a state penitentiary, and three of her cousins had done time in prisons. To Hailey, prisoners were lost souls in need of guidance, and she firmly believed that once someone had served his or her time, that person deserved an unprejudiced chance to begin again.

She had proudly defended Ali Rahman al Sallifi, his Warriors of God organization, and its rural New Jersey Kurmastan settlement precisely because they held the same outlook that she did when it came to these lost souls of society.

Hailey had never actually examined the group's specific religious teachings. As an agnostic, she personally wasn't interested—although she did recognize and respect that any religion was a form of philosophy that could be very helpful in turning around certain troubled men and women.

For her, it was enough to know that the group was a religious-based organization that gave the state's ex-cons direction, focus, and a halfway home after they left their prison lives. Montel always assured her of that. In fact, Montel had been very pleasant to meet with from the start. That was another reason she was a bit taken aback to find a different sort of man greeting her today.

His manner was very cold. And his skin was so very pale. The whiteness of it looked almost unnatural to Hailey, quite off-putting, but she hid her reaction and extended her hand.

The Albino ignored it. Instead, he simply dropped his large briefcase down on the edge of her desk and opened it. There was computer inside. He tapped a few keys, and the screen came to life. The Congresswoman noted that the satellite system quickly located a remote wireless connection and locked on to it.

"Ibrahim Noor sent me," the man began, speaking in a thin, raspy voice.

"Noor?" Hailey Williams said, frowning. "Not Ali Rahman al Sallifi?"

A tight-lipped smile of regret spread across the man's

ghost-pale features. "I'm afraid the Imam is quite busy with his clerical duties. Ibrahim Noor is handling political matters these days."

"I see."

Hailey sank back into her chair, waiting while the albino man stooped over the portable computer, long fingers drumming the miniature keyboard. Finally, he straightened up, turned the computer so it faced the Congresswoman.

"The site for the Palm Bank of the Cayman Islands is displayed," he said. "Please punch in the password to your account."

The woman's jaw dropped. "How do you know about that account?" she demanded, half rising from her chair again.

"Just enter the password, please," he repeated.

With a frown, the Congresswoman punched in the numbers. Her balance and a list of transactions came up immediately.

"Don't go messing with my account," she warned.

The man smiled again. "Ibrahim Noor has a proposal for you. He wants you to cancel your appearance with Reverend Ahern this afternoon."

"But . . . I don't understand . . . my meeting with the Reverend was precisely to smooth things over for the Warriors of God. It's been members of Reverend Ahern's congregation who've been complaining about activities at Kurmastan—"

"Ibrahim Noor desires to meet with the neighboring group *personally*," said the Albino. "What he does not desire is further *publicity* about Kurmastan."

"But publicity is the point!" Hailey argued. "My meeting was supposed to be covered by the local press. I was hoping to use it as the kickoff for my reelection campaign. To show my support for diversity. Tolerance. Why should I give up on it?"

"For money," the Albino said flatly. "A quite substantial amount of money, wired anonymously to your account. Money no one will ever have to know about. Not the Federal Elections Commission, not the Treasury Department nor the IRS."

Hailey frowned, considering this. "Why would Mr. Noor make such an offer? Surely there are strings attached."

The Albino shook his head. "It is a gift, truly. We only ask that you stay away from Reverend Ahern, and not join him on his visit to Kurmastan. Send your sincere regrets instead. In return, we offer you this token of our friendship—one million euros."

"Euros!" The Congresswoman shook her head. "I'm sorry, but I'd rather be paid in U.S. currency."

The man tossed his blond mane in an almost effeminate gesture of disdain. "In time you will thank Ibrahim Noor for his generosity and foresight."

Hailey narrowed her eyes. "Now why would I do that?"

The Albino offered her a thin smile. "Because in two weeks, Madam Congresswoman, a sheet of toilet paper will be far more valuable than United States currency."

11:57:41 P.M. EDT
Security Station One
CTU Headquarters, NYC

"Sorry, our satellite bandwidth is all tied up right now. Have a nice day."

Morris hung up the phone.

"Was that the FBI?" Jack asked.

"The Drug Enforcement Agency. Something about a cocaine shipment coming ashore on Fire Island. They wanted us to track it for them."

"Then the local DEA has lost satellite capabilities, too."

"Apparently." Morris touched his finger to his chin. "You know, Jack-o. None of these agencies are really thinking. If the situation was critical, they could always appropriate bandwidth from the civilian broadcast stations in the area. Practically all of them use the most powerful microwave tower in the city."

Jack sat up, alarmed. "Where?"

"Top of the World Trade Center, Jack."

"Can you tap into the WTC security system from this console?"

Morris shrugged. "Sure."

"Get to work."

While Morris keyed in the protocols, Jack summoned Layla Abernathy.

"Contact the Operations Control Center of the World Trade Center. Ask them if they've authorized any maintenance work near the microwave tower—specifically workers from Consolidated Edison."

Five minutes later they were scanning the streets around the twin towers for Con Edison trucks and men in blue uniforms.

"I've got nothing, Jack. Nobody on the streets. Nobody on the roof of the North Tower, where the antenna is located."

"Try the security cameras inside the maintenance shafts and freight elevators," Jack commanded.

Layla returned, and Jack faced her.

"The OC center at the World Trade Center has authorized no work on or near the microwave tower," she told him. "No one from Con Edison has passed through their security checkpoints today, either."

"Then who are these guys?" Morris replied, jerking his head at the monitor.

On screen, two men in Con Ed blue entered a freight elevator, accompanied by a man in a Port Authority policeman's uniform.

"The enemy," Bauer said grimly.

· ·

**THE FOLLOWING TAKES PLACE
BETWEEN THE HOURS OF
12:00 P.M. AND 1:00 P.M.
EASTERN DAYLIGHT TIME**

· ·

12:07:41 P.M. EDT
The Flemington Traffic Circle
Flemington, New Jersey

The silver BMW entered the roundabout, then took the
first exit onto New Jersey Route 12 west.

Cruising at sixty miles per hour, the Albino considered
his short and expensive interaction with Congresswoman
Hailey Williams.

*As predicted, the woman eagerly accepted the deal we
offered her. And why not? She's a politician—a whore for
money—like the rest of her ilk.*

Meanwhile, he slipped a disposable hypodermic needle

out of a black bag on the floor. Holding the needle high, he pressed the plunger until a tiny bit of golden fluid pearled at the tip. Then he thrust the needle into his forearm, chewing his lower lip as he pushed the steroid and stimulant cocktail into his veins.

If only I'd learned this simple fact earlier in life, he mused, shaking back his long white hair. *I wasted years as an assassin, only to find that buying a politician is so much easier than killing one.*

His heart began to race and sweat beaded his brow. The veins on his neck and forehead quivered. The Albino clutched the wheel and stepped on the gas.

On the road back to Kurmastan, he noticed the many outlet stores for which Flemington was noted, each a huge, gaudy temple dedicated to consumerism. They sold designer shoes, designer coats, furs, jewelry—even designer foods.

His thin lips stretched into a tight smile.

This will soon end. In another year, the average American will be content to eat garbage, live in a cardboard box, and wear rags on his back.

Slipping into the fast lane, the Albino tossed the used needle out the window and reached for the cell in his pocket. He punched speed dial on an international exchange. It took a moment for the connection to be made.

"Ungar Financial, LLC, Geneva," a woman said in a coolly efficient voice.

"I must speak with Soren Ungar," the Albino rasped. "Erno Tobias calling."

"I'll put you through immediately, sir."

12:39:51 P.M. EDT
North Tower
World Trade Center

Jack Bauer stood inside a stairwell on the 110th floor of One World Trade Center.

He wore the Con Edison uniform taken from the intruder he'd killed on the roof of CTU, blood from the fatal head wound hastily cleaned. Jack had to roll up the sleeves to hide the fact that the shirt was too small. The collar was still damp, and he fidgeted uncomfortably.

A steel door to the roof was in front of him. Beside him, Layla Abernathy used a digital photo of the dead man's tattoo as a model, drawing a stylized 13 on Jack's bared forearm. Jack knew about the number 13 tattooed on members of the multinational prison gang MS–13. But this tattoo wasn't a regular 13. Its design included a five-pointed star inside the bottom loop of the numeral 3 that suggested the star and crescent symbol of Islam.

Jack watched Layla sketch, wishing Tony had his back instead of a novice like this woman. But Tony was in Newark, and Layla was the only person he trusted from the New York office, so Jack had brought her along. While she worked, Jack lifted a cell phone to his ear.

"Where are they now, Morris?" he asked.

"The copper's pacing on the other side of your door," O'Brian replied from the security console at CTU. "The men in the utility company uniforms are at the base of the tower, climbing onto a ladder."

"Is the Port Authority cop real?"

"Don't know, Jack-o. I could ask, but that would tip the WTC security staff that they've got a problem, and you don't want that."

Morris paused. "My best guess is they're using the officer as cover. I suspect they were afraid to disable the cameras and arouse the suspicion of the OCC managers. But that pair of utility workers entered without signing in, and I observed the PA officer as he escorted them to the roof."

"Then he's working for the bad guys," Jack concluded.

"Finished," Layla said, displaying the phony tattoo to Jack. "Try not to sweat too much; I drew it with felt tip pens."

Jack nodded.

"I hope this works," the woman continued. "We don't even know what the 13 tattoo means. There's no match for it in CTU's database."

"It just has to fool them long enough for me to take them down," Jack replied. Then he spoke into the cell. "How far away is the tower from the door in front of me?"

"A good hundred yards, Jack. The roof slopes upward, and you'll have to climb onto a three-tiered metal platform to reach the base of the tower. There are steel support cables strung all over the roof, so be careful not to trip over one."

Jack frowned. "So charging the bad guys would not be a good idea. Don't worry, I don't plan to."

Bauer spoke to Layla while he slipped a hands-free headset over his ears and tucked the phone into the Con Ed uniform.

"Go down two flights, to level 108, and listen in to my

transmission. If something happens to me, alert the NYPD Bomb Squad and let them handle the bombers."

"You shouldn't do this alone," Layla insisted. "We can have a SWAT team up here inside of five minutes."

"I need to take one of them alive, for interrogation," Jack replied. "We're working in the dark. We need some solid intelligence."

"Good luck," Layla called as she descended the concrete steps.

"I'm about to move," Jack said into the headset. "Where's the officer now?"

"About two feet away from you. On the other side of the door. Why? Are you planning to charm your way past him?"

"No time for that," Jack hissed.

Jack clutched the metal handle, felt relief when he realized the door opened inward, which offered him a better chance to surprise the PA cop.

"Jack!" Morris cried, voice sharp in his headset. "The copper's leaning against the door right now."

Bauer yanked it open. A burst of sunlight and the roar of wind filled the dim stairwell. With a startled cry, the man in the navy-blue uniform fell into Jack's arms. Bauer immediately placed him in a chokehold and dragged the struggling man into the stairwell. The door closed automatically.

The man was young and Hispanic and smaller than Jack, but very powerful. While he struggled, Jack applied just enough pressure to render him unconscious, then let the limp form slide to the floor. Jack checked the man's arms but found no tattoo. The ID in his pocket pegged him as Hector Giamonde, a real PA police officer with just eight months on the job.

Jack heard footsteps and whirled, fist ready.

Layla jumped back. She clutched a Glock in her small hands.

"I told you to stay downstairs," Jack hissed.

"I heard a struggle, and—"

"Cuff him," Jack interrupted. "I'm going out."

While Layla strapped flex cuffs around the man's wrists and ankles, Jack slipped through the door.

Outside, high winds buffeted him, flapping the legs of his baggy pants and tugging at his hair. Jack blinked against the constant blast and scanned the roof.

He spied the intruders on a steel ladder. They'd climbed a hundred and fifty feet up the transmission tower. They were both focused on their ascent, and neither noticed the absence of the Port Authority policeman who'd been guarding their backs.

Jack bolted across the roof, leaping over steel cables, until he reached the metal platform that ringed the tower base. Still undetected, he ascended two levels of steps, wending his way around a dozen or more STLs and ENG receiver dishes. Amid an electronic hum mixed with the howl of the winds, Jack reached the bottom of the ladder.

The tower was a building in its own right, a square structure eighteen hundred feet high and perhaps a hundred feet around. The ladder in front of him snaked up the side.

Eyes squinting against the bright sunshine, Jack gripped

the steel rail and began to climb. After twenty rungs, he knew why the intruders weren't looking down. The vistas around him were incredibly vast, the height dizzying. Jack battled a constant wind that whistled in his ears and threatened to rip him off the ladder.

"Can you hear me, Morris? I need to know the location of the intruders."

The voice in his headset was drowned out by the gale. Jack muttered a curse and kept climbing.

He couldn't find the intruders now. He did come across three bombs taped to the tower wall—solid bricks of C–4 wired with detonation cords instead of timers. Jack ripped the cords out as he went.

About two hundred feet above him, between rows of saucer-shaped dishes, Jack saw a steel mesh platform that circled the tower. The men had apparently exited the ladder there, and moved to the opposite side of the transmission tower.

Jack continued his ascent until the platform was less than twenty feet above him. Here the climbing space narrowed because the ladder was sandwiched between two massive receiver dishes. As Jack moved between them, strong hands grabbed his throat and threatened to tear him from the ladder.

"*Te morati poginuti!*" the attacker cried.

Jack understood the language from his Delta Force missions in Eastern Europe. Rather than resisting, he threw up his arm so his attacker could see the tattoo.

"*Prekid JA sam jedan prijatelj,*" Jack rasped in Serbian. "*JA moći pomoć.*"

The big man saw the tattoo, heard Jack's words. Suddenly the pressure on his throat eased. Jack did not resist when the man grabbed his forearm and dragged him onto the top of a massive receiver dish, where he sprawled, gasping. The man loomed over him, stocky build, dark eyes, a once aquiline nose twisted by too many breaks.

"*JA sam jedan prijatelj*," Jack repeated, telling the man he was an ally.

Jack heard a grunt of surprise. At the same instant, he realized the tattoo on his forearm had smeared. The other man was looking at his own hand—the ink was now staining his fingers.

Before the big man could make a move, Bauer lashed out with his elbow, crushing his larynx. As the man's head jerked back, Jack grabbed him by his collar and flipped him from his perch.

The big man tumbled silently, arms and legs windmilling in the blasting winds. A hundred feet above the roof, the man struck a steel cable that severed his body in half. Jack looked away, spied another bomb, and ripped out the det cord. Then he grasped the ladder, swung himself onto the rungs, and continued his climb.

Grunting, he pulled himself onto the platform a moment later. There was no sign of the other utility worker, but Jack spied bundles of plastic explosives taped to the tower, and a detonation cord leading around the bend.

Jack drew the Glock and followed the wire. He turned a corner and came face to face with the bomber a moment later.

"*Tko biti te?*" the Serb cried.

The lanky blond man had just inserted cord into a brick of C–4. The tiny electronic detonator dangled from his utility belt. Now he reached for the button.

"*Prekid! Predaja zatim*," Jack cried, ordering the man to surrender.

The man grasped the detonator, lifted it. Jack had no choice. The Glock bucked, its blast muted by the howling wind.

There was an explosion of red. The detonator, along with the hand clutching it, tumbled over the railing. The force of the concussion slammed the man against the rail, and he tumbled over it, too.

He screamed once, before bouncing off an ENG dish.

"Damn it!" Jack yelled, punching the rail.

Though he had stopped the bombers, he'd failed to take either man alive. Jack was back where he'd started . . .

6:54:30 P.M. CEST
Ungar Financial, LLC
Geneva, Switzerland

Expressionless behind horn-rimmed glasses, billionaire currency speculator Soren Ungar held the phone to his ear, listening to the Albino's rasping voice speaking from thousands of miles away.

While Erno Tobias talked, Ungar stared at his own reflection on the glass surface of the desk. He'd worn a blank business mask for so many decades that his bland, angular face now seemed incapable of even a micro-expression.

Ungar believed that was for the best. One should always maintain control and hold one's thoughts and emotions tightly. It was vulgar, unseemly, *bourgeoisie* to do otherwise. Even now, the anger that seethed inside him never reached Soren Ungar's cold, dead eyes.

"This was an expensive mistake Ibrahim Noor made," Ungar interrupted. "Inviting that Congresswoman to his compound, today of all days, was a bit of insanity on his part."

"Noor had his reasons," Tobias replied. "Williams and the others were to be his gift. A blood sacrifice to those who remain behind. Slaughtered lambs for them to vent their rage before the final conflagration."

"Nevertheless, it was an error that cost me a million euros to remedy," Ungar said without a trace of rancor. "Noor and his savages can have the others to do with as they please. But I may need the Congresswoman's services in the future. It's never wise to squander an asset that could still prove useful."

Ungar paused. "Fortunately, I will only have to deal with these savages a little while longer, until they have served their purpose. When the bloodbath begins, America's attention will be focused on stopping the threat, and I can act freely. After the final attack on their financial center and my speech tomorrow, before the International Board of Currency Traders, the final nails will be pounded into the coffin of American hegemony."

"You will possess wealth beyond measure," the Albino rasped.

"More importantly, with Europe in ascendance, a sorry

century of dangerous technological inventions, vulgar consumerism, crass commercialism, and vile popular culture will finally end."

"This plan is not without risks. And losses. I assume that you have accounted for them," the Albino said evenly.

"The outcomes are worth the risks," Ungar replied. "A century ago, Europe ruled the world through its superior culture, its economic might, and its colonial ambitions. Then came the First World War, communism, fascism, nazism, and another war that obliterated all traces of the glorious Europe that was. The Second World War allowed those barbarians to enter the gate. It gave the Americans free rein over the fate of the entire world."

Ungar glanced up, at the painting of his great-grandfather, the man who'd catapulted his Swiss family to prominence in the banking industry.

"America's dominance ends now," he went on. "Though Europe can never beat the superpower militarily, there are other ways to bring defeat to your enemies."

"Yes, well . . . I'm going back to the compound and meet with Noor for the last time," the Albino said. "Then I'm heading to my apartment in Manhattan, where I'll prepare for the final strike in the morning."

"Very good," Ungar replied.

There was a long pause. "You're quite certain the other nations are ready to go along with this scheme?" the Albino asked at last.

"Europe is united and has once again become an economic powerhouse. It's only a matter of time before the euro outpaces the dollar in value. All I'm doing is expediting the inevitable," Ungar replied. "When I dump billions upon billions of dollars' worth of undervalued U.S. currency into the money markets, the Saudis and the Chinese will have no choice but to follow suit, and the sell-off will begin."

"Then the euro will replace the dollar as the world standard," the Albino concluded.

"And the United States will collapse into a mire of poverty from which it will never emerge. The balance of power will shift in Europe's favor once again, as it was meant to be."

The Albino chuckled. "A brave new world."

"Indeed," Ungar replied. "Who knows? In the twenty-first century, the poverty-stricken citizens of the new Third World America may welcome a modern wave of European colonialists. Then they can dine off the crumbs that fall from our tables."

1 2 3 4 5 6 **7** 8 9
10 11 12 13 14 15 16 17
18 19 20 21 22 23 24

. . . .

THE FOLLOWING TAKES PLACE
BETWEEN THE HOURS OF
1:00 P.M. AND 2:00 P.M.
EASTERN DAYLIGHT TIME

. . . .

1:00:32 P.M. EDT
Kurmastan, New Jersey

The eighty-eight martyrs squatted in subdued silence
inside the dining hall. Tables and chairs had been cleared
away and replaced by prayer rugs, dutifully positioned
so the supplicants would face Mecca. Old men and
young boys served them strong, bitter tea sweetened with
honey.

Farshid Amadani—the man they called "the Hawk"—
wisely abstained, though he waited with the rest for their
spiritual leader to address them from the raised platform
at the front of the room.

Earlier that morning, the martyrs had bid their final goodbyes to their families. They'd completed their ritual cleansing in the communal showers, and donned overalls and shoes that had never been worn. With skullcaps on their shorn heads, the men then proceeded to the mosque to pray.

Precisely at noon, Farshid Amadani had gone to the house of worship to collect them. Single file, he had led the procession out of the mosque and into one of the underground tunnels. He had marched them through a long, low-ceilinged corridor to a spacious chamber inside the main bunker.

There he had showed them what had been done to the infidel woman captured on their property the day before.

As their paramilitary trainer, the Hawk had been impressed by the martyrs' reactions.

He'd expected the older men—all felons convicted of violent crimes—to show no emotion when the miserable remains of the woman were displayed, and they did not disappoint him. But even the younger men, those who had not yet spilled blood, had hardened their hearts sufficiently to gaze at the grisly remains without flinching.

Truly these are the Warriors of God.

The Hawk noticed movement in the kitchen, and he knew Ibrahim Noor would soon appear. He settled onto his prayer rug and waited for their spiritual leader to arrive.

1:11:32 P.M. EDT
Warriors of God Community Center

From his vantage point behind a curtain that separated the dining hall from the kitchen, Ibrahim Noor watched his martyrs.

A powerfully built African American in his forties, Noor wore a skullcap over his shaven head. The prayer shawl on his broad shoulders did not cover the jailhouse tattoos that crisscrossed his bull neck, and his holy man's robes—a loose-fitting *shalwat kameez*—barely concealed the scars from multiple knife wounds and gunshots that puckered the flesh on his thick-muscled torso.

Noor waited for the powerful beverage to take effect before he deigned to make an appearance. Meanwhile the men nervously gulped cup after cup of the bitter brew, a concoction of tea laced with amphetamines and mingled with the same powerful steroids that had been pumped into his disciples since paramilitary exercises began many months ago.

The amphetamines were a stimulant created for, and then rejected by the NATO forces because they caused psychotic episodes. It had been supplied by Erno Tobias and his employer, the Swiss-based firm Rogan Pharmaceuticals. The food and water stored inside the trucks were laced with the same chemical. The dangerous potion would send his Warriors of God to the very edge of reason, where the urge to kill would be strong.

Already Noor observed the effects of the drug. After a few minutes the men began to perspire, then fidget on their prayer rugs. Voices became loud, almost shrill. Soon the drug-induced tension was palpable—then almost unbearable.

When the moment was right, Noor stepped through the curtains and mounted the platform. An almost fearful silence greeted him, all eyes following the massive man as he stepped up to the podium.

After an opening prayer, during which Noor seemed to slip into an almost mystical trance, the holy man opened his eyes again, and his intense gaze swept the room. There were men of many races present—Middle Easterners, Albanians, Afghanis, and Saudis among them—but the vast majority of the men in this room were African Americans, former inmates of the Federal and state prison systems.

"The Imam Ali Rahman al Sallifi sends his regards and his blessings to you, his *Shahid*, his Warriors of God," Noor began, his voice so low that men in the back of the room strained to hear him.

"The Imam wants you to know that with our actions and our sacrifices this day and in days to come, the world will take its first step on the long road to *Khilafah*, to a world ruled by Muslim law—"

Both cheers and imprecations greeted Noor's words. Men cried out in praise of God and the Imam, while they cursed the Great Satan America and her evil, godless allies. When the walls began to shake from their cries, Noor waved the men to silence, then his own voice boomed.

"To you, my *Shahid*, I repeat the words that Ali Rahman al Sallifi said to me when he came to me in my prison cell, ten years ago," Noor declared, his voice becoming louder with each word.

"This world does not want you, the Imam said. Because this world is diseased and decadent, it has no place for the Faithful. This world has no place for *you*, because you do not grasp for money, nor do you fornicate with tainted women. This world does not want you because of the color of your skin . . ."

Noor paused; his expression darkened.

"I wept when I heard those words because I knew they were true, and you know they are true, too. From the womb to the ghetto to the Great Satan's jails, that is the path the godless have set out for us! A path as deadly as the slavery they inflicted on our ancestors!"

Boos and catcalls greeted Noor's words.

"But do not despair, the Imam told me that day. Do not despair, Ibrahim, he said, because Allah wants you, and He has a special place in Paradise for all of His faithful servants . . ."

Noor's voice trailed off, until they feared he would say no more. But suddenly he cried out, the sound of his mighty voice shaking the rafters.

"It's *true*!" he roared, raising his arms and throwing his head back. "I know, for I have seen the place in Paradise reserved for each and every one of you! Your great mansion, your forty virgins, your seat at the One God's table."

The wild shouts swelled in volume, until they battered the ears of every man in the room. With difficulty, Noor waved the martyrs to silence.

"Today you will secure a place in Paradise. By defending the only true faith, you will take your place in a long line of martyrs," Noor continued. "Like our brothers in Palestine, in Sri Lanka, in Pakistan, in Egypt, and in Saudi Arabia, you will find favor with Allah, and you will never be forgotten."

Noor paused, as if to collect his thoughts.

"But you will not merely martyr yourselves," he continued, his voice tight with emotion. "You will become a warrior for the cause—a sword of God. And with that sword, you will take many thousands of infidels with you when you die. They will plunge into the fires of hell, while each one of you climbs to the very Gates of Paradise!"

The martyrs leaped to their feet, shook their fists in the air, and howled for the blood of the infidel.

"Your chariots await you!" Noor cried. "Go and smite the enemies of God. With each blow of your sword, cut out their lying tongues. Pierce their evil hearts with your spears. Open their throats with your knives! Blow them up with your explosives. Shoot them with your guns. Burn them with your fire!"

Faces contorted by hatred and anger, the narcotics magnifying their emotions, the men howled like maddened wolves.

"Go, Warriors of God," Noor shouted. "Shower destruction and death on our enemies and show no mercy toward the infidel's children or their women. Go! Go and smite the unfaithful. End this abomination and enslavement the West calls civilization. End it forever!"

"Yes!" Farshid Amadani cried when he heard his cue. He leaped in front of the podium, brandishing an AK–47 over his head.

"Come," bellowed the Hawk, "let us rain destruction down on the unfaithful!"

The martyrs burst from the Community Center and charged down Kurmastan's deserted main street. Crying for blood, they reached the factory and swarmed around their assigned trucks. Some ran final checks on the vehicles; others armed themselves from their cache of weapons.

The sound of roaring engines filled the hot afternoon. Diesel fumes belched, filling the compound with blue smoke. Then, one by one, the trucks rolled toward the gate.

As they rumbled through town, wives and children peeked out of their windows to watch the vehicles pass. They peered through dust kicked up by a hundred spinning wheels, hoping for a final glance at their husbands, their fathers, their brothers, their uncles.

Those billowing clouds hung over the tiny settlement long after the last truck rumbled through the security gate.

1:17:35 P.M. EDT
Central Ward
Newark, New Jersey

"I'm really sorry, Agent Almeida," the woman said, a frown curling her glossed lips. "On a good day, you can make this trip in twenty minutes, but that mess at the Holland Tunnel really set us back."

While she spoke, Rachel Delgado kept her eyes on the road. Tony Almeida, unaccustomed to riding in the passenger seat, mostly watched her.

"Don't apologize," he replied. "Anyway, the sign says that we're almost there."

Rachel slipped into the left lane. As she steered them onto the exit ramp, she gave Tony a sidelong glance.

"Next stop, Newark. My hometown."

They drove for a few minutes in silence. As in many urban areas, Newark's hospital was in the older part of town. Soon they reached a squalid street lined with graffiti-scarred bodegas, check-cashing outlets, liquor stores, and boarded-up businesses.

"Are you really from Newark?" Tony asked.

Rachel's eyes flashed with amusement. "Born and raised in University Heights, right here in the Central Ward. See that place with the tall fence and the barbed wire at the top? That's the junior high school I almost flunked out of."

She grinned. "Not the nicest community in America, maybe, but it's my hood."

Her expression was suddenly guarded. "I admit it wasn't easy. I made a lot of mistakes when I was young. But there were people who took an interest. Saw a future for me that I couldn't see."

"People?"

The silence hung heavy for a moment. "People," Rachel said at last. "Community groups. Mentors. Teachers. *People*. With their help, I got a college scholarship and a Get Out of Newark Free card."

At a traffic light, she faced Tony. "You have that look, you know."

Tony frowned. "Look? What look?"

"That swagger. Don't con a con man. You were a street kid, too, Agent Almeida."

Tony snorted, and a smile flashed across his guarded face. "Yeah. And call me Tony."

Rachel waited a moment, then two, for Tony to say more, but he stopped talking. Finally, she nodded. "Okay, Mr. Mysterious. I get it. Chitchat's over and it's back to business. There's the hospital, anyway."

Rachel twisted the steering wheel. Tires squealed in protest, and the van swerved into the visitors' parking lot.

1:26:06 P.M. EDT
The Novelty Inn, off Route 12
Clinton, New Jersey

Brice Holman stepped out of the shabby motel room, into the harsh glare of the afternoon sun. Head throbbing, he slipped a pair of dark glasses over his eyes, then popped the top of a small bottle of Advil with his teeth. He quickly gulped down the last three pills dry, then tossed the plastic bottle into a trash bin.

Holman had checked into the Novelty Inn a few hours before. As soon as he got to the room, he had showered and shaved. Still dripping, he tried to call Judy Foy again, and then again, but got only her voice mail. He wanted to call Jason Emmerick next, to see if the two "packages" had arrived on the Montreal to Newark flight, but it was just too risky.

Bad enough Emmerick and his partner, Leight, were

communicating with Judy nearly every day. At least the three of them had concocted a phony cover story about a smuggling ring working out of Newark International to cover their tracks.

If Holman tried to contact Emmerick, it would set off alarms at the Bureau and prompt an investigation that might compromise, or even expose the rogue operation.

Better to wait for the rendezvous at noon, Holman had decided. He could talk to the two FBI agents then.

But noon came and went with no sign of Emmerick or Leight. When Holman finally relented and called them, he got voice mail and left no message.

By one P.M., Holmen knew something had gone wrong. Either the situation at the compound was exploding, and Foy, Emmerick, and Leight were caught up in it. Or his Deputy Director and the two FBI agents had been taken into custody by their superiors, the rogue operation exposed. If that was the case, they were looking for him right now.

Either way, Holman was effectively alone. He knew he had to act, had to get inside that compound in Kurmastan. Unfortunately, there was only one way to do that, now, and it involved endangering civilians who might already be in danger.

His decision made, Holman hurriedly dressed in fresh clothes and left the motel room. His destination was the Nazareth Unitarian Church in Milton, New Jersey, where a group led by United States Congresswoman Hailey Williams and the pastor, Reverend James Wendell Ahern, were scheduled to travel to the compound and meet with one of its leaders, Ibrahim Noor.

As Holman guided his Ford Explorer out of the motel parking lot, he watched a truck rumble down Route 12, heading west. Holman realized the vehicle was from Kurmastan when he saw the Dreizehn Trucking logo on the unpainted aluminum trailer.

Holman wondered if the truck was carrying cardboard containers, or a more deadly cargo, like the one he'd seen earlier. If he was lucky, he'd know in a few hours.

Minutes later, Holman spied another Dreizehn Trucking trailer roar past him on the highway. This time he managed to snap a few pictures with the secure CTU cell phone camera, including a close-up of the license plate, before the truck roared around the bend and out of sight.

With a grim feeling that something ominous was stirring, Holman headed for the tiny town of Milton, on the banks of the Delaware River.

1:32:14 P.M. EDT
Security Station One
CTU Headquarters, NYC

As soon as Jack Bauer returned to CTU Headquarters, he cleaned up and changed back into his own clothes. Sandy hair still damp, he summoned Morris and Layla to the security station.

"The bombers were Serbian," Jack declared.

Morris appeared skeptical. "Serbs working with Muslims? That doesn't make sense."

The screen behind O'Brian displayed images of personnel from the NYPD Bomb Squad. The officers were swarming the roof and ascending the microwave tower on One World Trade Center, collecting the bombs that Jack had defused.

"I know about the religious tensions in Eastern Europe better than anyone," Jack said. "But those men were Serbs. I know because I spoke to one of them in his own language."

Jack rubbed his forearm, where traces of ink still lingered. "That man definitely recognized the 13 tattoo, and took me for an ally because I had one on my arm. It fooled him, long enough for me to get the drop on him, anyway."

"Yet neither of these men had the 13 tattoo on any part of their bodies," Layla observed. "Neither did the PA policeman."

Morris shook his head. "Curiouser and curiouser."

"What did you learn from that Port Authority cop?" Jack demanded.

"He admitted his guilt immediately," said Layla. "He claimed that he took a bribe to give those men access to the roof. They told him they were putting a device on the tower to steal cable signals."

"And the idiot bought it?" Morris cried.

Layla shrugged. "He didn't appear to be particularly bright."

Jack glanced at the security camera images of the bomb squad at work. "There's more to this than a bunch of paramilitary fanatics on a compound in New Jersey. We have to find out what the 13 symbol means and how it's connected to the compound at Kurmastan. And we need to know who's paying for out-of-town attack teams like the Serbs, and the hit men who tried to assassinate my team this morning."

"You think it's all connected?" Layla asked.

Bauer ignored the question, posed his own. "Do you know of any mystical, cultural, or political meaning to the number 13 in the Islamic faith?"

Frowning, Layla closed her laptop. Jack sensed her anger.

"Is something wrong with my question?"

Layla nodded. "Earlier, you asked me why I was here in New York, and not at Langley, using my language skills to monitor the chatter among Middle Eastern terrorists."

"That's right, I did."

Layla's dark eyes remained fixed on the laptop. "Here's my honest answer," she said. "These people on the compound, and the imams who inspire them, they are atavisms, perverted throwbacks to the seventh century. Medieval monsters who hearken back to a dark and terrible time. Their beliefs are an affront to reason. Frankly, as a Muslim—former Muslim, in my case—they are an embarrassment."

"You've lost your faith, then?" Jack asked.

Layla looked up. "I've *rejected* it, Special Agent Bauer. My religion. My heritage. All of it."

"Listen," Jack said. "My last name. Bauer. It means 'farmer' in German."

"So?" Layla replied.

"So I'm German. Should I be ashamed?"

She blinked. "Ashamed of what?"

"The Nazis? They brought Europe to its knees. They

are responsible for the Holocaust. That's my heritage, according to your logic."

Layla shook her head. "That's not a reasonable comparison," she replied. "For starters, nazism was a political movement, not a religious jihad. And the only American religious community with roots in Germany are the Amish. And as far as I know, the Pennsylvania Dutch are not a pack of paramilitary fanatics."

Morris chuckled. "She's got you by the bollocks on that one, Jack-o."

"As an American, I choose to live in *this* century," Layla continued. "And as a woman, I have no desire to spend my life in a burka, or in an arranged marriage, or traded for a goat."

"There are bad seeds in every race, creed, and religion," Jack argued.

"Please, not *that* lecture," Layla said. "I've heard it enough. From my stepfather. From my mother, too, a woman who should know better."

Jack opened his mouth. Layla silenced him with a raised hand.

"You won't change my mind, Agent Bauer." Her expression was resolute. "And for the record, we'll get along better if you don't even try." Then Layla Abernathy rose, unplugged the laptop, and tucked it under her arm. "If you need me, I'll be in my office."

1:53:46 P.M. EDT
Newark General Hospital

Tony Almeida folded his arms as the doctor briefed him. The physician was young, barely out of residency, but from his attitude, Tony sensed the man had already seen it all. While he spoke, the diminutive Asian American peered through the door, at the woman stretched out on the hospital bed.

"Ms. Foy's car was broadsided by a pickup truck," Dr. Lei said. "A stolen pickup truck, according to the police. She has seven stitches above her hairline to close a gash in her head. I've just checked the X-rays and there's no sign of a fracture, so at worst she's suffering from a concussion. That's the extent of her injuries, except for a few bruised ribs.

"She was fortunate, Mr. Almeida. Very fortunate. The air bag saved her life. I'm keeping her here overnight, for observation, but I'll most likely sign her release papers in the morning."

Tony nodded. "I need to speak with her immediately."

Dr. Lei shrugged. "She's on pain management, but otherwise she's alert. Just try not to get her too excited."

"Got it, doc," Tony replied. Dr. Lei moved on to his next patient.

Tony signaled Rachel Delgado, who was waiting at the nurses' station. They entered the room together.

Judith Foy appeared small and pale and frail on the huge hospital bed. Her head was propped, and an IV tube ran from a bottle into her arm. Her shaggy red hair stuck out from under the bandages wound around her head. Tony noticed some swelling around her nose and eyes—probably the results of the air bag deployment.

"Deputy Director Foy. I need to speak with you," Tony began.

The woman's eyes narrowed. "Who the hell are you?" she demanded in a surprisingly strong voice.

"My name's Almeida. I'm from CTU."

"Then why haven't I ever seen you before?"

"I'm from Los Angeles Headquarters."

"Oh, right. The consultants from the West Coast." The woman's deep azure eyes drifted to Rachel Delgado. "I've seen you before."

Rachel nodded. "At the orientation meeting a few weeks ago, Deputy Director. That was during our first tour of the new facility."

"Delgado, right? You're in Security."

Rachel nodded.

"I need to speak with you," Tony said. "About the ongoing operation that you and Director Holman are involved in. The *rogue* operation."

The woman shifted in her bed. "I don't know what you're talking about," she said evenly.

"We know that it involves the New Jersey settlement called Kurmastan," Tony continued. 'We know at least two agents from another government agency are involved—illegally involved."

Judith Foy's eyes shifted like a trapped animal. Then she faced Tony. "I'll talk," she said. "But only to you. Agent Delgado has to go."

"Agent Delgado is a security agent from your own division."

"She's out, *now*, or you both can leave and I'll do my talking to a lawyer. It's up to you." Judith Foy crossed her arms and turned her head, to stare out the window.

"I'll be at the nurses' station," Rachel said.

When she was gone, Tony closed the door behind her and returned to the side of the bed. Deputy Director Foy looked up. Tony could see the pain and trauma etched on her face.

"I'm sorry I had to do that, but I'm taking orders directly from Brice Holman," Judith Foy began. "Holman told me not to trust anyone at CTU New York. He said there were several security breaches at our temporary offices in Battery Park. And then last week, when Holman transferred his files to the new mainframe, there was an attempt to raid his personal database and crack his private surveillance files."

She touched her head, winced. "After that, Brice added many levels of additional locks to thwart more attacks."

"That's all you know?" Tony asked suspiciously.

"There have been other leaks . . ."

Her voice trailed off when she saw the doubt on Tony's face. "You don't believe me," she said.

"Who are the agents you're working with?"

Judith Foy seemed to ponder Tony's question, then nodded as if she'd made up her mind about something. "Their names are Jason Emmerick and Douglas Leight. They both work out of the New York office of the FBI."

"Where are they now?"

"I have no idea."

Tony frowned. "Where is Brice Holman?"

She shook her head. "I couldn't tell you."

"Why were you in Newark today?"

Judith Foy told Tony about the two men who arrived on the flight out of Montreal, how she and the FBI agents followed the men when they split up—she on the tail of one car, Emmerick and Leight on the other.

"How did you know these men were coming to the United States in the first place?" Tony asked.

"The FBI picked up some chatter between Ibrahim Noor and a guy named Farshid Amadani, a.k.a. the Hawk. Amadani is a known terrorist and a paramilitary instructor. Lately he's been acting as sort of go-between for the Warriors of God. The big guys, Ibrahim Noor and al Sallifi himself, never leave the compound. It was Special Agent Emmerick who passed the intelligence on to Brice and me."

"Do you know the names of the two men who got off the airplane?" Tony asked.

"One was Amadani himself, whom—surprise, surprise—we didn't even know was coming back to the country. The other man was traveling under the name Faoud S. Mubajii, supposedly from Quebec. But that identity could be a phony. I didn't have time to run a check on him."

Tony sensed anger and frustration in the woman's voice; he also believed she was telling the truth, though it wasn't his call to make.

"Can you describe him?" Tony asked.

"I can do better than that," she replied. "I shot pictures—

even some close-ups—at the airport this morning. The digital camera is in my purse, which was in my car—"

"Then it's in the hospital property room," Tony said.

"Get it, Agent Almeida. Before someone else does."

"Someone else? Like who?"

"Listen, what happened to me wasn't an accident. They knew I was following them and they set me up to be killed. They might try to get my stuff next—or they might try to kill me again and succeed this time."

Tony nodded. "All right, I'll get the camera."

"Get my cell phone, too. I have Emmerick's and Leight's numbers stored inside. If you don't believe what I told you, you can talk to them and they'll back me up. At this point, I don't think secrecy matters anymore."

The woman touched the IV needle in her arm. "I think something bigger is going on," she said.

"I'm gone." Tony moved to the door.

"One more thing, Agent Almeida . . ."

He paused, one hand on the doorknob.

"I have a cyber lock on the camera's digital contents. If you try to retrieve the data without my password, you'll lose it all."

Tony nodded. "At least I know where I stand."

"I've been an agent too long to trust anyone," said Foy.

In the busy hallway, Tony saw Rachel Delgado. The moment she noticed him, she closed her cell phone.

Who was she speaking to? Tony wondered.

"Do you have a weapon?" he asked, walking up to her.

"Standard nine-millimeter." Rachel held up the bag on her shoulder.

"Guard Deputy Director Foy's door," he commanded. "Don't let anyone in or out except Dr. Lei and the nurses—and then I want you with them the whole time."

"What's going on?"

"Just do it," Tony replied. "I'll be right back."

1:59:16 P.M. EDT
Property Room
Newark General Hospital

The property room was adjacent to the hospital morgue, and the two departments shared the same security desk, which Alexi Szudamenko found suitably moronic.

Sure, some of the stuff in the property room was probably valuable, but who would want a corpse?

With his Russian father and Polish mother, Alexi had emigrated from Krakow with his parents in the early 1980s, when he was just a boy. But even after twelve years living in nearby Jersey City, he still didn't quite understand why Americans did some of the things they did.

Like guard dead people.

Alexi pulled the collar of his dark blue security uniform tight. It might be a warm spring afternoon outside, but down here in the basement things got chilly. The reason for the arctic temperatures was cold air seeping out of the morgue's massive refrigeration unit. The constant risk of frostbite made this particular security posting unpleasant. But at least Alexi didn't have to deal with the public, which was infinitely worse than sitting between drawers full of dead people and a wall of steel lockboxes for eight hours a day.

At least it was quiet. So quiet that Alexi sat down behind the security desk and pulled the latest issue of *Live Nude Girls* out of the drawer. He was just about to open the cover when the intercom buzzed.

Sighing, the big man tossed the glossy magazine back into the drawer and crossed to the door. Running his hand through his light brown hair, he punched the intercom button. "Yes?"

"I need to see someone in the properties department," a voice replied. Alexi looked up at the security monitor. A dark-haired Hispanic man stood on the other side of the door.

Alexi threw the lock and opened the door. "Can I help—"

The silenced weapon barked twice. Alexi stumbled backward, but eerily, he remained on his feet despite the twin holes over his heart.

The man stepped through the door and closed it behind him. Then he shot the guard again.

This time Alexi's knees gave out and he dropped to the tiled floor, one leg out, the other folded under him.

. . . .

THE FOLLOWING TAKES PLACE
BETWEEN THE HOURS OF
2:00 P.M. AND 3:00 P.M.
EASTERN DAYLIGHT TIME

. . . .

2:02:06 P.M. EDT
Security Station One
CTU Headquarters, NYC

Jack summoned his team to the security station for a brief-
ing by Morris O'Brian. He leaned with folded arms against
a desk while the cyber technician spoke.

"This morning, when Brice Holman refused to answer
our friendly phone calls, I followed CTU protocol and
issued a trace command on his cell phone."

"A trace command? What's that?" Layla interrupted.

Morris glanced at Jack, then smiled indulgently. "I used
the unique identifiers on Holman's phone to trace its activ-

ity. Nothing happens when the man's phone is turned off, of course. But as soon as he turns it on, the trace commands imbedded in the telecommunications grid automatically attempt to triangulate his position, and then forward the data to me."

"So what have you got?" Jack demanded. He moved behind Morris's chair to stand over the man.

Peter Randall was there, too, doe-eyed behind his round glasses. Despite his boyish demeanor, Randall had assumed responsibility for internal security in Tony Almeida's and Rachel Delgado's absence.

In the last hour, he'd proved to be a valuable asset. Randall had determined the intruders killed on the roof of CTU Headquarters had entered through the parking garage, and his security team also found the bodies of the murdered guards behind some parked cars.

Now they were hunting a third accomplice, clad in a good copy of a CTU uniform. He had been taped fleeing the scene by the reactivated security cam inside the parking garage, around the same time the firefight broke out on the roof.

"Here's the skinny, Jack-o," Morris replied. "At twelve twenty-eight this afternoon, Holman activated his phone for approximately thirty-nine seconds—not long enough to triangulate his position with any sort of accuracy, but I did learn that the low-power transmission from his cell went to a switch in the farming community of Alpha, New Jersey—"

Layla interrupted again. "A switch? What kind of switch?"

"Darling," Morris said patiently. "In mobile lingo, or as you call it in the colonies, in *cell phone* lingo, a switch is a transmission tower."

"So Director Holman is in Alpha, New Jersey?"

"I didn't say that, luv. I said his cell phone signal came to the tower in Alpha. But you are correct, in a sense. Director Holman is not far away. Cell phone signals are weak. CTU's phones are better than most, but they only have a range of thirteen kilometers."

Morris looked up at Jack Bauer, who peered over his shoulder at the grid map up on the HD computer monitor.

"About twenty minutes ago, Holman tried using his phone again. It was only activated for fifty-two seconds, but this signal went to different place . . . a tower in Clinton, New Jersey. Using the location of the prior call and this one, I was able to triangulate his position. Assuming he hasn't moved, I know where Holman is."

"Where?" Jack demanded, though he thought he already knew the answer.

"He's in a town called Milton, New Jersey. A picturesque little community on the Delaware River. According to our geographic database, parts of the Erie Canal still exist in the area—"

"Cut the regional history tour and show me the map."

"All right, Jack-o." Morris tapped a key, and a flashing red dot appeared on the grid. "That's Milton."

Jack nodded. "Where's Kurmastan?"

Layla moved behind him while Morris tapped another key. Instantly a second blip appeared, nearly on top of the first.

"Now we know where Director Holman is," Layla said. "But what is he doing there? And why hasn't he responded to our calls?"

"We're going to find out the answer, right now." Jack faced Peter Randall. "Where are your choppers?"

"Two blocks away," Randall replied. "There's a secure compound on the banks of the Hudson River. The detention block is there, too."

"Alert them," Jack said. "Tell them to prep a helicopter, and get clearance for an immediate takeoff. Tell them they're carrying two passengers to Milton, New Jersey."

Jack turned to Layla. "You'll need your weapon for this trip. And tactical assault gear, too."

The woman's lips parted in surprise. "You're taking me?"

"You wanted fieldwork, didn't you?"

"I . . . I'll secure my gear from the armory," Layla stammered.

2:16:06 P.M. EDT
Property Room
Newark General Hospital

It took Tony a while to locate the property room. Finally, he cornered an orderly in the ER and asked him where to go.

"Through that door over there and down one flight. You make a left and follow the corridor. The property room will be on your right. You can't miss it. The sign on the door says morgue."

Tony frowned. "Morgue?"

The orderly shrugged. "That's the way it is, mon."

Tony thanked the man and entered the stairwell. He took the stairs two at a time, the heels of his shoes clicking hollowly in the cavernous space.

At the bottom of the steps, Tony bumped into a youth in a white smock.

"Sorry," he muttered.

The dark-haired Hispanic did not reply. Hands in his bulging pockets, he hurried up the stairs. Tony shrugged off the encounter and followed the corridor until he spotted the door to the morgue. To his surprise it was ajar, cool air from the massive refrigerators streaming into the stuffy corridor.

Suspicious, Tony slipped his hand into his jacket and drew the Glock from its holster. He peered around the open door, into the room. A security guard was sprawled on the floor. Tony moved forward, examined the guard. *Dead.* Then he noticed the banks of steel lockers lining one wall.

The one marked "Room 424" had been pried open. The axe used for the job lay on the floor. Tony stepped around the corpse and examined the contents of the small square locker. Agent Foy's purse, wallet, and CTU ID were still inside, but her cell phone and the digital surveillance camera were both gone.

Tony cursed, recalling the man who'd bumped him. Glock pointed at the floor, he chased after him, certain the Hispanic youth was the culprit.

In the corridor, Tony collided with a nurse. "Call the

police," he told her. "The security guard in the morgue has been shot."

2:19:36 P.M. EDT
Administration Level B
Newark General Hospital

The woman saw the gun clutched in the dark-haired man's hand, and her eyes went wide. The man turned his back on her, raced up the stairs and out of sight.

Alarmed, the nurse proceeded to the morgue and pushed through the door. Only after she saw the man on the ground, and checked his pulse, did the woman use the emergency phone to call the security desk.

She reported the murder, and gave the security chief a description of the dark-haired man she'd bumped into.

"He still has the gun! I saw it . . ."

2:28:42 P.M. EDT
On the road to Kurmastan, New Jersey

Inside the church bus, Brice Holman sat beside a scare-crow of a woman named Mrs. Hocklinger. During the entire trip from the Nazareth Unitarian Church of Milton, New Jersey, she'd spoken only once. As they pulled out of the church parking lot, Mrs. Hocklinger used the con-descending tone of an elementary schoolteacher to order Holman to fasten his seatbelt.

Now, as the minibus rumbled along a narrow rural road, the Reverend James Wendell Ahern closed the issue of *Sojourners* magazine he'd been reading and tapped it against his knee.

"I'm really surprised to see anyone from the press here today, Mr. Holman," the Reverend said, turning to face him. "Outreach to other faiths and other cultures doesn't sell newspapers, I'm told. And since the Congresswoman had to cancel at the last minute—"

"Good riddance, I say," an older man interrupted from the back row. "We all know Congresswoman Williams is in bed with these people. She's defended that crazy mullah or wallah or whatever they call him—"

Reverend Ahern raised a hand. "The Imam's name is Ali Rahman al Sallifi, Mr. Simonson."

The older man sneered. "If you know his name, then you know this Sallifi character is wanted by the law in his native country. He's a terrorist."

Reverend Ahern offered the man a patronizing smile. "You have to understand, countries like Egypt and Pakistan have repressive governments. Imam Ali Rahman al Sallifi tried to practice his personal brand of Islam in peace, but was forced to flee. That's why he came to America, for the right to practice his faith without persecution."

Simonson waved a dismissive hand. "Fine. I'll wait and see what the Grand Poobah has to say for himself."

Ahern fixed his wide-eyed stare on Brice Holman. "You see what I'm up against. There's a tragic mistrust of the stranger, the other, even among the members of my own flock."

"Yet you strive always to be a unifying force," Holman said. "That's why New Jersey Cable One sent me here, to cover this story."

"You brought no cameras," Ahern noted.

"I didn't want to be too . . . intimidating," Holman lied. "I'll certainly conduct on-camera interviews later, with you and perhaps Ali Rahman al Sallifi, if he'll speak with us."

"He agreed to meet with my group today, which is certainly a breakthrough. Imam al Sallifi is a private man, very spiritual."

Holman raised an eyebrow. "So you've met the Imam?"

"I'm told," Ahern amended. "I've met with the Imam's disciple, Ibrahim Noor, several times. He's a fascinating figure. A former gang leader and convicted felon who found redemption through faith. His is a story we can all learn from."

"Indeed," Holman replied.

"Excuse me, Reverend Ahern," Mrs. Reed called from behind the steering wheel. "I think that's our turn up ahead."

"Yes, that's the turn, Emily," the Reverend declared, "We're to make a left and follow the road for about a mile, until we see the gate."

Mrs. Reed nodded and slowed for the turn. Reverend Ahern faced the other passengers in the minibus.

"Again, I want to apologize on behalf of Congresswoman Hailey Williams," he said. "She was quite eager to make the trip, but legislative duties prevented her from joining us."

Brice Holman shook his head. *If the Reverend had half a brain, he'd know Congress is on spring break—which is why Congresswoman Williams is in her home district, instead of Washington.*

Whatever's going on here stinks, thought Brice. *But at least it will get me inside that compound.*

Beside Mrs. Hocklinger, a teenager named Danielle Taylor fidgeted nervously. Holman had originally estimated her age at fifteen or sixteen, but upped it when Reverend Ahern mentioned she would be attending Columbia University in the fall.

Dani was here because of an incident that had occurred several months ago.

Her dog had broken from its leash and wandered into the compound. Dani had gone in after it, and found the dog dead—shot—and two men with guns standing over the corpse. When she demanded to know why they had killed her pet, one of the men sneered and declared that "soon all dogs will die."

Instead of being intimidated, Dani had filed animal cruelty charges against those two men. A court date was still pending.

The minibus swerved onto a narrow road that was pitted and bumpy. Emily Reed switched to low gear, and they climbed a short rise. At the crest of the hill, the front tire bounced off a particularly deep pothole.

"With all the taxes they charge us, you'd think they could fix these roads," Mr. Simonson grumbled.

"It's the trucks from the cardboard factory," Mr. Cranston explained. "Those semis really tear up the highway."

Joseph Cranston told Holman he was a retiree from New York City, who used to be an engineer for the Bridge and Tunnel Authority.

"I really hope to get a look inside that factory," Cranston continued. "It's the oldest paper fabrication facility in the country."

Abby Cranston pointed. "Look, there's the front gate."

"Does that man have a gun?" Emily Reed cried.

Reverend Ahern swallowed hard. "Slow down and I'll have a word with him."

But as the bus approached the gate, the old man with the rifle slung over his shoulder smiled and motioned them forward. Another man limped out of the guardhouse, offering them a toothless grin. He carried no rifle, but there was a .22-caliber handgun tucked in the belt around his *shalwat kameez*. Together, the two men swung the chain-link and barbed-wire gate open to admit them.

Ahern visibly relaxed. "I told you they were expecting us."

Holman studied the guards as the bus passed through the gate.

In weeks of surveillance, he'd never seen the main gate guarded by anyone but tough-looking former felons in their prime, all of them Americans. But these two guys looked Middle Eastern, and they were probably pushing eighty.

Reverend Ahern pulled a copy of Ibrahim Noor's e-mail out of the pocket of his black shirt. As he read, he adjusted his clerical collar.

"Just go straight ahead until you reach the Community Center," he told the driver.

The bus bumped through the center of town. To Holman the place seemed abandoned. Of course, the men were probably working at the factory, but the women should have been out and about.

Finally, a man with a rifle slung across his back stepped in their path, waving his arms.

"I think he wants us to stop," Ahern said.

The bus halted in a cloud of dust, in front of a large building made of unpainted cinder blocks. The aluminum screen door opened, and a woman in a black burka exited the building. Though her features were obscured, she carried a bundle of flowers in her tattooed hands.

"That's nice," Mrs. Cranston said.

Emily cut the engine, and Reverend Ahern opened the sliding door. Before he could step out, a howling mob of people burst from the Community Center and charged the bus. Another mob rushed out of the communal baths next door. They were women, mostly, along with a smattering of young boys and girls and old men. The males had guns. The women carried knives, clubs, axes.

The mob swarmed the bus, threatening to tip the vehicle over on its side. Reverend Ahern was assaulted and pummeled into unconsciousness. Emily Reed tried to restart the engine and drive away, but an old man fired an ancient pistol at her through the windshield. The bullet struck her right eye, killing the woman instantly.

Brice Holman kicked the first person to reach for him. The woman howled and fell to the floor. Clawing and screaming like animals, the rest of the pack crushed her in an effort to get at the passengers.

Holman heard Dani scream. Mr. Simonson lunged at the women attacking the teenager, knocked them aside. Then someone stuck the man in the throat with a machete. He went down spewing blood.

Holman lashed out again, his fist striking flesh. Then someone struck him on the back of the head and his world went dark . . .

2:39:06 P.M. EDT
Newark General Hospital

Tony Almeida ducked behind a pillar and observed the white-smocked kid he fingered for the murder of the guard. The Hispanic youth was standing near the ER, talking into a cell phone. No doubt he was reporting his situation, which was dire.

Fifteen minutes ago, Tony discovered that hospital security and the Newark Police had sealed the hospital exits, effectively trapping the murderer inside the facility.

Almeida had located the punk at around the same time, but decided not to move against him in the crowded lobby. Tony watched while the killer drifted over to an emergency fire exit, preparing to push through. He got a surprise when the door suddenly opened from the outside, and two uniformed cops entered—and walked right past him.

The close call obviously spooked the youth. Still on the phone, he slipped into a nearby stairwell. Tony followed, pausing at the steel door long enough to turn off his own cell—the last thing he needed was the phone to ring.

As soon as he entered the stairwell, Tony heard the man's muffled voice, his footsteps on the stairs. Cautiously, Tony climbed, Glock in hand. It took five flights before he finally caught up with the kid. The youth had just ended his call and was heading back the way he came.

Tony leveled his gun on the punk, who stumbled backward, tripping on the steps. The kid fell onto the fifth-floor landing.

"Don't move or I'll shoot," Tony said evenly.

On his back, the kid threw up his arms. He couldn't have been more than seventeen or eighteen, and he seemed very frightened. Tony had to remind himself that this fresh-faced kid was old enough to murder a security guard in cold blood, then steal evidence of a possible terrorist plot.

Tony slowly approached him. "Show me your weapon and get up," he commanded.

Eyes twitching, the kid shook his head. "I already dumped the gun. In a garbage can," he said, getting to his feet. The youth had high cheekbones; narrow, catlike eyes; and so many twitches, Tony thought he might be overdosing on cocaine.

"Colombian?" Tony asked, one hand covering him while the other rifled through the pockets of his white smock.

Head shaky, the youth nodded. Tony located Foy's digital camera and cell phone and pocketed both.

"Okay," Tony said. "Now we're going downstairs."

Tony gestured with his Glock. As soon as the barrel wavered, the Colombian bolted. As the teenager raced up the final flight of stairs, Tony drew a bead at his broad back—but didn't pull the trigger.

Better to take him alive. CTU can't interrogate a dead man.

Deep inside, Tony knew the truth. He didn't want to cap someone so young.

Taking the stairs two at a time, Tony reached an emergency exit and burst through the door, expecting to come out on the roof. Instead, he emerged on a narrow, dead-end catwalk six stories above the parking lot.

When the Colombian heard the door open, he whirled to face Tony. The youth was panting, his face shiny with sweat—almost as if he was coming off some kind of drug high. Tony aimed the Glock at the punk's heart.

"Come on, kid, give it up," he called. "This time I will shoot."

The youth wavered. Then he yanked the smock off his shoulders and leaped onto the rail. As the white coat fluttered to the concrete below, the youth threw up his arms.

"No! Wait!" Tony cried.

Stumbling forward, Tony spied a tattoo of the number 13 on the Colombian's forearm. He dropped the Glock and reached out to snatch the youth—too late.

Without uttering a sound, the Colombian dived headfirst off the catwalk. A moment later, his body slammed into a Cadillac parked in the physicians-only lot. The impact crumpled the roof and triggered the alarm.

Tony pulled the cell phone out of his pocket to call Agent Delgado, but as soon as he activated it, he discovered an urgent message from Morris O'Brian back at CTU Headquarters in New York.

Frowning, he played it back.

2:59:28 P.M. EDT
Room 424
Newark General Hospital

"I understand," Rachel Delgado said into her cell. "I'll take care of everything here. You don't have to worry about it."

Rachel had been lingering outside Deputy Director's Foy's hospital room for almost an hour. Scrupulously following Tony Almeida's last command, she hadn't let anyone in or out of room 424.

Now she'd received new instructions. Agent Delgado closed the phone and tucked it into her purse beside the 9mm handgun. She scanned the area.

The doctors had made their rounds; the nurses had administered the afternoon meds. Most of the staff was gathered around the nurses' station, waiting for the shift change at three-fifteen. With luck, Rachel Delgado would be finished by then. Finished and long gone.

Rachel peeked through the tiny window in the door of the private room. Judith Foy was asleep, her bandaged head lolling on the pillow. Quietly, she slipped through the door and approached the bed.

Rachel dropped her purse in the chair and leaned close, to examine the woman. Foy was definitely asleep. Her breathing was even, and she was snoring a little.

Circling the bed, Rachel looked around for the right tool for the job. She grinned when she fingered the IV tube running from the clear plastic bag into Judith Foy's arm.

Rachel gently disconnected the plastic tube at the flow

meter joint. Then she pulled the long tube free from the IV bottle. While the solution trickled onto the faux-hardwood floor, Rachel wrapped the plastic around both hands, to create a garrote.

Rachel paused for a moment while an orderly drifted past the door, heading for the nurses' station. When the man was out of sight, Delgado loomed over Judith Foy.

In one quick motion, Rachel slipped the strangling cord around the sleeping woman's throat and pulled it tight . . .

. . . .

THE FOLLOWING TAKES PLACE
BETWEEN THE HOURS OF
3:00 P.M. AND 4:00 P.M.
EASTERN DAYLIGHT TIME

. . . .

3:00:00 P.M. EDT
CTU Heliport
Hudson River

In his right hand, Jack Bauer clutched the cell phone to his head. With his left, he covered his ear to shut out the high-pitched whine of the turboshaft engines.

He was standing on a concrete pier at the edge of the water. A Sikorsky S–76 "Spirit" helicopter idled behind him, its wide, composite blades cutting the humid air. A barge streamed up the Hudson, leaving a roiling wake as it passed.

"Any word from Tony?" Jack asked Morris back at CTU Headquarters.

"We've got a problem on that score," Morris replied. "Apparently a man fitting Agent Almeida's description is wanted in connection with the murder of a security guard at Newark General Hospital."

Jack cursed. "That has to be a mistake."

"You'd think so, wouldn't you? Except that the Newark Police received an *anonymous* tip five minutes ago. And the tipster gave Tony's name. Our boy's been framed, Jack-o."

Jack's mind raced. *Another leak at CTU. But who's the mole?*

"You've got to warn him," he ordered Morris.

"I have, by voice mail," Morris said. "We haven't been able to reach Tony *or* Rachel Delgado, the agent who accompanied him to Newark. Frankly, I fear the worst."

"Almeida can take care of himself," Jack said, dismissing that problem for now. "I want you to keep monitoring Brice Holman's signal. I'll keep this line open for any updates. I'll need to know his exact location once I reach Milton."

"Better move, Jack. Or Holman might not be there when you arrive."

Jack glanced at the idling helicopter and cursed again. "We're leaving right now," he told Morris. Then he ended the call.

He walked up to Layla Abernathy. She stood on the tarmac, blinking against the dust, her hair twisting in the wind. A heavy duffel bag was slung over her shoulder. As Jack approached, she lowered her own cell phone.

"I'm still trying to get clearance," she explained. "I'm on hold with the Deputy Mayor's office."

Jack reached up, his hand covering her fingers. He closed the phone in her hand. "We've waited twenty minutes. That's already too long—"

"I can't convince the authorities, Agent Bauer!" Layla shouted to be heard over the noise. "If they thought it was a real emergency, we'd get immediate clearance. But—"

"We're going," Jack said. "Now."

He took the bag from her shoulder, tossed it into the cabin. Then he guided Layla through the hatch. The interior of the S–76 Spirit was almost spacious—large enough to seat an assault team of eight, along with their special equipment.

Jack thrust Layla into a seat. "Strap in," he commanded.

Then he moved to the cockpit.

The pilot and copilot wore dark blue CTU flight suits, and helmets with visors and interior headsets. The man in the pilot's seat had a CTU Rapid-Strike Team patch on his chest, and a Glock on his belt. His name tag read "Fogarty."

"Take off," Jack said.

"We can't, sir," Captain Fogarty replied. "We've been denied clearance—"

Bauer's eyes flashed angrily. "Take off now. On my authority."

"Sir, I can't. I could lose my job—"

"Listen," Jack rasped. "Director Holman is in danger. There's already been an attempt on Deputy Director Foy's life. She's in a hospital now and I don't know her condition. Unless you want to be responsible for the death of your boss, I suggest you take off immediately."

Fogarty frowned, then shifted his unhappy gaze to the copilot. "Prepare for takeoff," he said.

The whine of the turboshaft increased in volume. With an abrupt lurch, the helicopter lifted off the pier and swooped over the river. The landing gear retracted before the aircraft banked and shifted direction, heading due west at a hundred and fifty miles per hour.

3:02:21 P.M. EDT
Room 424
Newark General Hospital

Lucky break, Tony Almeida mused, seeing the birthday party at the nurses' station. *First one I've had all day.*

Two doctors, three nurses, and an orderly were laughing and talking and eating cake. Best of all, they were not paying attention to him.

Tony moved quickly down the hall, toward room 424.

Now that he was a hunted man, Tony knew he had to proceed with caution. When he didn't see Rachel Delgado outside the room, he increased his pace.

Tony knew the enemy who had dispatched the Colombian might have sent another assassin to finish off Judith Foy. If Rachel got in the way, they'd kill her, too. Tony's heart pounded.

What if I'm too late?

He reached the room and quietly slipped through the

door—then Tony heard a muffled cry. He turned and saw Judith Foy on the bed, legs kicking, hands clutching at the tubing embedded deep into the flesh of her throat. Rachel Delgado stood behind the woman, the plastic garrote wrapped around her hand.

She heard Tony's surprised gasp and looked up, just as Tony lunged across the bed.

With no time to finish the woman off, Rachel slammed her elbow against Judith Foy's temple, stunning her. Then she released the plastic strangling cord and deftly avoided Tony's grip.

Stumbling backward, Rachel ripped the top of the IV pole away from its base. Using the heavy stainless steel rod like a club, she swung at Tony's unprotected head. Tony ducked low, the pole slicing the air above his scalp.

Tony could easily shoot Rachel—but the sound of the shot would bring the whole floor running for this room. Trying to explain his actions to the police would be a waste of time—and might prove fatal. There was obviously no one he could trust, not even the local authorities. Tony knew it was possible he'd end up dead for "resisting arrest."

He had only one recourse. He had to finish Rachel off quietly, then get Deputy Director Foy out of the hospital to a safe location.

Clutching the pole in her right hand, Rachel feinted a few times, then swung again. This time Tony was ready. Dropping his left arm and holding it straight against his body, he stepped into the blow, leading with his left shoulder. Tony was suddenly so close to the woman that Rachel couldn't strike him with the pole. Her forearm struck Tony's shoulder instead.

Tony popped his right hand, slamming the woman under her chin.

As he struck, he lifted his left arm, curled it around Rachel's right. He added some pressure and she released the club. The steel pole clanged to the floor. Tony squeezed harder, until he heard the snap of bone. Rachel gasped and her arm went limp.

Tony spun the dazed woman around and encircled her neck with one arm, clapped his other hand over her mouth to muffle any cries. Her platform shoes kicking wildly, Rachel was dragged into the tiny bathroom.

Once inside, Tony calmly applied pressure until he snapped Rachel Delgado's neck. Panting, he let her limp body slide to the tile floor. Then he stepped over the corpse and hurried back to the bed.

Judith Foy's gown was disheveled, and Tony threw a sheet over her. Then he helped a dazed Agent Foy untangle the plastic cord from around her neck. The tender flesh was bruised and red and she was gasping, her face flushed.

"Why did she try to kill you?" Tony whispered.

For a moment, Judith Foy ignored the question. Tony thought it was because she didn't have an answer. Finally, she looked up from the bed, and her eyes met his.

"CTU's been compromised," she rasped. "I warned you. And I'll bet she's not the only traitor."

"We've got to get out of here."

"I don't have any clothes," Foy protested.

Tony checked Rachel's corpse, realized the dead woman

was two sizes smaller than the Deputy Director. Then he found a blue hospital robe hanging behind the bathroom door. He ripped it off its hangar and tore away the sanitary plastic wrapping.

As he left the bathroom, Tony stopped dead in his tracks. During the struggle, the buttons on Rachel Delgado's three-quarter-length sleeves had popped. On the forearm he'd broken, Tony spied a familiar tattoo—a stylized number 13.

"Son of a bitch."

"What?" Foy croaked, swinging her naked legs over the side of the bed.

"Never mind." Tony tossed her the robe, then he snatched Rachel Delgado's purse from the chair and tossed it to the woman, too. While she dressed, he went to the door and peered through the window. The way seemed clear. He faced the woman, saw the fear that haunted her eyes.

"Don't worry. I'll get you to a safe place," Tony vowed.

3:48:52 P.M. EDT
Community Center
Kurmastan, New Jersey

Brice Holman awoke with a start, screams battering his ears. He felt hands gripping him, and he opened his eyes.

He was sitting upright in a metal folding chair, ropes loosely circling his arms and torso to hold him in place. He was in a large room with unfinished walls and a low ceiling.

He moaned and shifted in the chair. Someone struck him in the face with a balled fist. Brice saw stars—then, when his vision cleared, scores of wild, mocking eyes stared at him from behind black burkas.

Fists punched and prodded him. A woman gouged the flesh of his cheek with long fingernails. Holman ignored the pain as he tried to stare through the crowd, looking for Reverend Ahern and the rest of the passengers from the bus.

Then an old man stepped onto the platform, a pitchfork in his wizened hands. He shook the implement in the air, and Holman nearly gagged when he saw Emily Reed's ruined head impaled on its prongs.

Holman strained at the ropes. They were meant to constrain him, but the ropes had been applied carelessly, and he easily freed his left hand. He slipped it into his pants pocket, felt around, then smiled grimly.

The crazy fools didn't take my cell phone!

While the women danced around him, and the old men brought in another trophy—the grisly remains of Mr. Simonson's head—Brice opened the phone inside his pocket and pressed the speed dial button, sending out a call to CTU Headquarters in Manhattan.

Holman heard a scream. The crowd parted long enough for him to see Mrs. Hocklinger, bound and helpless. An old man had cut the woman's throat with a shard of broken glass. The woman twitched in her chair, her blood spilling onto the bare concrete floor. The flow soon ceased, and her eyes rolled back. When Mrs. Hocklinger was dead, a twelve-year-old boy attacked her throat with a hacksaw.

An amplified voice boomed, filling the room. Holman looked up to see a large man stride onto the platform, dressed in robes and a prayer shawl. Holman noticed prison tattoos on the man's arms and neck.

The mob began to chant. "Noor . . . Noor . . . Noor . . ."

"The day is now at hand," the man cried, silencing them with a gesture. "Your husbands, sons, uncles, and brothers have departed this compound and will never return. Now I will tell you what bold and daring things they are going do to bring about *Khilafah!*"

Awestruck cries greeted his words. The women tore at their clothing, their hair. The old men and young boys howled like hungry animals. The room stank of sweat and blood.

Amid the chaos, another figure mounted the platform. A striking contrast to the muscular African American, the newcomer was tall, lanky, and very pale. The Albino's colorless eyes watched the mob impassively while the man named Noor continued his speech.

"On this day, the prophecy has been fulfilled. Twelve trucks—twelve chariots of death—have left this compound, to sow death and destruction against the infidel!"

Brice clenched his teeth, his mind roiling.

I hope to God someone at headquarters is monitoring this call. I don't want to die for nothing . . .

"This is Allah's punishment on the unbeliever. We are the sword of God, the vessel of his wrath," the male voice declared, before the rest of his message was drowned out by a cheering mob.

"What do you make of it?" Peter Randall asked.

Morris O'Brian shook his head. "You *are* recording."

Randall nodded. "Every word, every sound, since the call came in."

"Good," said Morris. "We're going to have to put it through filters and screen out the background noise in order to decipher the main speaker's words. Didn't he say something about chariots of death and seeds of destruction?"

"I think so," Randall replied.

"In my experience, that sort of talk is never good." Morris rubbed his hand through his short, wiry hair. "And Holman hasn't spoken during the entire call?"

"No. Director Holman never said a word. But I know he wants us to find him now."

Morris blinked. "How's that, mate?"

"He's reactivated the GPS chip. We can easily pinpoint his location. Brice Holman is in Kurmastan . . ."

1 2 3 4 5 6 7 8 9
10 11 12 13 14 15 16 17
18 19 20 21 22 23 24

· ·

**THE FOLLOWING TAKES PLACE
BETWEEN THE HOURS OF
4:00 P.M. AND 5:00 P.M.
EASTERN DAYLIGHT TIME**

· ·

4:00:06 P.M. EDT
Over Kurmastan, New Jersey

Jack Bauer closed his cell phone and peered through the helicopter's window. Green hills dotted with farmhouses sped by. Plowed fields, barns, and silos rolled under the aircraft's belly.

Layla was studying him from across the aisle. She'd changed out of her business suit, into the tactical equipment she'd taken from the armory—blue overalls, a weapons belt with an assault knife, and a 9mm strapped to her waist. Her dark hair was pulled into a bun, and in oversized assault gear, she appeared small and frail.

"Who called just now?" she asked.

"Morris O'Brian," Jack replied, his voice grim. "They located Brice Holman. He's in Kurmastan."

Layla let out a breath. "That's not all, is it?"

"No. Your boss is in trouble." Jack unfastened his seat-belt and moved to the cockpit.

Fogarty greeted him with a nod. "We've been circling the area for almost thirty minutes, Agent Bauer. We're nearly down to our reserve fuel. Either I land soon, or we're diverting to Phillipsburg or Easton to replenish."

"I want you to land inside the compound and let us out," Jack said. "Then you can divert to the nearest airfield, refuel, and wait for further orders."

The pilot and copilot exchanged looks. "Then you've located Director Holman?" Fogarty asked.

"He's in Kurmastan, and his life may be in danger," Jack replied.

Fogarty peered through the windshield. "We can land near the center of town. There's enough open space for me to—"

"No," Jack said. "You have to put us down where we won't be spotted. Maybe half a mile away from the settle-ment. Somewhere in the woods."

"You'll have to hike to get to main street, Agent Bauer," Fogarty warned. "The hills around here can be steep. You'll lose valuable time."

Jack frowned. "Can't be helped. I don't have numbers. My only weapon is surprise."

Fogarty nodded. "We'll do what we can to back you up, sir," he said, then shifted his gaze to the control panel, where real-time images of Kurmastan were displayed on the digital map screen.

Jack looked, too, and counted himself lucky that CTU New York still had satellite capabilities. After the concerted bomb attacks earlier in the day, no other law enforcement agency on the East Coast had access to orbital surveillance. Right now, a satellite was beaming these pictures of the landscape around the compound to the helicopter's computer.

"I think I can put you down here," Fogarty said, tapping the screen.

Jack studied the map. "It's a shallow valley surrounded by trees. What about the rotors? Do you have enough space to bring this thing down safely?"

"It will be tight, but it's the best place to land," the Captain replied. "Chances are they won't see us behind this hill, and you'll have a whole line of trees to use for cover as you move toward town."

Fogarty paused. "With luck, you probably won't encounter anyone until you reach this stretch of mobile homes. If you do, you may have a fight on your hands."

Jack nodded, memorizing the landscape.

Fogarty gripped his arm with his free hand.

"Are you sure you want to do this, Agent Bauer? I mean, you and Agent Abernathy aren't exactly a strike team."

"I've already ordered Morris O'Brian to dispatch a tactical team to the scene," Jack replied, his tone resigned. "But we're not waiting. We're going in now, even if there's only two of us."

4:21:43 P.M. EDT
Community Center
Kurmastan, New Jersey

Brice Holman shut out the shouts and screams, the sound of Reverend Ahern's pleading voice as he begged the mob to spare him.

His attention was focused on the old Albanian man with the 9mm Uzi in his wrinkled hand and spare ammunition clips tucked into the belt of his tattered robes. The weapon was tarnished and pitted, and Holman wondered if it was truly functional, or merely for show.

I can take that bastard down, he mused. *All I have to do is get close to him, or trick him into getting close to me. But I'd hate to come up empty, stuck with a gun that doesn't shoot.*

Ibrahim Noor and the albino man were long gone. They'd slipped through the curtained door and had not returned. Soon after they departed, the slaughter began. Now, on the podium, Ahern's ravings about interfaith harmony and reconciliation morphed into howls of tortured agony. Bound tightly to a sturdy wooden chair, shirt ripped, clerical collar hanging limply, James Wendell Ahern struggled vainly while two boys, no more than eleven years old, took turns ripping at his throat with a rusty saw.

Holman looked away.

Among the swirling, bloodthirsty throng, he caught brief glimpses of the Cranstons. The woman hung limply from her ropes, and though Mr. Cranston bled from scores of wounds, he was still conscious.

Dani Taylor had been screaming for several minutes. The young women of the compound seemed to derive a special relish in her torment. They punched and kicked the teenager, smeared the makeup they found in her purse on her face, and tore at her clothing.

A particularly vicious slap from a heavyset black woman tipped her chair over, and the girl vanished in a swarm of flapping robes and kicking feet.

Holman strained against his own bonds, until loops of rope sagged onto his lap and tumbled to the blood-soaked floor. He was free now, but pretended to be trapped while he scanned the room, searching for a way out.

An abrupt silence ensued when Ahern stopped screaming. A moment later, the crowd gasped when an older boy displayed the Reverend's head, the eyes still twitching in their sockets. The youth swung the grisly trophy by its hair, then tossed the head on top of the stack piling up in the corner.

Several women gripped Mrs. Cranston, and Joe protested, cursing a blue streak and vowing to kill them all. The old man with the Uzi stepped in front of Mr. Cranston's chair and fired it in the air, to silence the old man.

Holman almost smiled. *That relic still works! And now I know how to get that bastard clutching the Uzi over here to me.*

Two burly women untied the ropes and hauled Abby Cranston out of her chair. She was alive, but only semiconscious. Blood trickled from her nose and ears, the signs of head trauma. Mr. Cranston cried out again. This time women wielding rakes and hoes beat him senseless.

As women in burkas surged past him, carrying Mrs.

Cranston by her arms, Holman shot out his foot and connected with an ankle. A robed woman cried out, then whirled and struck him.

With one eye on the old man, Holman began to curse the woman, then he launched into a string of unspeakable blasphemies calculated to enrage his captors.

It worked.

The old man rushed to his side. But he didn't aim the Uzi at the ceiling. He placed it against Holman's temple.

Brice refused to be silenced. His taunts became more vicious, until the old man twisted the gun to pummel him with its butt—then Holman moved.

He shot out his arms, one grabbing the old man's bony wrist, the other his wattled throat. Holman squeezed until the man's throat was crushed. Then he yanked the gun out of the man's dead fingers.

The women reared back, but one young boy lunged for him. Still partly ensnared by the tangling ropes, Holman shot the youth in the face.

A woman howled, dropped to her knees beside the corpse. The rest of the robed wall seemed to withdraw. Holman spotted a man clutching a double-barreled shotgun and killed him, too. Another armed man fumbled with the rifle on his shoulder, and Holman blew the top of his head off. Finally, Holman shot the kid who'd brandished the Reverend's head—just because he felt like it.

The woman beside the dead boy clawed at Holman's shoes, and he kicked her aside. Waving his Uzi at the quaking horde, he grabbed clips of spare ammunition from the dead man's belt.

Holman was about to bolt for the exit when he saw Dani Taylor on the floor. Her chair was broken, and she'd untangled herself from the ropes. Now she was struggling to rise.

"Wait . . . Take me with you," she pleaded.

"Come on, then," Brice yelled.

A woman lunged for Holman, and he shot her at point-blank range. Enraged howls greeted the move, but the mob retreated.

Brice grabbed Dani's hand. It was slippery with blood, but he managed to haul the girl to her feet. He pushed Dani behind him and nudged her toward the nearest exit.

"Wait," Dani gasped, snatching the shotgun from the dead man's grip. Brice was surprised when she waved the weapon at their captors, effectively covering his back.

"You know how to use that?" Brice called.

"I live on a farm. I can fire a shotgun," Dani replied.

Another woman took a swing at Brice with a rusty rake, and he shot her, too. Robes flapping, the dead woman spun backward, into the arms of her comrades.

Dani and Holman bolted through the door, into the harsh afternoon sun. They were on main street, where Holman hoped to board the church bus. But the vehicle had been tipped over on its side.

Cursing, he grabbed Dani's arm and they dashed down the dusty street.

"I want you to go that way," Brice said pointing. "Get to the woods beyond those mobile homes and you'll have a chance to get out."

Dani took a step forward. Brice gripped her arm.

"Take this," he cried, shoving his cell phone into the girl's pocket.

"What is it?"

"Intelligence," Holman cried. "Images, recordings. Give it to the FBI. Do you understand? The FBI. Don't trust anyone from CTU—"

"Huh?"

"CTU. The Counter Terrorist Unit. They've been compromised. Promise me you'll give that phone to the FBI and no one else."

The girl nodded, Brice noticed a chunk of blond hair had been yanked from her scalp. "The FBI, I got it," she said nervously.

Holman pushed her. "Go!" he commanded.

Dani took off in a run toward the line of mobile homes in the distance. Holman whirled to face the Community Center. Legs braced, he aimed at a pair of angry women and an old man who stumbled through the door.

He fired once, bringing down the man. Then Brice fled the scene, fumbling with a clip to reload.

Cries battered Holman's ears as an enraged mob streamed out of the Community Center. Someone fired a shot that whizzed over his head. They chased after him, and Holman swerved onto the road that led to the factory.

Good, you dumb bastards, he thought. *Follow me and Dani will get away clean . . .*

4:49:48 P.M. EDT
Joe On the Go
Newark, New Jersey

In the cool darkness of the brick-lined coffeehouse, Tony Almeida studied the woman across the table while he sipped his fourth espresso. Judith Foy fidgeted in her chair while she nursed her third iced tea.

The Deputy Director was wearing a navy-blue tracksuit, no-name sneakers, and a knockoff New York Yankees cap meant to hide the bandages on her head. Tony was no fashion guru, but he had grabbed what he thought was appropriate at a discount store on a shabby block of clothing and apparel shops in the Central Ward, while Judith Foy cowered in the hospital gown, inside the stall of a McDonald's restroom.

Securing clothing was their first priority after the escape, and Tony had handled that situation well and efficiently. He was having less success convincing the Deputy Director of the New York Division to turn over the intelligence she'd gathered to analysts at CTU Headquarters.

Every time he broached the subject, Agent Foy changed the topic of conversation. Now she peered across the table with an expression that bordered on admiration.

"You're quite resourceful, Agent Almeida. The way you whisked me out of the hospital . . . It was some of the quickest thinking I'd ever seen."

"Call me Tony," he said.

While she spoke, his gaze continued to scan the coffee shop. So far, the only other patrons were a pair of college coeds bemoaning their romantic life, and a man in a jacket and tie pounding on the keyboard of his laptop.

"What are you thinking, Tony?" Judy said. "Wish I could tell. But for the last hour, your expression covered the emotional spectrum from A to B."

Tony arched an eyebrow. "You caught me at a bad time."

Judy Foy shook her head. "I caught you at a very good time. You're one of the best agents I've ever seen. You were smart to grab the wheelchair and put me in it. When you put on those green scrubs, even I thought you were part of the medical staff. Then you triggered the fire alarm, pushed me right past the police guarding the door, along with the rest of the evacuees . . . makes me wish you worked for me."

Tony ignored her praise. "Too bad about Delgado's car. We had the keys. We could have been in a safe house by now, if the police hadn't cordoned off the parking lot."

"Don't worry about it," Foy said. "You recovered my cell phone and camera. That's what counts."

"Not if we don't get the information to CTU."

"We've been over this, Agent Almeida."

"Look," Tony said. "You can trust Jack Bauer. He's from Los Angeles, not New York. He never even heard of Kurmastan until today."

Foy shook her head so vigorously, her scarlet ponytail whipped back and forth. "I don't know your boss from Adam, or who this Bauer chose to trust," she replied. "He can unwittingly help the traitor if he shares information with the wrong person."

"Maybe we got the traitor," Tony argued.

"Rachel Delgado was a mole," Foy replied. "But I doubt she's the only one. I don't trust Brice's assistant, either."

"Agent Abernathy?"

Foy nodded. "I told Holman about my suspicions, but he laughed them off . . ."

"What if we call Morris, forward the intelligence to him—"

"We've been through this, Almeida. Any data we forward to your friend will have to go through CTU New York's network. I'm convinced the traitor has access to the data dump. The bastard will see the intelligence as soon as it comes in—maybe even delete it before your friend has a chance to retrieve it."

The woman stared through the window, at the rush hour traffic building outside.

Tony calmly sipped his espresso, but inside he was cursing. Judith Foy had ordered him not to use his cell phone, and almost made him deactivate his GPS chip, until she realized CTU New York didn't have Tony's telecommunications signatures in their database and couldn't track him if they wanted to. The woman was so cautious, it bordered on paranoia. She even tossed Rachel Delgado's cell into a storm drain, along with the woman's car keys, purse, and wallet. Foy kept only the dead woman's cash and her Glock.

"If only your friend Morris had a laptop," Foy said. "Something not connected to the mainframe."

Tony struck the table with his fist, rattling the espresso cup on its saucer. "That's it!"

"What?"

Tony leaned across the table, speaking softly. "Before we left Los Angeles, George Mason gave Jack Bauer a briefcase computer with all the codes and mission protocols inside. Only we never even cracked it because things went Code Red in a hurry."

"So?"

"What if we forward the intel you collected to *that* system, then alert Morris to open the files inside the briefcase computer, effectively cutting CTU New York out of the loop."

"That might work. But how are you going to transmit the data?"

Tony shrugged. "There's an internet café around the corner and down the block. We rent a computer for an hour and download the information."

"But you still have to contact this Morris person. If you call him, even on a public phone, that could compromise everything."

Tony shook his head. "I won't be contacting Morris. Someone from CTU Los Angeles will. Someone Morris can't ignore."

• •

THE FOLLOWING TAKES PLACE
BETWEEN THE HOURS OF
5:00 P.M. AND 6:00 P.M.
EASTERN DAYLIGHT TIME

• •

2:04:17 P.M. PDT
CTU Headquarters, Los Angeles

Chloe's expression soured when the phone warbled. Irritated by the interruption, she pushed her disheveled blond hair back from her face and returned to work. The phone rang again.

"How am I supposed to get anything done around here?"

No one replied, because no one wanted to work near Chloe.

The phone rang again, then again. Finally, Chloe snatched up the receiver.

"What?" she said sharply.

"Chloe? This is Tony Almeida. Listen, I need you to pass along some information to Morris—"

Chloe's mouth twisted into a frown so deep, it threatened to deconstruct her face. "Why? That doesn't make sense. Morris is in New York with you. Why can't you pass along your own information?"

"It's a long story," Tony replied.

Chloe glanced at her watch. "I see." Her tone was disapproving. "Well, I really don't have time to hear it. You seem to have all the time in the world, but some of us actually have to work for a living."

"Give me a break, Chloe."

"Give *me* a break. I can only guess it's happy hour on the East Coast. Have one on me."

"Don't hang up!" Tony cried. "This is a matter of national security. Have you heard about the bombs?"

"If you're talking about the ones that disabled satellite capabilities in the Mid-Atlantic states, then yes, I've heard about them. In fact, I'm in the middle of analyzing a list of—"

"My information might have something to do with those attacks," Tony said. "All you have to do is forward some data in an e-mail attachment to Morris O'Brian's ISP account, then tag it with something personal so he reads it right away. Can you do that?"

Chloe's face scrunched up again. "I don't know. That little British creep took me out a couple of times, then he stopped calling—"

"Chloe, please."

"Oh, all right!" She rolled her eyes. "But how in the heck

can I tag the e-mail so Morris will read it right away?"

Tony sighed. "You'll figure something out . . ."

5:27:36 P.M. EDT
Inside the Warriors of God compound
Near Kurmastan, New Jersey

Jack Bauer took the lead as he and Layla Abernathy followed the tree line along the top of a gentle slope. Between breaks in the foliage, Jack caught a glimpse of the mobile home park. Even from this distance, the trailers seemed decrepit, with rusty and pitted walls, broken windows, and missing doors.

The late afternoon sun was scorching—so hot that Jack signaled Layla to hunker down in the shade for a moment. She removed her cap and wiped sweat from her forehead. Jack loosened his body armor to let some air through. They both gulped water from plastic bottles.

Layla glanced at her watch. "We've been hiking for half an hour, ever since we debarked from the chopper. We must be close now."

Jack rose and used micro-binoculars to scan the area below.

"We're almost there," he replied. "I can see the compound. There's no sign of life, no one on the streets or—"

Jack fell silent.

"What do you see?" Layla asked.

"There's a minibus in the middle of main street. It's lying on its side, windows broken."

The cell phone went off in Jack's pocket. "Morris?" he answered.

"News, Jack," O'Brian began. "I'm still tracing Holman's phone, and he's close by. He's moving up the hill due south of your position. Maybe three hundred yards away."

Jack swung his binoculars around and scanned the next hill. All he saw were trees and thick brush.

"Are you sure?"

"Positive, Jack-o."

Jack closed the phone. "Wait here," he whispered to Layla, handing off his phone. "If I'm not back in ten minutes, call Morris."

Layla took the phone and nodded. A moment later, Jack faded into the thick brush.

5:33:14 P.M. EDT
Inside the Warriors of God compound

Dani had been spotted somewhere near the mobile homes. She never noticed anyone as she passed the cluster of ramshackle old trailers, but someone must have seen her and put the alarm out. Almost as soon as she entered a heavily wooded stretch, Dani heard excited voices—both women and boys—followed by the sound of several people crashing through the brush.

Still clutching the shotgun in her sweating hands, Dani ran until she was too exhausted to continue on. Finally, she dived into a thicket at the base of a hill, hoping to elude the hunters. Cowering in the brush, knees curled under her, the teenaged girl fought panic and tried to control her rasping breath.

Suddenly the traumatic events of the past few hours overwhelmed her. Dani felt a knife through her guts and she heaved. Then she began to tremble uncontrollably. Tears filled her eyes and dug canals through the filth and caked blood that stained her cheeks.

Dani sobbed once, then clapped her hand over her mouth—too late, for a moment later the branches parted above her head and a young man cried out.

"She's here!"

Startled out of her fear trance, Dani looked up. The youth loomed over her. He was maybe fourteen. Round face. Deep brown eyes. His triumphant grin exposed a missing front tooth. He wore a frayed T-shirt and a hemp necklace around his thick, sweat-stained neck. He lifted a baseball bat—

She shot him in the chest with both barrels. The kid was blown off his feet by the impact, and bounced off the trunk of a tree.

The explosive double blast shocked Dani, and the recoil was more than she could handle. The stock slammed against her shoulder; the smoking gun flew from her hands.

Moaning, Dani clutched her bruised shoulder and stumbled to her feet. Without a second glance, she stepped over the dead boy and scrambled up the hill.

5:36:27 P.M. EDT
Inside the Warriors of God compound

Jack Bauer heard the shotgun blast and took off. Leading with his Glock, he ran through the trees until he reached the edge of a shallow valley. Crouching among a cluster of trees, he immediately spotted the injured teenager moving up the hill.

Where's Holman? Jack wondered.

At the base of the hill, three women in black robes clustered around a figure sprawled on the ground. Jack heard anguished cries and wailing. Then the trio spotted the blond girl. Brandishing pitchforks and kitchen knives, the woman hiked up their robes as they climbed the hill.

The teenager glanced over her shoulder, saw the women, and picked up her pace. In another minute, she would reach his position.

Jack slipped the Glock into its holster and ducked behind the thick foliage. When the girl reached the trees, Jack reached out, snagged her, and pulled her to the ground in one smooth motion.

The girl screamed and fought him.

"I'm a friend," Jack hissed. "I'm here to rescue you."

Still the girl struggled. Part of her wanted to believe him—Jack could see it in her eyes—but she was beaten bloody and half mad. Too terrorized to trust anyone.

Jack heard voices, peeked through the leaves and saw the women. They were almost on him. Holding the girl down with one hand, he drew his Glock with the other.

The women reached his position a moment later. They stopped in their tracks when they spied Jack.

"Get down on the ground now!" Jack cried, reluctant to fire.

One of the women surprised him by hurling a kitchen knife. Jack deftly avoided the blade, then shot the woman in the head. As she toppled, the others reared back. Then both women fumbled for their belts. Only then did Jack notice their bulging robes, and the detonation cord dangling from their waists.

Jack aimed—but before he could fire, a volley of shots cut the women down. Layla Abernathy stepped out of hiding, a smoking Glock gripped firmly in both hands.

"I thought I told you to stay put," said Jack, one hand pinning the teenaged girl on the ground.

"I heard the shots," Layla replied. "I thought maybe you were in trouble."

"Check the dead women. I think they're wearing explosive belts. Be careful not to set one off."

Jack looked down, into the teenager's eyes. By now, she'd stopped struggling against him. "Are you calm?"

The girl nodded and Jack released her. She sat up and rubbed the reddening flesh on her bare shoulder.

He examined the girl. One sleeve of her sweatshirt had been torn away; the other hung by a few threads. Dried blood caked her thin arms, covering bruises and gouged flesh. She had a black eye and a swollen nose, and chunks of her hair had been torn out by the roots.

Though she was fairly banged up, Jack concluded the physical wounds were superficial. Her psychological condition was another matter.

"You were right, Agent Bauer," Layla said. "These

women are all wearing explosive devices—bricks of C–4, connected to a detonation cord."

She frowned. "Two of them had IDs. Both are . . . *were* born in the United States. And none of these three dead women are of Middle Eastern descent." The notion seemed to confound Layla Abernathy, but Jack didn't have time to deal with her existential dilemmas right now.

Jack addressed the teenager. "Who are you? What were you doing inside the compound?"

Danielle Taylor told them her name and where she lived. Then the harrowing story of her captivity came tumbling out of her mouth. She told them about the church group, the torture, and the beheadings. Near the end of her tale, she mentioned a Mr. Holman, the man who helped her escape.

"Holman?" Layla interrupted. "Brice Holman?"

Dani nodded.

Before Jack could silence her, Layla spoke again. "Holman is an agent for the Counter Terrorist Unit of the CIA," she told Dani. "I'm from CTU, too. Brice is my superior."

Dani instantly paled, and Jack could see the look of fear and panic return to her eyes. He also sensed the girl was hiding something. He knew the only way she would open up was if he somehow earned her trust.

"Forget about that," Jack said gently. "We're here to help. My name is Jack Bauer. I'm—"

Then the ground trembled under their feet. As one, thousands of birds burst out of the trees and took to the sky as the rumbling roar of multiple explosions battered their ears.

Dani cried out. Layla dropped to the ground, clutching her head.

Jack whirled, seeing a dozen blasts and plumes of black smoke rising from the center of Kurmastan. On the opposite end of town, flames lit up the sky above the old paper factory.

More explosions followed. Several clapboard homes blew apart, sending debris leaping into the afternoon sky. Then a mobile home erupted, bursting asunder like a shoe box stuffed with firecrackers.

Trailers went up in smoke and flames, the eruptions continuing for almost thirty seconds before the cacophony finally subsided. As Layla hugged the earth, smoke billowed over their position. It stank of cordite, scorched metal, and burned flesh.

"*Inshallah*," Layla muttered from the ground.

Jack crouched over Agent Abernathy. "Stay here," he told her. "Call Morris and tell him to send backup. We'll need tactical teams and a medical unit." Jack pointed to the teenager. "Take care of the girl, too—"

"What are you going to do?" Layla demanded.

"I'm going down there to find out what the hell is happening."

. . . .

THE FOLLOWING TAKES PLACE
BETWEEN THE HOURS OF
6:00 P.M. AND 7:00 P.M.
EASTERN DAYLIGHT TIME

. . . .

6:05:50 P.M. EDT
Security Station One
CTU Headquarters, NYC

Morris O'Brian watched flickering, real-time satellite
images of the shattered town. Thick smoke crossed his
monitor screen like a creeping black smudge. Flames
licked the walls and roof of the rambling factory.

He was tempted to alert the local firefighting
authorities—though in that isolated region of rural New
Jersey, Morris wasn't sure what resources were actually
available.

It wasn't his call, anyway, so Morris didn't make it.

Jack Bauer had called for backup and Morris obeyed—dispatching two tactical assault teams and a medical unit. Estimated time of arrival: twenty-eight minutes and fifty-five seconds, according to his threat clock.

"The last chopper's just lifted off from the heliport," Peter Randall informed him. "No problem with clearance this time."

Morris nodded—then his cell phone beeped. *Bloody hell? Who's calling me on my personal line?*

But it wasn't a call. His ISP had just alerted him to an urgent e-mail waiting in his cache. Morris looked around for the briefcase computer he had brought with him that morning, found it behind the door where he'd left it when he started work on the troubled security system.

He dumped the briefcase on his desk and opened the lid. He wiped his thumb over the fingerprint sensor, and got clearance to proceed. His ISP protocols and passwords were programmed into the computer, and Morris had the "urgent message" on screen in seconds.

The e-mail came from Chloe—the kinky bird from the computer department he'd been dating on the sly. Morris read the tagline, and his knees turned to jelly.

"Oh god," he moaned, dropping into a chair. "She's pregnant?"

6:22:06 P.M. EDT
Kurmastan, New Jersey

As Jack descended into the valley, he entered a pall of smoke. Passing the ruins of the mobile homes, he saw everyday signs of human habitation among the ruins—refrigerators turned on their sides, doors wide, spilling their contents, burst mattress smoldering in the sun, a shattered baby crib, torn cereal boxes, broken dishes.

There were no signs of life, but plenty of signs of death. The grisly remains of the citizens of Kurmastan were all around him.

Jack circled one of the intact mobile homes. Sheets of opaque plastic had been hung in place of windows. The door was unlocked, and Jack opened it. Inside he saw three filthy bunks, an aluminum sink filled with dirty Styrofoam plates, plastic utensils, and swarming ants. The tiny bathroom was crammed with empty ammunition boxes, all brand-name sportsman shells purchased legally, over the counter.

When Jack exited the cramped trailer, a braying goat stumbled into his path. Startled, he watched the frightened creature bolt for the forest, spindly legs kicking up dirt.

Crouching low, leading with the weapon he clutched with both hands, Jack moved along Kurmastan's main street. He saw a small market, blown apart now, fruits and vegetables scattered on the scorched and blackened street. Here the smoke was choking, and Jack had to cover his nose and mouth with a tattered prayer shawl soaked in the streaming flow from a shattered water pipe.

There were many bodies around the blasted Community Center, some of them intact. Jack examined two of the corpses and discovered they'd been shot—probably by Brice Holman in the escape Dani had described.

Jack wondered where Holman was now, if he was dead or alive.

He holstered his Glock, wiped smoky tears from his eyes with the sleeve of his CTU tactical assault uniform. It was clear that the people of Kurmastan had committed mass suicide, after savagely attacking the church group and slaughtering almost everyone. But Jack had more questions than answers.

Why were Dani's captors, and the ones who chased her up the hill, all women, children, and the elderly? *Where are all the men?*

Cautiously, Jack peered through the door of the smoking Community Center. The stench of death permeated the place, but, mercifully, the roof had collapsed, so he couldn't see much.

He circled the ruined building. In the back, he found two large Dumpsters that had been tipped over in the explosions. The smell of rotting food mingled with charred flesh, adding to the unbearable conditions.

Jack stopped in his tracks when he suddenly heard a human sound—a mad, tittering laugh.

"Hello?" Jack called.

More laughter followed, and Jack trailed the echo until he spied a six-foot pit reinforced with logs—the entrance to an underground bunker. Jack heard the laughter again, and knew it emanated from that earthen pit.

Reluctantly, he descended into the trench and entered the bunker. Inside, he found a long tunnel lined with wooden support beams. He found a light switch and tested it, but the generator was either destroyed or inactive and the naked bulbs remained dark. Jack paused, waiting for his eyes to adjust. The underground bunker was ten degrees cooler than the temperature outside, and smelled of raw wood and freshly turned earth. There was another odor, too, a kind of chemical smell Jack couldn't identify.

He heard the mad chortling again. In this eerie place, the deranged voice set Jack's flesh crawling. He slipped the emergency light from his utility belt and pinned it to his shoulder holster. Crouching, he proceeded along the dark, low-ceilinged tunnel.

After fifty paces, the tunnel ended with a spacious underground chamber. Large chemical barrels lined the walls. Jack played the flashlight beam over the plastic drums. All of them came from Rogan Pharmaceuticals, LLC. According to the labels, the barrels contained one of three substances—Hyperdrine, Androne, and something called Virilobil.

Curious, Jack squinted to read the fine print on one of the barrels. Then he heard the tittering laugh, this time right behind him. He played the flashlight beam into the shadowy corner and discovered he was not alone in the darkness.

Chains rattled as the other man threw up emaciated arms to ward off the harsh light. He moaned, and Jack saw a long, unkempt beard crawling with lice. The man's hair was long, too, and hung in dull ringlets from a dirty scalp.

His fingernails were curved into filthy yellow talons.

The captive's flesh was sallow, and there were chafing sores on his wrists and ankles where he'd been chained. Despite the man's horrible condition, Jack recognized him from the photos in the secret Kurmastan files. This wretch was Imam Ali Rahman al Sallifi, the supposed leader of this community.

The man trembled under the light, in the throes of some type of drug fugue or madness, Jack didn't know which. Only one thing was clear. This man had not been the spiritual leader of these people for a long time.

So who did control Kurmastan? And why did their leader have the compound destroyed, his followers commit mass suicide?

The bound figure shifted, and a new stench curled Jack's nostrils. The old man was lying in his own offal.

"It's inhuman. Not even an animal should be treated like this," Jack muttered, moving to free the man. But as soon as he approached al Sallifi, the old man howled and lunged at him, raking the air with filthy claws. Jack cursed and stumbled back.

He waited a moment for the man to settle down, then Jack took a cautious step forward. Al Sallifi charged again, snarling as he strained against the rattling chains that bound him to the wall.

Knowing there was nothing more he could do, Jack quickly fled the bunker, into the smoke-shrouded afternoon.

Outside, he heard the roar of turboshaft engines, the steady beat of helicopter blades cutting the air.

The reinforcements had arrived.

Too impatient to wait for the strike teams, Jack headed back up the hill, through the ruined mobile home park, to the grove where he had left Layla Abernathy and Dani Taylor.

6:49:57 P.M. EDT
In the woods above Kurmastan

Layla Abernathy watched the CTU helicopters circle above the blazing compound, before setting down in a cyclone of smoke and burning embers.

She glanced at her wristwatch, wondering why Jack Bauer had not yet returned. Layla fished for the micro-binoculars on her belt, but before she peered through them, she glanced at Dani. The girl was squatting on the soft loam, legs folded under her. Then Layla recognized something shiny on the ground beside the girl, something that had fallen out of the pocket of her pants.

"Is that Brice Holman's cell phone?" Layla asked.

Dani jumped as if startled, then snatched up the phone. "No, it's mine."

"That phone belongs to Brice," Layla insisted. "That's what CTU was tracking when Jack found *you.*"

She stared at the girl, her mind roiling. Holman could very well have the key to all this chaos locked inside that device. Digital recordings. Surveillance logs. Photographic images.

Layla knelt down beside the teenager. "You have to give me that cell phone," she said urgently.

"No!" Dani cried.

"This is a matter of national security." Layla reached for the phone.

Dani screamed, and the two women struggled. Layla was petite, but better trained. In a few deft moves, she had the girl pinned to the ground.

"Give me that phone," Layla demanded. "I can't let some moody adolescent jeopardize innocent lives."

Suddenly a shadow fell over the women. Layla looked up, just as a foot lashed out and struck her temple.

Without a sound, Layla toppled to the ground and stayed down. Dani slid out from under her, looked up at the newcomer.

"Mr. Holman!" she cried. "You're alive."

Brice Holman stumbled, then slumped to the ground. "Barely," he grunted, clutching his belly. Dani saw black blood seeping through his shirt.

Dani threw her arms around Holman. He touched her arm reassuringly, then stared at the still form on the ground.

"Judy warned me," he said to the unconscious Agent Abernathy. "She was sure you were a mole. I thought it was Rachel Delgado, but I guess Foy was right . . ."

Then Holman grunted and clutched his gut with both arms. "Won't be long now," he rasped.

Another figure entered the clearing. Holman looked up, into the barrel of Jack Bauer's Glock.

"Who are you?" Jack demanded. "What did you do to Agent Abernathy?"

Dani hurled herself between the two men. "This is Mr. Holman. The man who helped me!"

Bauer lowered his weapon. "I've been searching for you all day."

"You're Jack Bauer? From the Los Angeles unit?"

Jack nodded.

"Forgive me if we don't shake hands. I'm holding my guts in place at the moment." Holman winced again. "Listen, we have to talk, Bauer, and fast. I don't have much time . . ."

"I'll call the paramedics," Jack said. "There's a medical unit hovering around here somewhere."

Brice Holman took his cell from Dani Taylor's hand and offered it to Jack. "Use my phone."

1 2 3 4 5 6 7 8 9
10 11 12 **13** 14 15 16 17
18 19 20 21 22 23 24

. . . .

THE FOLLOWING TAKES PLACE
BETWEEN THE HOURS OF
7:00 P.M. AND 8:00 P.M.
EASTERN DAYLIGHT TIME

. . . .

7:04:49 P.M. EDT
In the woods above Kurmastan
Hunterdon County, New Jersey

Flickering flames still rose from the ruined town. In the debris-strewn streets, helicopters idled and armed silhouettes moved through the billowing smoke. Down in the valley, the shadows deepened—the sun would set in an hour or so.

Jack used mini-binoculars to watch the medical team move among the mobile homes. Following his GPS signal, they were making their way up the hill to perform triage on Director Brice Holman. After personally examining the man's ravaged abdomen, Jack didn't think they would make it in time.

Sprawled on the ground, head cradled in Dani Taylor's lap, Brice grinned, but the amusement never touched his pain-ravaged eyes.

"Turns out a pitchfork can kill you as dead as a nine-millimeter," he grunted.

Also on the ground, Layla Abernathy groaned and stirred, but her eyes didn't open. Jack ignored the traitor. He had secured the woman's wrists and ankles with flex ties, so she wasn't going anywhere.

Brice Holman's intense gaze locked with Jack Bauer's.

"Twelve trucks, Bauer. All of them with the Dreizehn Trucking logo," Holman said ominously. "Between eighty-five and a hundred fanatics aboard them. If the forces are divided equally . . . Hell, you do the math, Bauer. I'm too damned tired. But I have lots of intelligence inside that phone. The access code is Bin 666 Charlie seven—that's the word *seven* spelled out in letters, got it?"

Jack nodded. Holman relaxed, slumping against Dani Taylor. The teenager had never left his side, even when Bauer exposed the deep puncture wounds and tried—vainly—to staunch the bleeding.

"Listen, Bauer, these trucks are packed with deadly cargo. Guns. Ammunition. Explosives. Maybe chemical and biological weapons, too. One truck left the compound early this morning. The rest later, maybe the early afternoon. They fanned out in all directions . . ."

Holman winced against the pain. When he spoke again, his voice was weaker, his tone more urgent. "You've got to stop them. Send out a nationwide bulletin, alert all

Federal, state, and local law enforcement agencies. Track them down. Use satellites. Raid truck stops and diesel fuel dumps—whatever it takes."

Holman groaned, and fresh blood stained the bundled cloth he clutched to his guts. "It's up to you now, Bauer. There's no one else who can stop these terrorists. Nobody but you."

Bauer nodded. "I'll stop them, Holman. I swear it."

The medical team arrived at that moment. They dragged a protesting Dani aside, then began to work over the man.

Bauer stepped to the edge of the hill and tugged Holman's cell out of his pocket, dialed up CTU New York.

"O'Brian here."

"It's Jack, Morris. Prepare to receive data."

"Ready."

Jack punched in Holman's security code, located the intelligence cache, and pressed the send button.

Behind him, Jack heard Dani sobbing. A paramedic appeared at his shoulder.

"I'm sorry, Agent Bauer," the woman said softly. "We did what we could, but Director Holman lost too much blood. He's gone . . ."

7:18:50 P.M. EDT
Security Station One
CTU Headquarters, NYC

Morris O'Brian downloaded the contents of Brice Holman's cell phone. After opening the files in his briefcase computer, he copied the data, bundled it with the information retrieved from Judith Foy's cell, then forwarded complete data packages to the Central Intelligence Agency in Langley; FBI Headquarters in Washington, D.C.; and CTU Los Angeles for further analysis.

He also sent them the cleaned up audio of the mad, ranting speech by Ibrahim Noor, which was picked up from Holman's cell phone and processed at CTU New York.

Then Morris went to work analyzing the photographic images shot by Deputy Director Judith Foy at Newark Liberty Airport that morning.

Thanks to Chloe's alarmingly titled e-mail—a false alarm as it mercifully turned out—Morris had been able to retrieve Agent Foy's intelligence data, which had been sent as an attachment.

Now Morris worked with the surveillance photographs on his screen, using the CTU known-terrorist database to analyze facial features for a match. Within fifteen minutes, he'd come up with a potential equivalent.

He called up the personnel file of the known terrorist and his alias and made a closer comparison. Suddenly Morris's angular face broke into a grin of triumph.

"As the old lady at the church bazaar said—*Bingo!*"

"Pardon me?" Peter Randall called from the next station.

"Never mind, back to work," Morris said. "Nothing to see here, mate."

Morris placed the two photographs side by side for a final eyesight comparison. "Got you," he whispered.

The man posing as Canadian structural engineer Faoud S. Mubajii, from Montreal, Quebec, was really a Saudi Arabian scientist named Said al Kabbibi.

Morris scanned the man's file. Kabbibi's list of known terrorist affiliations was as long as the degrees after his name. According to the database, Kabbibi was a doctor of medicine, Harvard; a doctor of pharmacological sciences, MIT; a doctor of biochemistry, Berlin University, who hung out with members of the PLO, the Taliban, and the Republican Guard in Iraq.

Back in the 1980s, Kabbibi was so well known inside the intelligence community that he had an official handle: "Biohazard Bob."

As it turned out, Kabbibi had dropped out of sight for more than a decade. The last time anyone saw him—anyone being agents of Britain's MI–5—Biohazard Bob Kabbibi had been a guest of Saddam Hussein, the current dictator of Iraq. The scientist apparently resided in some opulence, inside a villa near an Iraqi army base on the outskirts of Baghdad.

Not coincidentally, that villa was less than a kilometer away from a state-of-the-art biological warfare facility.

7:28:51 P.M. EDT
Carlisle, Pennsylvania

Luddie Kuzma rolled his vehicle into a remote spot on the edge of the sprawling truck stop parking lot. He powered down the window and cut the engine. The night was more comfortable than the afternoon, but it was warm and becoming humid. Still, Luddie welcomed the fresh air streaming through the window after hours spent with a rattling air conditioner.

Massaging his neck, Lud savored the silence—at least he did until a trailer truck rumbled past his van and rolled to a halt, air brakes hissing in protest.

He watched as the man in the passenger seat jumped out and helped guide the big truck into a parking spot between a moving van and an Ethan Allen furniture truck. He noted with interest that the newcomer lacked backup alarms—as annoying as those beepers were, they were also a requirement in most states. The vehicle had a small logo that Lud strained to read.

DREIZEHN TRUCKING

The license was local, too. The vehicle was based in New Jersey.

Yawning, Lud forgot about the truck and glanced at the illuminated dial of his plastic sports watch. *Not even eight o'clock yet, and it's already been a long day—too long to get right back on the road.*

Lud tilted his seat back, stretched out his legs. At five foot three, and nearly two hundred pounds, he was built like a sandy-haired fireplug. But nine hours behind the wheel would wear out anyone's knees, even a midget's.

At fifty, Luddie was the oldest livery driver in the Allegheny–Lehigh Valley Medical Alliance.

Today he hauled a kidney from Allegheny County Hospital to Easton Medical Center. He hadn't a clue where the organ came from, or who the lucky recipient would be. But that was par for the course. Luddie was only a driver. It was none of his business. He'd delivered the organ to

Easton General on time, earned his three hundred bucks plus gas, and now he was on his way back to his dinky apartment on Pittsburgh's South Side, home since the wife divorced him two years ago.

Lud balled up the empty bag of Bon Ton pork rinds and tossed it into the trash bag on the floor. With a contented sigh, he released his seatbelt and shoulder strap, pulled his Pittsburgh Pirates cap over his eyes, and settled back. In seconds he was snoring . . .

The loud bang of a metal door shocked him back to consciousness.

Startled, Lud bolted upright, momentarily disoriented. He glanced at his watch and realized he'd been sleeping for about twenty minutes. Then he looked around for the source of the sound.

It was the vehicle from Dreizehn Trucking. The double cargo doors were wide open, and several men were crawling around inside.

"What the hell are yo'uns doing?" he muttered suspiciously.

For a moment, Lud thought he was witnessing a robbery in progress. But when he discerned the deadly nature of the hauler's cargo, he realized the truth was even more nefarious.

In the dim light of the trailer's cavernous interior, Lud saw a wall lined with fully stocked weapon racks—machine guns, assault rifles, shotguns, boxes of grenades—the kind of stuff Luddie Kuzma had handled in Vietnam.

There was more. A black youth aboard the truck started handing down bricks of plastic explosives wired to timers.

Lud ducked lower in his seat, scanned the parking area around him. Fifty yards away, he spied another man on his knees, using duct tape to connect one of the bombs to a tanker truck full of gasoline.

Heart racing, Lud pondered his next move. If he started his engine, or even made a move, they would spot him— and he realized with mounting panic that all the men were wearing sidearms, too.

Before he could decide on a course of action, Lud saw a figure loom in his rearview mirror, heard the click of a bullet sliding into its chamber.

He turned, looked up—

7:48:37 P.M. EDT
Carlisle, Pennsylvania

Vernon Greene strode across the parking lot, toward the cargo bay of the Dreizehn truck, the gunmetal-gray USP Tactical still smoking in his right hand.

"I found some cracker sleeping inside that van. Didn't you scope the place first?" he demanded.

The man in the truck shrugged, handed down another bomb to a youth, who clutched it to his chest as he raced away.

"My boys clipped two guys sleeping in their trucks and some bitch in a Caddy. So what if they missed that one. You got him, right?"

Greene unscrewed the silencer and tossed it inside the trailer.

"Tell your boys to step it up. We're leaving in five minutes."

Three minutes later, the last of the men returned to the truck and piled inside. Vernon Greene closed the door behind them, then hopped into the cab.

"You ready to hit the big target?" he asked.

The driver nodded, nervous sweat beading his leathery skin. "I can get us to the U.S. Tactical Training School in twenty minutes."

"Go," Greene commanded. "Let's get scarce before this place blows sky-high."

The diesel engine roared, belching smoke. One minute later, the Dreizehn truck rumbled down the exit ramp and away from the sprawling truck stop. The driver ignored a red light and swung onto the main road. In the process he clipped a Pennsylvania State Police car and turned the vehicle completely around.

The trooper behind the wheel couldn't give chase—the front of his car was shattered, and he had an injured partner to deal with—but he immediately used the radio to report the Dreizehn truck, and its plate numbers, to the State Police barracks less than a mile away. He also requested an ambulance.

While the driver tried to revive his partner, the world exploded around him. Ears battered by the noise, bathed in an eerie orange glow, he watched as a dozen explosions rocked the truck stop, one after the other. The diesel pumps blew in a stupendous blast, sending a roiling, burning mushroom cloud into the darkening sky.

Then the gasoline pumps erupted, spewing burning

liquid upward like a blazing fountain. Diners and staff hurried to the windows to view the commotion—just in time to die as bombs placed at each of the food court's four corners brought the entire structure down on top of hundreds of customers and employees of a dozen different fast-food chains.

Then a gasoline tanker that was rolling toward the police car exploded. The tank leaped into the air and split asunder, sending thousands of gallons of burning gasoline spilling down the ramp like a river of volcanic lava.

Behind the wheel, the state trooper threw up his hands to protect his face as a fireball streaked toward the windshield of his crippled vehicle. The window exploded into tiny, cutting shards. Then the billowing flames engulfed the car and filled the interior, instantly incinerating the two occupants.

1 2 3 4 5 6 7 8 9
10 11 12 13 **14** 15 16 17
18 19 20 21 22 23 24

. . . .

THE FOLLOWING TAKES PLACE
BETWEEN THE HOURS OF
8:00 P.M. AND 9:00 P.M.
EASTERN DAYLIGHT TIME

. . . .

8:01:29 P.M. EDT
Kurmastan, New Jersey

Jack Bauer stood in front of the burning cardboard factory, his form silhouetted by the crimson glow. Emergency
lights flickered around him, flashing from a dozen fire
trucks hastily summoned from the surrounding communi-
ties in response to one of the worst fires northwestern New
Jersey had ever witnessed.

In the middle of the smoking chaos, Jack collared a fire
chief. Water dripped from the fireman's helmet, to mingle
with the sweat on his smoke-blackened face.

"I need to get inside that factory," Jack cried over the roar of the blaze.

"Ain't gonna happen, buddy," the chief replied. "That fire is going to burn itself out. There's not enough water to smother it. We're pumping the wells dry as it is."

Jack looked around. Professional fire companies from Clinton, Phillipsburg, and Milford had joined volunteer units from Alpha, Milton, and Carpentersville to battle the roaring blaze. Though the old factory was by far the largest conflagration, houses and mobile homes were also engulfed in flames.

Suddenly a section of the factory roof collapsed. Rolling flames gushed out of the shattered windows and gaping doors. Cursing, Jack turned his back on the holocaust.

Any evidence the terrorists might have left inside that industrial building was incinerated now. Except for the intelligence provided by Judith Foy and the late Brice Holman, CTU was flying blind—unless they could get something out of Ali Rahman al Sallifi.

Jack ran among the emergency vehicles until he reached a CTU medical helicopter. The chief medical officer noticed Jack's arrival and faced him.

"I'm about to dispatch Imam al Sallifi to CTU for evaluation, Special Agent Bauer," the man said.

"What's his condition now?"

"Offhand, I'd say he was suffering from a drug-induced psychosis, but I couldn't tell you what drugs were pumped into him. He's also violent. My team had to tranquilize him before we could drag him out of that cave. He's dehydrated and malnourished, too."

"Will al Sallifi be able to talk?"

The medical officer shrugged. "In a few days, perhaps. But I doubt they'll get much out of him."

"How's the girl?"

"Danielle Taylor has been traumatized, but physically she'll recover."

"Take her back to CTU for debriefing," Bauer commanded. "And tell Security to turn Agent Abernathy over to the interim director—"

The officer blinked. "I didn't know we had an interim director."

"He's en route from Washington."

The officer yanked the helmet off his head and ran a gloved hand through dark, sweat-damp hair. "Layla Abernathy is asking to speak to you."

Jack's cell phone chirped.

"No time. Take Abernathy back to Manhattan. Let the interim director deal with her."

Bauer waved the officer away, then pressed the cell phone to his ear. "Bauer."

"It's me," Morris replied from the security console in New York.

"What have you learned?"

"First, I've identified someone from Brice Holman's surveillance photos. A fellow with bad dentures called 'the Hawk,' a warrior-hero from the Afghan war against the Russians. A couple of years back he became a terrorist. Been busy since then, in Milan, London, Hamburg. The usual things. Anarchy and murder."

"What's he doing in America?" Jack wondered aloud.

"Haven't a clue," Morris said. "But he has had past contact with the compound in Kurmastan. I also located a dossier on Ibrahim Noor. Smooth operator. Good at public relations. Despite local complaints about his compound, Noor has scored some success with the local politicians. He even endorsed the winning congresswoman for the district in the last election."

"Where did Noor come from?" Jack asked.

"He's made in America, Jack-o," Morris replied. "A product of the mean streets of Newark, New Jersey—"

"Newark!" Jack cried. "Where Foy was ambushed. Where Tony is holed up right now."

"Nice coincidence—"

"If it *is* a coincidence. Tell me more."

"Noor was born Travis Bell, in University Heights, forty-two years ago. Bell was a former gang leader and drug dealer from Newark. He was the prime suspect in several murders, and a rising star in the cocaine trade. And get this, Jack. Travis Bell had his own gang, named after the address where he grew up. Number Thirteen."

Jack let out a breath. "The tattoos—"

"On the late Rachel Delgado's arm, too, according to Tony Almeida," Morris replied.

Jack stroked his forehead, lost in thought.

"Listen, Morris. Forward everything you have about Ibrahim Noor and Travis Bell to Tony in Newark. I don't care how he does it. Just tell him to dig up all he can about the Thirteen Gang. Find out if they're still active and who their leader is now."

"Consider it done."

Jack hissed. "Tell me how a street thug like Travis Bell ends up a spiritual leader?"

"Well, Jack-o, it seems Mr. Bell converted under the spiritual guidance of Ali Rahman al Sallifi, while he was serving a ten-year sentence for a drug conviction."

"Converted to Islam, you mean?" Jack said.

"No, I don't," Morris replied. "They might use the jargon—jihad, *Khilafah*, and all that—but what Ali Rahman al Sallifi was preaching wasn't Islam at all. It was more like something out of Jim Jones and the Kool-Aid drinkers in Jonestown."

Morris paused, "The Warriors of God is a *cult*, Jack. Pure and simple. Ali Rahman al Sallifi and Ibrahim Noor set *themselves* up as prophets, or maybe even gods. They preached violence, not spirituality. And now their deluded followers have gone on some kind of insane rampage."

"No," Jack said. "Not insane. There's a reason behind this attack. It's not random because too many elements are involved—Mangella in Little Italy, the Albino. Someone is pulling strings here. There's some ultimate goal in mind. We just haven't figured it out yet."

He heard voices on the other end of the line, then Morris vanished for a moment. "Are you there, Morris?"

"Sorry, Jack," O'Brian replied. "We've just received word of a terror attack in Pennsylvania. A State Police car was run off the road by a truck, and he reported the license plate of one of the vehicles registered to the paper factory in Kurmastan. A minute after receiving that initial report, the truck stop where the squad car was wrecked blew up—multiple bombs with many estimated casualties."

Jack cursed.

"A nearby tank farm went up, too," Morris continued. "Now half the town of Carlisle is burning."

In the ruins of Kurmastan, Jack blinked, faced the blazing factory again. He tried to imagine an innocent American town reduced to this smoldering inferno around him. Then Jack caught his breath.

"Did you say Carlisle?"

"You got friends there, Jack?"

"That's the home of the new Special Operations Tactical Training School, part of the Army War College. Ryan Chappelle is lodging at the barracks right now. He's in the middle of a nine-week training seminar on counterterrorist tactics."

"No wonder it was so quiet in the L.A. office," Morris quipped.

"Are you tracking that truck now, Morris?"

"I am," Morris replied. "After the blast, I positioned a satellite over that section of Central Pennsylvania, and homed in on the bloody bastards."

Anticipating Jack's next request, Morris called up the location of the training school on his monitor. He whistled.

"Good instincts, Jack-o. That truck is making a beeline for the SOTTS. It should arrive in half an hour or so."

"Alert the school, warn them what they're up against. And see if you can reach Ryan personally."

"I'm on it, Jack," Morris replied. His fingers flew across

the keyboard as he entered the codes to send out the dispatch.

In Kurmastan, Jack felt the heat from the smoldering ruins. "They've struck first," he said softly. "Before we could stop them."

"We'll get them," Morris insisted. "We're using highway surveillance cameras to check license plates. Every state and local police department has been alerted. Dr. Guilling has arrived here in New York. He's shifting satellites over the eastern seaboard. It's only a matter of time—"

"Did you say Dr. Guilling was in New York? I thought Ted was at Langley," Jack said.

"The new director brought him along. In fact, nearly everyone has been replaced with the interim director's people. They marched in here like a conquering army and swept the place clean." O'Brian chuckled. "It's a wonder I kept my job."

"I'm boarding a helicopter now," Jack said. "Locate those trucks, and relay their coordinates to me as soon as you get them."

8:38:25 P.M. EDT
Special Operations Tactical Training School
Security Gate

As soon as Ryan Chappelle got the warning from CTU, he alerted the rest of the men in his barracks that they were about to be attacked—for real. The men immediately sprang into action.

"If this operation is successful, it will be the fastest ambush ever mounted in the history of counterterrorist operations."

The speaker was Joe Smith. Like the other instructors at the counterterrorism seminar, Smith was an active duty special operations soldier. and the name he was using was an alias.

"If it doesn't work, we're all going to be in trouble for raiding the armory without proper authorization," said William Bendix. The tall African American had the body of a pro wrestler and a shaved head. He wore a utility vest, sans shirt, and a briefcase-sized magnetic mine was slung over his broad back.

"As senior officer, I'll take responsibility. If this is a bust, it'll be my neck under the hatchet."

Smith spoke with quiet authority and a southern drawl. He clutched a Heckler & Koch UMP .45 with a twenty-five-round magazine in his large hands, and several concussion grenades were hooked to the belt of his black denim pants. A big man, he had stained his face and hands with shoe polish that rendered him nearly invisible in the darkness. Smith crouched behind a decorative stone fence, watching the well-lit road that led from the front gate at the bottom of the hill, right up to the main building.

"This whole thing sounds loco to me, man," said Ben Johnson, a Hispanic standing close to Smith. "Mad cultists driving trucks of death? Come on. Someone at Langley must have had an Austin Powers moment to feed us that kind of intel."

His teeth white against a face streaked with dark paint, Johnson held a Colt Commando in his scarred fist.

"You've got it wrong. The threat is real," protested Ryan Chappelle, the Regional Director of CTU Los Angeles. "You heard about the blasts in Carlisle, and you read the alert that came over the military wire. And I spoke to one of my operatives, personally. This intelligence is solid—from one of my best agents. Though I don't like Bauer personally, his job performance is—"

"Bauer? Are you talking about *Jack* Bauer?" asked a man who called himself Martin Eden.

"That's correct," Chappelle replied. "Jack was Delta Force before he came to CTU . . . Perhaps you knew him."

Eden flashed Chappelle a feral grin. "Nope. Never heard of no Jack Bauer. And, for the record, Delta is an *airline*."

The men around Chappelle chuckled. Ryan frowned, not understanding why the others were laughing.

"Yo, check the gate," the man named Moe Howard called from his position near a bronze statue of colonial hero Robert Rogers, the founding leader of America's first special ops unit, back in 1756.

Joe Smith squinted in the distance. "I see lights. Looks like a truck. Let's see what the driver does."

Martin Eden raised night vision binoculars. "It's an eighteen-wheeler with a long trailer. Logo's too small to read from here. D . . . R . . . something. Wait a minute! The truck just smashed through the front gate. Now *that* wasn't friendly."

"Take position, everyone," Joe Smith commanded.

A half-dozen men fanned out down the hill, vanishing in the shadows among the trees and brush of the land-scaped hillside.

"What do you want me to do?" Ryan Chappelle whispered.

"You came here for some hands-on counterterrorism experience, so I'll hand you this." Joe Smith thrust a Glock into Ryan's limp grip. "If I point at something and say 'shoot there,' you do it. Otherwise stay out of the way."

Ryan chewed his lip and gave the man a nod.

The truck was rumbling up the hill now, close enough for Ryan to hear the growl of its diesel engine. He tucked the gun in his belt and lifted his micro-binoculars.

Under the streetlight, Ryan thought he saw a dark figure dart into the roadway beside the truck. If it was one of the special ops men, he was gone before Ryan could be certain.

Suddenly Chappelle was blinded by a yellow flash—an explosion that blew the back wheels off the trailer. The cab kept moving, dragging the tottering cargo bay with it, until a second explosion went off under the engine block. That blast blew off the front tire, shattered the truck's windows, and sent the engine cover flying into the air.

"The squids were right," Martin Eden said in the tone of a professional evaluating a new product. "Those magnetic mines blew the hell out of that truck. I'd love to see what they do to a boat."

On the narrow road, the semi's blasted cab came to an abrupt halt when the axle dug into the asphalt. Then its trailer jackknifed, and the whole rig tumbled on its side, breaking in half as it smashed a section of the stone fence.

The din faded, and for a long moment all was silent. Then the cargo doors opened with a loud bang. Red tracer fire cut through the night. Men rolled out of the truck, into a fusillade of fire and a rain of concussion grenades. Howling, the terrorists fell, one by one, until there was no one left alive.

In the darkness around the ribbon of road, voices cried out. "Clear!"

"Clear here."

"All clear!"

"Anybody hurt?" Joe Smith called. A chorus of negatives greeted him. Only then did he realize the ambush was over—and he hadn't fired a shot.

Martin Eden rose from his hiding place and ran toward the wreck, Ryan Chappelle on his heels. Other men emerged from hiding and swarmed over the smashed truck, checking the bodies, then the contents of the cargo bay.

"I got nine unfriendlies down, no survivors," Moe Howard declared. "There are some maps and stuff in the cab. Might be intel. Might be crap."

"I don't know about intel, but there are enough guns and ammo here to start a war," Larry Fine said, shaking his head.

"There must be a ton of C–4, too, manufactured with easy-set timers and ready to go," Smith observed, his facade of calm suddenly cracking.

As they fumbled through the wreckage, reality began

to dawn on all of them as the magnitude of the threat was slowly revealed.

Finally, Martin Eden faced Ryan Chappelle. "Jack Bauer says there are eleven more trucks on the prowl just like this one, right?"

"That's right."

Eden frowned. "Then God help us."

1 2 3 4 5 6 7 8 9
10 11 12 13 14 **15** 16 17
18 19 20 21 22 23 24

. . . .

**THE FOLLOWING TAKES PLACE
BETWEEN THE HOURS OF
9:00 P.M. AND 10:00 P.M.
EASTERN DAYLIGHT TIME**

. . . .

9:10:20 P.M. EDT
Eight hundred feet above Interstate 495
New Jersey

Jack Bauer leaned through the door of the CTU helicopter, wind tearing at his hair. His right hand gripped the exit bar. His left clutched a thick rope attached to a winch on the side of the fuselage.

A six-lane highway rolled under the belly of the racing Sikorsky, a long ribbon of glowing headlights against a crowded urban landscape. In the distance, Bauer could see the Manhattan skyline glittering against the violet sky.

"You're telling me one of the trucks is down there?"

Jack yelled into his headset. His heart was racing and he was ignoring a cold sweat.

"Yes," said Morris.

"I need confirmation!"

"Right," said Morris. "I'll forward the satellite feed to the navigational computer inside your chopper. Give me a moment . . ."

"I've got the target on-screen now, Agent Bauer," Captain Fogarty informed him seconds later.

Jack strained to hear the voices over the throb of the pounding rotors. He released the rope, increased the volume on his headset, and twisted the earphone tighter.

"This truck was holed up in the parking lot of Giants Stadium since early afternoon," Morris explained. "About an hour ago, Meadowlands security finally got suspicious and dispatched officers to check out the vehicle. Two guards were killed; a third is in critical condition and not expected to live. And the truck, as you can obviously see from my tracking, got away from them."

"And you're positive you've locked on the right vehicle?" Jack pressed.

"The survivor managed to get the license number," said Morris. "The truck's from Kurmastan."

The increasingly bizarre pattern of attack puzzled Jack. A highway rest stop. A gas farm. Then a failed assault on a military training school.

"Why did they stop at the stadium?" Jack asked Morris. "Did they plant explosives there before they left?"

"Unlikely. The New Jersey State Police and the bomb-sniffing dogs have been going over every inch of the

Meadowlands Sports Center. They're still looking," Morris answered. "But so far they've found nothing."

"Why would the terrorists hole up in a parking lot?" Jack wondered aloud. "Could they be on some kind of schedule?"

"I've no idea," Morris replied. "But we've got this vehicle locked. I'm watching a live satellite feed of the truck right now. You're practically on top of it, Jack-o."

Jack gazed at the river of headlights below. "Can you guess where they're going?"

"Into the Lincoln Tunnel," said Morris.

Jack instantly pictured thousands of commuters, driving under the Hudson, rolling into the heart of Manhattan. He flashed on midtown, Broadway, Times Square, theaters, restaurants, all jammed with tourists, office workers, families—innocent targets.

Jack's jaw clenched. "I need to stop that truck before it gets to the tunnel."

"*You?*" said Morris. "Jack, listen to me. I can have a local SWAT team at the tunnel exit in ten minutes—"

"No. The men in that truck know they're hunted. They'll react like trapped animals at any sign of the authorities. And there's a risk of collateral damage if the police respond recklessly."

"Jack, let the authorities handle it."

"What if that vehicle is a truck bomb they plan to detonate inside the tunnel? It will be Oklahoma City times ten."

Captain Fogarty called to Jack from the cockpit. "What do you want to do, Bauer?"

"Where's the truck now?" Jack asked.

"It's two hundred feet under us. I'm watching it with our belly camera right now," the pilot replied.

"Good. I can make a fast-rope descent. If I can get on the back of the trailer, I can—"

"Fast-rope out of a moving chopper?" Fogarty cut in. "You're nuts, Bauer—"

"I've done it before," Jack insisted. "Get me down to an altitude of fifty feet. All I need is a wide open space, a short stretch of highway without high tension wires or an overpass."

Fogarty shook his head. "I don't like it, but if you're serious, I can put you over the ramp."

"What ramp?"

"The Jersey interstate ends in a long, curved downhill ramp that leads to the tollbooths. There are no overpasses, no electric lines or telephone cables, either. Traffic may even slow a little as it backs up at the toll plaza. Even then, we won't be hovering. We'll be moving at forty or fifty miles per hour."

Jack had learned helicopter assault tactics in the Army, and he'd used those skills on many Delta Force missions. Swinging on a fast-rope wasn't a problem for him, though he knew it would be a lot tougher from a moving aircraft.

"Listen, Fogarty, I can do this." Jack's tone was sure. "Your job is to get me over that truck."

"Weehawken is two minutes ahead. After that it's the ramp and the tunnel," Fogarty's copilot warned.

Fogarty grunted. "Okay, Bauer, you win. Get ready to move when I give the signal. We'll reach the ramp in approximately two minutes. After that, you'll have about a minute to make your descent before we'll have to pull up."

Bauer nodded. "Do it."

Adrenaline feeding his veins, Jack slipped a new clip into the Glock, then tucked the weapon into its holster. The few doubts he had burned away as he focused on the details, inspecting the fast-rope on the chopper. Because it wasn't anchored to the ground, the fast-rope had to be thick, heavy, and long to prevent it from being jerked around by the tremendous down draft from the rotors. This rope looked good. It was at least fifty millimeters in diameter and it was more than one hundred feet long— more than sufficient for a descent.

Gloves were essential in a descent like this, otherwise friction could strip his palms raw. Fortunately there were gloves and knee pads among the chopper's stores, though Jack could find no helmet—not even a hockey-style head protector like the ones he'd worn in Delta.

"Bauer, we're beyond the last overpass and dropping now. Get ready to move," Captain Fogarty warned in Jack's ear.

Jack inhaled, his heartbeat slowing as he took control of his breathing and his impatience, focused on his actions. The chopper's sudden descent made his stomach lurch. He ignored the discomfort, clipped a deadweight to the end of the rope, and tossed it through the open door. The cord quickly unspooled to a length of sixty feet. He locked the winch, slipped the gloves over his hands, and seized the thick cable.

Jack could see the truck now, its shape outlined by four dim lights on top of the trailer.

"Go! Go now," Fogarty cried.

Still clinging to the rope, Jack stepped out of the helicopter. He dangled for a moment, the rotor blades throbbing above, the traffic roaring below, the pilot's voice lost in the howling maelstrom.

Buffeted by the merciless downdraft, Jack waited for the chopper to line up over the vehicle. Then the rope began to spin. Without hooks or a safety harness, there was nothing to hold Jack to that lifeline but the strength of his grip. Now the wild movement threatened to throw him off. And the spinning would only get worse the longer he hung there.

Captain Fogarty swooped low and positioned the chopper directly over the speeding truck. Still twisting in the wind, Jack aimed his feet at the swaying silver trailer far beneath the soles of his boots.

Finally, Jack eased his grip on the rope and began the descent . . .

9:20:29 P.M. EDT
Interstate 495, at the Weehawken Exit
New Jersey

Inside the rumbling trailer, the members of the Warriors of God cult heard the rotors beating over their heads. Farshid Amadani—the Hawk—felt three pairs of eyes watching him expectantly, waiting for him to issue a command.

"Have they found us, Hawk?" one man asked, his voice trembling with emotion.

"They found us at the stadium, my friend. It was only a matter of time before they tracked us down," the former mujahideen replied, his tone resigned.

The throbbing intensified as the helicopter descended upon the rumbling truck. Inside the trailer, the air was hot and suffocating, tinged with the chemical taint of explosives.

"Turn out the lights," the Hawk commanded.

In a moment, the interior of the cavernous trailer was plunged into darkness. Amadani used a dim emergency flashlight pulled from his black utility vest to climb the stacked crates of C–4. He moved with caution, careful to avoid the crisscrossing detonation cords.

In the dull glow of the crimson light, the Hawk unlocked the roof hatch and cracked it. The slipstream whooshed around his ears, filling the stuffy trailer with a blast of fresh air.

Peering through the hatch, the Hawk saw the belly of the helicopter above him, a long rope dangling down. He frowned when he spied a single man in a blue battle suit hanging from the door. Amadani quickly closed the hatch before the other man spotted him.

"We are about to be boarded," the Hawk warned.

The men cried out.

"Remember we are warriors! Martyrs for the jihad!" Amadani bellowed, his fierce words drowning their laments.

"I shall swat this flea," the Hawk said. "You will follow

the *alternative* plan and detonate this vehicle inside the Lincoln Tunnel."

The men nodded. Grim-faced, they began to arm the explosives.

Still perched on the crates, the Hawk touched the pocket of his combat vest. He considered using his cell to inform Ibrahim Noor that they'd been discovered, that this truck would not be in position to destroy the Brooklyn Bridge at dawn and provide the necessary diversion for Noor's final, devastating strike. But he didn't make the call. Why should he? Noor and his foreign allies were monitoring the situation from a secure location, and they would know he and his men had failed. Any call he made now might be tapped and traced by their enemies.

Better to keep the infidels fumbling in the dark, the Hawk decided as a sudden thump sounded above him.

Clutching a USP Tactical in his scarred hand, the Hawk muttered a final prayer for himself and his warriors. Then he opened the hatch . . .

9:22:53 P.M. EDT
On the 495 ramp to the Lincoln Tunnel

Jack Bauer landed with a bruising crash, facedown on the top of the speeding trailer. Battling the relentless slipstream, he hugged the ridged aluminum while he brought his legs up under him. He climbed to his feet the same way he used to mount a surfboard, using his arms for balance.

But instead of smelling a cool ocean breeze, Jack choked

on hot exhaust fumes belched by the cab's twin stacks. He lurched forward, through the smog, toward the cab and the man behind the wheel. The roof had evenly spaced ridges, and they helped Jack maintain his balance as he stumbled to the front of the trailer.

Meanwhile the truck rolled down the center lane at a good clip, cars, buses, and other trucks flowing around it. Over Jack's head, the staccato beat of the whirling rotors intensified when Captain Fogarty pulled up and banked over the Hudson. In seconds, the helicopter was no more than a dark silhouette against the glistening skyline.

Jack planned to smash his way into the passenger compartment and take out the driver. Once he gained control of the vehicle, he could swerve away from the tunnel and its traffic, neutralize the other terrorists in a remote location—or simply drive the whole damned rig into the Hudson River if he had to.

He'd almost reached the cab when Jack heard a clang. A roof hatch opened directly in front of him, and a figure emerged clutching a handgun. Jack recognized him immediately, from the surveillance photos Morris had forwarded to his PDA—Farshid Amadani, a.k.a. the Hawk.

Before the terrorist could take aim, Jack launched himself at Amadani. The velocity of Jack's charge carried them both over the edge of the trailer. They landed on top of the cab with a loud crash; a roof light shattered under the Hawk's battered spine. Jack, who was cushioned from the fall by the other man's body, heard Amadani gasp, smelled his sour breath.

Jack groped for the weapon, his fingers closing on the

man's wrist. The Hawk fought, refusing to release his handgun. He sank his yellow teeth into Bauer's shoulder and bit down. Jack howled and slammed his right fist into the man's abdomen, his left still clutching the man's wrist. Amadani cried out and pushed Jack aside. Together they rolled off the roof of the cab and slammed onto the engine's hood.

Still grappling, Jack was on the bottom now. The hot metal scorched his back. The noise battered his ears. Jack glimpsed the startled face of the driver, the USP Tactical waving at him through the windshield as the men struggled to control the weapon.

Jack slammed his knee into Amadani's groin—and the gun bucked in the man's hand. The Hawk fired twice. Glass shattered, and Jack heard a howl. Still struggling, he glanced at the driver through the broken windshield. The man was clutching the steering wheel, crimson gore gushing from a ghastly head wound. Meanwhile the rig rolled on, increasing speed as it descended the incline.

The Hawk saw the driver, too, and his eyes went wide. Jack used the opening to strike back. He brought up his knee again, to deal another punishing blow to his foe's genitals. Then he used both legs to toss the Hawk aside. The man's gun bounced off the hood, and tumbled onto the pavement.

Amadani flew off the hood, too, but the sleeve of his utility vest snagged the rearview mirror, and the Hawk ended up dangling helplessly. He'd banged his head on the way down, and blood poured from a gash in his forehead.

In the cab, the unconscious driver slumped forward, his

foot depressing the gas pedal. The truck lurched sideways and careened into the guardrail. Sparks flew as the semi roared forward. Chunks of concrete fell from the crumbling guardrail.

Jack rolled onto his stomach. Ignoring the truck's searing hot hood under his chest and belly, he reached for Amadani.

"Take my hand!" Jack cried.

Panting, the Afghani sneered and spit blood. "I am not afraid to die," he cried.

Jack's fingers closed on the collar of the man's combat vest. "You don't have to be a martyr."

"Yes. I do," the Hawk replied.

As Jack tugged on the man's vest, the former mujahideen threw up his arms and slipped free of the garment. The rig bounced once as Amadani was swept under the rolling wheels.

Jack scrambled to his feet, then cringed when a bullet punched a hole in the hood. Another armed man had appeared on the roof of the trailer.

Jack reached for his Glock—and the vehicle lurched violently, as the guardrail broke under its weight.

Time to go.

Still clutching Hawk's vest, Jack leaped off the out-of-control cab and slammed down on the luggage rack of a passing SUV. His arrival so surprised the driver that the woman braked, nearly throwing Jack under the wheels of a giant commuter bus.

Jack hung on, and watched the big rig rip through the steel guardrail and tumble off the curved ramp. A moment later, he heard a second thunderous crash when the truck slammed into the ground far below.

9:59:21 P.M. EDT
CTU Headquarters, NYC

Peter Randall closed the office door and sat down behind Layla Abernathy's desk. He adjusted the round glasses on his bland, boyish face, then went to work.

First he sorted through the stack of papers until he located the most current threat report. Then Randall activated Layla's computer and typed in the woman's secret password. When he was inside her system, he slipped a thumb drive into the USB port.

It took less than a minute to download the data into Agent Abernathy's secure files, and another minute to alter the times and dates on the file folders. Finally, Randall deleted the computer's log, erasing any sign of tampering, and put the computer back to sleep again.

Threat report in hand, Peter Randall left Layla's office and returned to Security Station One.

"I have the threat report you requested," he said.

"Great," Morris O'Brian replied. "Hand it over, mate."

. . . .

THE FOLLOWING TAKES PLACE
BETWEEN THE HOURS OF
10:00 P.M. AND 11:00 P.M.
EASTERN DAYLIGHT TIME

. . . .

10:03:07 P.M. EDT
Detention Block
CTU Tactical Center, NYC

Layla Abernathy shivered. She wanted to cover herself,
but her arms and legs were shackled to a steel chair bolted
to the floor. A chain around her throat kept her back rigid,
her head erect.

She sat in the center of a large chamber, her surround-
ings dark, cold, and damp—almost medieval. The con-
tours of the detainment room's gray walls seemed to defy
geometry, a mad tangle of arches, angles, and shadows like
something out of the German Expressionist films she'd

watched in graduate school. There was no sound, except for the echo of dripping water.

They'd taken Layla's overalls and all the tactical gear she'd carried to Kurmastan, left her with only a white T-shirt and the spandex bicycle pants she'd worn underneath. She listened while a security team searched through her gear, which was spread out on a steel table behind her. Layla couldn't imagine what they were looking for and she didn't ask.

No point. They wouldn't answer me anyway . . .

Soon the guards left Layla alone, and there was nothing to listen to but the slow, maddening drip.

Then a loud clang startled her. Somewhere close by, a steel door opened and closed. Layla heard two pairs of footsteps clicking hollowly in the nearly empty cell. One man stopped at the table, and Layla heard a metallic click, like a latch being opened.

The second man loomed over her. He was thin, almost skeletal, with high cheekbones, sunken eyes, and thin, expressionless lips.

"Do you know who I am, Agent Abernathy?" the man asked in a quiet, calm voice.

Layla shook her head. She'd been holding her body as still as possible, trying to keep her mind clear and focused. Now her lower lip began to tremble.

"My name is Christopher Henderson. I'm now in charge of the New York Division. Do you understand me?"

"Yes," Layla said, cursing the tremor in her voice.

A strong hand seized her shoulder and an alcohol swab swiped her forearm.

"No," she gasped.

Layla tried to move but was pinned like a butterfly on display. Her mouth was parched, her heart thumped in her chest. She barely suppressed the urge to scream.

"This will hurt a little," Henderson warned.

Layla winced at the needle prick.

For a moment, she felt nothing. Then her limbs began to tingle as if they were on fire, burning from the *inside*. Layla jerked wildly as her muscles tensed uncontrollably, and she strained at her bonds. Moaning, Layla chewed her lip and tasted blood. The pain intensified, until it felt like her heart was pumping boiling lava through her veins.

Finally, Layla cried out. In a moment, the pain eased.

"That was only the beginning," Henderson said. "How much more agony you'll endure depends on whether or not I'm satisfied with the answers you give me. Do you understand?"

"Yes," Layla rasped.

"Good," Henderson said, his tone obscenely cheerful. "Let's begin . . ."

10:41:54 P.M. EDT
Under the 495 ramp to the Lincoln Tunnel

Jack Bauer examined the mangled wreckage in the glare of spotlights. Emergency beacons flashed around him. A number of local fire companies as well as the New Jersey State Police Bomb Squad had converged on the scene. When Jack showed them his CTU ID, they allowed him to pass through the police line to view the devastation.

The truck from Kurmastan had plunged almost two hundred feet off the ramp and slammed into a Conrail switching station. The cab had been crushed beyond recognition; the dead driver was still inside. Though its tank had ruptured, and the smell of diesel fuel permeated the area, there was no fire. Still, firemen spread flame-retardant foam on the spillage to reduce the chance of accidental conflagration.

When it struck the switching station, the trailer had cracked open like an eggshell, spilling its deadly contents onto the railroad tracks. The aluminum shell was so twisted, Jack could hardly make out the Dreizehn Trucking logo on its hull. Plastic-wrapped bricks of C–4 were scattered like confetti. The cargo bay had been stuffed with enough explosives to bring down the roof of the Lincoln Tunnel, or level much of Times Square, if either attack had been part of the terrorists' plan.

Among shattered crates of C–4 and an armory of guns and ammunition, Bauer counted two mangled bodies. A third corpse dangled from the top of a nearby telephone pole, where the crew of a Weehawken Fire Department ladder truck was preparing to bring it down.

Across from the tangled wreck on the railroad tracks was Waterfront Terrace Road. Its large marina complex and luxury restaurant were now being evacuated via the Hudson River. Jack could see a fleet of police and fire boats bobbing in the dark water, the lit-up Manhattan skyline rising beyond.

Jack turned away from the glare, gazed at the liquid

crystal display on the PDA in his hand. The device had once belonged to the Hawk. Jack had found it, along with a cell phone, in the pocket of the man's black utility vest, which Jack now wore over his blue jumpsuit. Bauer had already forwarded the contents of the device and the Hawk's cell phone to Morris O'Brian for further analysis.

While he awaited the results, Jack studied a series of road maps stored in the PDA's memory. He was interrupted when his own cell phone vibrated.

"Bauer."

"It's me," said Morris. "You're looking at the maps?"

"Yes," Jack replied. "There are six of them—"

"That's right, Jack-o," Morris interrupted. "Two match the routes taken by the truck that hit Carlisle, and the vehicle you just took down—"

"So the other four maps might indicate the routes taken by other trucks that we have yet to locate," Jack said, thumbing through the PDA's index.

"*Might* is the problem," said Morris. "It's such a troublesome little word."

"*Might* is what leads are made of," Jack replied.

"Good point."

Jack squinted at the tiny screen. "Looks like one map outlines a route to Atlantic City. And another's going to a location outside of Rutland, Vermont."

"There are two trucks heading for Boston, too." Morris paused. "Director Henderson has ordered me to alert the proper state and local authorities. Thanks to you, we have a chance of stopping these trucks. A good chance."

But Jack remembered what Brice Holman had said

before he'd expired. He'd seen twelve trucks, *twelve*, loaded with armed men, leaving Kurmastan that morning.

Which still leaves six more out there—somewhere, Jack thought, *if I want to trust Holman's intel, and I have few doubts on that score . . .*

Morris seemed to read his mind. "Don't worry, Jack. You'll stop them."

Jack shook off his anxiety and redirected Morris. "What about the contents of Farshid Amadani's cell phone?"

"Nine numbers are stored there," Morris replied. "Eight of them are for cell phones with bogus accounts."

"And the ninth?"

"An unlisted number for the West Side apartment of one Erno Tobias, a citizen of Switzerland. Mr. Tobias is an executive officer for Rogan Pharmaceuticals."

Jack flashed back to the stockpile of steroids and amphetamines at Kurmastan. They'd all come from Rogan Pharmaceuticals.

"I've just pulled up the passport photo for Mr. Tobias from the State Department database, and I'm forwarding it to you," Morris continued. "You might recognize him."

The PDA beeped in Jack's hand, and he retrieved the digital image. Surprise struck him at the sight of the pale white face.

"It's the Albino," Jack said. "The man who killed Fredo Mangella in Little Italy."

"I have an address," Morris announced. "Nice digs, too. It appears Mr. Tobias occupies an apartment on Central Park West."

The address flashed on the PDA screen.

"Got it," said Jack. "I'm going there now."

10:56:25 P.M. EDT
Security Booth
General Aviation Electronics
Rutland, Vermont

On this wood-lined stretch of Route 4, just a few miles from Pine Hill Park, rush hour occurred three times a day, coinciding with the shift changes at the massive General Aviation Electronics manufacturing plant.

At seven A.M., three P.M., and again at eleven P.M., a steady stream of cars, pickups, and minivans flowed off Columbian Avenue, onto a short driveway that led into the access-restricted parking lot.

Because of the classified nature of the devices manufactured here, which included vital components for the U.S. military's fleet of high-performance jet aircraft, there was only one way in or out of the plant. That road was straddled by a gated security booth and manned by two armed guards.

While there was always a delay at rush hour, tonight's was worse than usual because of a security alert issued by the Federal government less than thirty minutes earlier.

Most days, gaining admittance to the employee parking lot was a simple process. The electronic pass glued to the workers' windshields allowed them to be waved through. But tonight the two guards inside the glass booth had been instructed to stop each vehicle and check the IDs of all occupants. The security officers were also advised to be on the lookout for suspicious vehicles, especially large trucks.

It was Officer Darla Famini and her partner, Archie

Lamb, who were taking the heat for the delay, mostly from workers rolling in at the last minute for the night shift.

"Come on, Darla, what's the problem?" complained a corpulent man behind the wheel of a late-model GM pickup. "You ought to know me. I'm your damned cousin."

"Sorry, Billy," Darla said, handing him back his employee ID. "Tonight we have to check everybody. We have a situation."

"*Situation?*" Billy rolled his eyes. "We haven't had a situation since Ronald Reagan was President."

Darla frowned. "We've got one tonight."

Billy adjusted his ball cap. "Lucky me. I'm at the end of the line."

"You have plenty of time to clock in," Officer Famini replied, waving him through.

As the gate went up, Billy glanced into his rearview mirror. "Here comes someone else you can harass," he said. Then he pulled away in a cloud of exhaust smoke.

Darla watched two headlights bounce up the driveway. Her partner appeared at her shoulder.

"That's a truck," said Archie Lamb.

The night sky was clear and cloudless above Rutland, the stars and planets sharply bright. Darla could make out the vehicle, too.

"Aren't we supposed to be on the lookout for big trucks?" Archie asked.

"Put the flashers on," Darla said.

Archie hit the button, and red warning lights lit up around the booth.

"He's still coming," said Darla.

Archie pointed. "Looks like he's speeding up."

"Contact the night supervisor!"

While Archie dialed the number, Darla punched another button on her console. Long, metal spikes popped out of the pavement. If the truck tried to pass through the gates now, its tires would be shredded.

She expected the driver to see the spikes and slow his vehicle, but he didn't. The truck kept right on coming, its headlights filling the booth. At the last possible instant, the vehicle swerved away from the tire-shredding spikes sticking out of the roadway and crashed right through the security booth.

The flimsy structure exploded into shards of glass and shattered lights; Darla and Archie were killed instantly; and the Dreizehn Trucking vehicle continued on, through the parking lot. Because of the shift change, the lot was jammed with cars and employees. The truck barreled through them, running down those who reacted too slowly.

The big rig rolled right up to the massive steel doors to the plant—and smashed right through them. Then a white flash lit up the night. With a single deafening blast, the General Aviation Electronics plant was leveled. Eight hundred men and women, fully two-thirds of the plant's workforce, were murdered.

The blast was so powerful, it blew the leaves off trees and turned over cars on Route 4. Miles away, windows in homes and businesses near Rutland's famed historic district were shattered.

Flames quickly spread to a nearby battery factory, where

a half-dozen chemical tanks ruptured, spewing millions of metric tons of poisonous fumes into the air.

As the cloud of toxic death spread, birds fell from the trees, their feathered carcasses dropping onto lawns and streets. Hundreds of people, tucked into their cozy homes for the night, succumbed immediately. Minivans and SUVs ran up into yards and through fences as their drivers instantly perished.

In the next few minutes, many more would die as a hellish orange glow spread out over Rutland, smothering the night sky, extinguishing every last point of light in the clear, cloudless heavens.

1 2 3 4 5 6 7 8 9
10 11 12 13 14 15 16 **17**
18 19 20 21 22 23 24

. . . .

THE FOLLOWING TAKES PLACE
BETWEEN THE HOURS OF
11:00 P.M. AND 12:00 A.M.
EASTERN DAYLIGHT TIME

. . . .

11:03:26 P.M. EDT
Ivy Avenue at Beacon Street
Newark, New Jersey

"God go with you," the old man said in Spanish.

"*Gracias, Padre,*" Tony replied. Then he turned from
the scarred metal door, glanced up and down the deserted
block, and ducked into a shadowy alley.

This broken-down neighborhood had been a thriving
area once, housing union workers for the nearby industrial
section of the city. But the industries were long gone now,
along with the well-paid jobs. The buildings around him
appeared abandoned, too; but Tony knew, from the amount

of discarded hypodermic needles and heroin wrappers scattered around, there had to be a shooting gallery somewhere on this block.

Ahead, in the darkness, he sensed movement—a figure stepped out of a doorway, walked toward him.

"Well, Almeida?" whispered a woman's voice. "Get anything?"

Judith Foy was still wearing her tracksuit and ball cap. She'd been hiding in the alley, staying out of sight while Tony conducted a quiet discussion with an old, white-haired priest.

Tony rubbed his soul patch. "Yeah," he said. "I got something. An address."

He'd been looking for intel on the Thirteen Gang. CTU had nothing in their database, but apparently they were still active here in Newark. And since Tony couldn't simply go to the Newark Police, flash his CTU ID, and ask for a file, he set out to do his own legwork.

He'd noticed fishes painted on the sides of buildings, like graffiti, with Spanish words scrawled inside, and he knew these were markers, leading illegal aliens to a Catholic rescue mission, where they could get help if they were in trouble with authorities, the law, or anyone else.

It was late, but Tony figured an underground rescue mission would have someone guarding the door 24/7. Sure enough, after only two sharp knocks, the heavy, battered door had cracked open.

He'd spoken to the priest in street Spanish, telling him he was trying to help his girlfriend, whose son had gotten involved with a gang. "Please, I have to find him. He may be in danger of overdosing on drugs. Can you tell me where the Thirteen Gang hangs out in this area?"

The priest was quiet for a long minute, just staring at Tony. Finally, he said, "I don't believe your story."

The priest said he'd heard enough confessions to hear in man's voice when he was lying. But he said that he felt in Tony's spirit and saw in his eyes that he was not an evil man.

Tony assured the priest that what he was doing was for the good of many—and he wouldn't reveal where he'd learned the information. The priest gave him the address, and they'd bid each other good night.

"Sounds like you're pretty familiar with life on the streets," Foy observed.

"Yeah, well . . . talking the talk helps."

Tony had steered clear of gangs and drugs while growing up on Chicago's South Side, mostly because his eyes were always fixed on a career in the Marine Corps. But he'd still lived on the streets—and if you wanted to keep on living, you knew whom to trust, whom to avoid, and whom to go to for information without fear of reprisals.

"So what did the man tell you?" Judith asked.

"That the Thirteen Gang has a crib on Crampton Street, three blocks away. An old brick house with a steel door painted red, all the windows boarded up so it looks abandoned."

Foy nodded. "I remember that location. We passed it half an hour ago. Come on, I know the way . . ."

11:49:56 P.M. EDT
The Beresfield Apartments
Central Park West
New York, New York

Jack Bauer stood on the corner of West Sixty-fourth and
Central Park West, staring at the eighth floor of the Beresfield Apartments. The landmark building sat across the
street from Central Park, and beside the New York Society
for Ethical Culture.

The ornate, terra-cotta trimmed structure had been
constructed in the 1930s, according to the bronze plaque
set above the cornerstone. The plaque also stated that the
Beresfield was the home of the wealthy and influential,
but Jack Bauer was interested in only one of the building's
occupants: Erno Tobias, an executive for Rogan Pharmaceuticals.

Jack needed to surprise Tobias if the man was home, or
thoroughly search the Albino's apartment if he wasn't. But
getting inside wasn't going to be easy. It was close to midnight, but many of the apartments were still brightly lit.
The Beresfield boasted both a doorman and a desk clerk.
Going through the front door was not an option.

Fortunately, the Beresfield was an old building, with an
outmoded security system that relied too heavily on the
men at the front door, and not enough on modern technology. Jack saw no cameras or motion detectors outside
the lobby door, or at the service entrance on Sixty-sixth
Street.

Jack had already decided to enter through the service

entrance. It was tucked behind an eight-foot cast-iron fence, in a shadowy alley between the Beresfield and the building behind it. All he had to do was climb the fence, pick the lock, and he would be inside. But he was forced to wait a few minutes while a chain-smoking, anorexic-thin woman finished walking her poodle. She did at last, flouting the pooper-scooper law by leaving the dog's dump at the base of a fire hydrant. As soon as the woman's stick legs disappeared around the corner, Jack moved.

With stealthy smoothness, he climbed the fence and dropped into the dimly lit alley. Hidden in the shadows, Jack used his Tac Five, CTU's version of a Swiss Army knife, to begin probing the lock. Before he even touched it, the steel door opened.

"Madre de Dios!"

The pudgy woman took a step backward when she saw the stranger looming in the doorway. Jack raised his hands to calm her.

"Estoy apesadumbrado que le asusté," Jack said, apologizing for frightening her. *"Trabajo aquí, también."*

The woman smiled, and Jack knew she'd accepted his lie, believed he was an employee for one of the wealthy residents, too.

"Buenas noches," she said, pushing past him.

"Buenas noches a usted, señora," Jack replied.

MetroCard in hand, the woman hurried through the cast-iron gate, heading toward the subway entrance on Broadway. Jack stepped through the door and closed it behind him.

He walked down a long corridor with peeling green

paint on the walls, fluorescent lights buzzing above. A
freight elevator stood at the end. Beside it was a door to the
stairs. He took the steps, avoiding the chance of a security
camera inside the elevator.

The staircase felt wider than his living room back in
Los Angeles, with marble steps and brass railings that
shone dully. Jack's footsteps echoed as he climbed. At the
eighth floor, he opened the door a crack and checked the
hallway.

Empty.

Jack left the stairwell and searched for apartment 801.
There were only four apartments on this floor, and he
found Tobias's quickly, placed his ear against the darkly
polished mahogany. The television was on, a car com-
mercial, then the channel changed—someone was inside.
Jack considered knocking but rejected the idea. Instead, he
drew out his Tac tool and went to work on the lock.

Eleven seconds later, the tumblers fell into place and
the lock clicked. Jack pushed through and closed the door
behind him. He stood in a large, well-appointed foyer. The
lighting was muted, the walls paneled with dark wood. An
antique table held an abstract sculpture. Jack pressed his
spine to the wall, drew the Glock from its holster. Clutching the weapon with both hands, he moved to the next wall
and peered down a long hallway lined with framed oil
paintings.

He was about to move when his eyes were drawn to an
object that had been carelessly tossed on an elaborately
carved end table—his own Glock, taken by the Albino
that morning, at the restaurant. Jack shifted the weapon

he'd borrowed from Morris to his right hand, slipped his
own gun into the empty holster with his left.

Jack moved cautiously down the hall. The television
continued to blare from the living room—now it was
turned to the Serbian News Network. Hearing the familiar language made Jack pause. He waited for the channel
to change again, but minutes passed and the somber Serb
anchor continued to drone her monologue.

The Albino speaks Serbian . . .

The realization made Jack consider something almost
impossible. Memories came over him. He flashed back to
the war in Bosnia. His Delta Force missions. Operation
Nightfall.

Jack remembered the stories of *Određeni član bled
ubica*—the Pale One.

Could it be . . .

Jack peered around the corner, into the living room. The
furnishings in here were sparse—Danish modern—sitting
on a parquet floor. A sliding glass door looked out on a
balcony and the park beyond. At only the eighth floor, Tobias's view of Central Park was basically a sea of treetops.
Across the park, the windows of Manhattan's East Side
skyscrapers glowed like stars above a dark, leafy sea.

On a table, a desktop computer displayed financial news.
A large-screen TV mounted on the wall was still tuned
to Serbian television, and Jack spied the satellite dish attached to the balcony's railing.

Finally, he saw the Albino. The man was lounging in
a chair of cream-colored leather, legs crossed, clad in a
silk robe. His white hair was damp from a shower, and he

appeared to be dozing off—then Jack saw the hypodermic needle clutched in his pale hand.

Jack slipped past the man, searched the kitchen and dining room, and found no one else. Glock raised, Jack returned to the living room and boldly entered.

"*Led pa Sneg!*" Jack shouted, addressing the Albino as "Ice and Snow," the name the Pale One's victims had given him.

The Albino's colorless eyes opened wide, not with confusion but recognition. He moved to rise, and the robe's lapels parted, revealing a small black tattoo of a snarling dog on his milky chest. That's when Jack knew for certain: Erno Tobias, the Albino, was the Pale One.

As the brutal war criminal got to his feet to move forward, Jack took aim above the kneecap, avoiding the artery, and fired.

Howling, Erno Tobias dropped back into the chair. He clutched his leg to stanch the bleeding. Still shocked by the attack, the Albino looked up, and their eyes met.

"Remember me?" Jack asked.

11:53:46 P.M. EDT
Security Station One
CTU Headquarters, NYC

Morris O'Brian watched the screens, where real-time images out of Atlantic City displayed the firefight at the Ali Baba Casino from several different angles.

He tapped his keyboard, moved the mouse, and the

speakers came to life, broadcasting chaotic radio trans-
missions from varied sources.

". . . Shooter on roof. Return fire . . ."

". . . We have multiple victims inside the casino. Need
medical teams . . ."

". . . He's taken a hostage. Bring in the sniper . . ."

"Officer down! Officer down!"

Peter Randall stood at Morris's shoulder, watching
the screens in rapt attention. The phone rang and Morris
grabbed it.

"O'Brian."

"It's Jack. I'm inside Erno Tobias's penthouse."

"Was the little bugger at home?"

"Affirmative," Jack replied. "I'm about to have a talk
with him. But first I want to send you the contents of the
Albino's computer."

Morris frowned. "Another data dump?"

"A large one."

Morris fed Jack the access codes for a large cache in the
CTU database. "Everything you send, I'll copy and forward on to the analysts at Langley."

"Have the police found any more trucks?" Jack asked.

"There's mixed news on that front. Rutland, Vermont's
been hit. A truck bomb went off at a factory. We don't
know how bad it is yet, but authorities anticipate many casualties . . ."

Morris heard Jack exhale.

"But there's good news, too," he added quickly. "The
New Jersey State Police and the local SWAT team stopped
a truck outside a large casino in Atlantic City. The bomb's

been neutralized, but several armed terrorists escaped into the casino. The firefight's still under way."

The silence on the other end of the line was heavy.

"Have you learned anything from Mr. Tobias?" Morris asked.

"I'll get back to you on that," Jack said, and the line went dead.

. . . .

THE FOLLOWING TAKES PLACE
BETWEEN THE HOURS OF
12:00 A.M. AND 1:00 A.M.
EASTERN DAYLIGHT TIME

. . . .

12:00:20 A.M. EDT
Near 1313 Crampton Street
Newark, New Jersey

"For a gang-banger's crib, this place seems pretty dead,"
Tony said.

He and Judith Foy were on the stoop of an abandoned
building on the opposite side of the street. Their surveillance had revealed a complete lack of activity at the Thirteen Gang's headquarters.

"Usually these places have a lively nightlife," said Tony.
"Punks coming and going. Women. Parties. The occa-
sional gunplay. This crib's way too quiet."

Tony shook his head. He'd even paced the block twice, looking for any signs of life. But all the doors and windows along this blighted block were boarded up and covered with graffiti—including the massive garage door on the empty warehouse at the end of the block. There was not even a crack dealer in sight, and no car had driven down this street in almost thirty minutes.

"You're sure this is the right place?" Foy asked.

Tony shrugged. "Priests tend not to lie. And the one I talked to wasn't afraid of me. He could have just sent me away with no information."

"Still, he could have—wait a minute." Foy gripped Tony's arm and pulled him back, into the shadows.

"That Hummer at the end of the block," she whispered. "I think I recognize it. From Kurmastan."

Tony saw it, too. The black vehicle had swung onto Crampton Street two blocks away. Now it moved slowly toward the row house with the red door. Judith Foy gripped the digital surveillance camera, hoping to snap pictures of the Hummer's passengers.

What happened next surprised them both. Instead of continuing down the block, the Hummer cut a sharp left at Peralta Storage, the supposedly abandoned warehouse on the corner. The garage door that seemed to be boarded up tight began to rise. Bright fluorescent light streamed out of the interior of the warehouse. Tony spotted equipment, holding tanks, men in white lab coats.

Though the angle wasn't good, and they couldn't see very deep into the garage, Foy managed to snap a few pictures. Meanwhile the Hummer rolled into the hidden space and the door closed behind it, plunging the block into darkness once more.

Crouched in the shadows, Tony and Judith exchanged puzzled glances.

"What's with the lab equipment?" Foy whispered. "Do you think the gang's manufacturing crystal meth?"

Tony shook his head. "I've seen meth labs before and they're not that complex. There's a state-of-the-art research lab inside that supposedly deserted building." He paused and rubbed the back of his neck. "What the hell are they doing?"

12:13:12 A.M. EDT
Eighth Floor, Beresfield Apartments
Central Park West
New York, New York

Jack Bauer tightened the tourniquet with a yank. The Albino grunted, chewed his lower lip. The crimson flow from the ghastly wound in his leg slowed, but didn't stop. Jack knew Erno Tobias could easily bleed to death if he wasn't careful.

Too bad.

"The generals thought you were an urban myth," Jack said, tugging on the electric cord wrapped around the man's arms. "But the Bosnian refugees I spoke with all swore you existed. They're the ones who named you Ice and Snow."

Bauer had addressed his captive in Serbian. Hearing his native language spoken by an American enemy seemed to throw the former assassin off balance, which was exactly what Jack wanted. Bauer also hoped the Albino might slip and say something he might not in his adopted tongue. So far, that hadn't happened.

Time to step up the pressure.

Jack faced the man. "After Victor Drazen was killed—"

The Albino spat on the hardwood floor at Jack's feet. "Murdered, you mean—"

"Neutralized," Jack cut in. "The NATO forces seized his records, and there you were. No name, just a description. *Određeni član*—the Albino. Another document called you *Određeni član bled ubica*. The Pale One . . ."

Jack saw the hunted look in the man's pink-rimmed, colorless eyes and knew he was wearing the Albino down.

"You were a member of Drazen's Black Dogs," Jack continued, gesturing to the man's tattoo. "We wondered why every moderate politician who worked for peace ended up dead. Then we discovered it was *you* who assassinated them."

"They were traitors! Corrupt internationalists who allowed violent invaders to flourish inside our borders. You can pretend the refugees were innocent, that they didn't invade our towns, murder Serbs, burn our churches. You can pretend, but I know the truth—"

"And now you're helping those same 'violent foreigners' sow destruction in America."

The Albino smiled though his pain. "I would call that irony."

Jack slapped him hard, then knelt down and spoke softly into his ear. "That's ancient history. Let's talk about your current operation. Why are you helping Noor?"

"The enemy of my enemy is my friend." The Albino snorted, licked blood off his lip. "Now you have them in your backyard. Let's see how you like it—"

Jack fought the urge to strike him again. Instead, he grinned coldly. "You blew it, Tobias—or whatever the hell your name really is. Even at the restaurant in Little Italy, I had no idea who you were, where you were from. But when I ran into that Serbian hit team at the World Trade Center, I started to get the picture. The people at Kurmastan are just pawns. Someone else is pulling the strings."

Jack grabbed a handful of the man's white hair and yanked his head back. "Who are you working for?" Jack yelled. "Who's pulling the strings and why?"

Jack released the man and the Albino hung his head.

"I hurt," he said softly.

Jack's fists clenched. He thought of the Black Dogs, all the murders, rapes, and carnage they'd committed in Serbia. He thought of Kurmastan and those trucks of death, rolling down America's highways now.

"If you don't tell me what I need to know," Jack promised, "the pain is going to get a whole lot worse."

12:23:47 A.M. EDT
Security Station One
CTU Headquarters, NYC

The phone rang. Morris O'Brian's eyes never left the monitor as he snatched the phone off its cradle.

"O'Brian."

"It's Tony."

"Ah, the prodigal son."

"Listen, Morris, we found the Thirteen Gang's headquarters. It's located at 1313 Crampton Street, Newark—"

"1313?" Morris interrupted.

"Yeah."

"You're serious?"

"*Listen*, we found something else, too."

Morris winced. On the monitor, three Atlantic City police officers had just cut down a terrorist who'd ignored repeated commands to drop his weapon.

"What . . . what did you find?" Morris asked, turning away from the bloody sight on the screen.

"We don't exactly know," Tony replied. "There's some kind of laboratory or drug factory or something inside the Crampton Street warehouse, which is supposed to be abandoned. A garage door opened up and Judith Foy shot a couple of surveillance photos. But we have no way to analyze the images on this end."

"Can you send them along? Or is Deputy Director Foy still worried about leaks?"

Tony sighed. "I've convinced her the leaks have been plugged, but we don't have a PDA. I can send the images to you through my cell phone, but they're bound to lose some resolution."

"I know. Wish our technology was better. Maybe in a few years—"

"Morris! We don't have a few years."

"We can enhance the digital images on this end, Tony, make your pictures as good as new. Just send them along."

O'Brian gave Tony a phone number to use for the data

dump. After he hung up, Morris faced Peter Randall. "We've got some intelligence coming in. It will be dumped in cache twenty-two. Digital images. I'm rather swamped here. Can you analyze them?"

"Sure, I'll be glad to, Mr. O'Brian," Randall replied. "I'll do the work at Security Station Two, if you don't mind. Less distractions . . ."

"Good lad," Morris murmured, his eyes drifting back to the live feed of the firefight in Atlantic City. But as soon as Peter Randall was gone, Morris reached for the phone.

12:56:18 A.M. EDT
Eighth Floor, Beresfield Apartments
Central Park West
New York, New York

"A name," Jack Bauer demanded.

"It will do you . . . no good . . ." The Albino's voice was weak. He let out a moan of agony, blood streaking his pale face. "You can't stop . . . what's about to happen."

"A *name*." Jack coolly dug the kitchen knife deeper into the man's ravaged wound.

The Albino cried out, perspiration beading his forehead.

"A name." Jack probed even deeper, hitting bone. "NOW!"

"Soren Ungar!" the Albino blurted out. "His company, Ungar, Geneva, LLC, is the real owner of Rogan Pharmaceuticals."

"And it was Rogan that provided the drugs that drove the men and women of Kurmastan mad?" Jack hissed, twisting the blade.

"Yes!" the Albino shouted.

Jack yanked the knife back, dropped it on the hardwood floor. "Why?" he asked.

The Albino shook his head.

"Talk!"

The Albino was breathing hard. "Before I tell you," he gasped, "I want a pardon. Signed by your President. Forgiving all my past crimes."

Looming over the man, Jack shook his head.

"You're an *international* war criminal. A fugitive from justice. They want you at the Hague. It's out of our government's hands—"

"You can fix this!" the Albino insisted.

"I can't, and I won't," Jack replied. "No bargains."

To Jack's surprise, the Albino actually shrugged under his bonds.

"As you Americans are fond of saying, you can't fault a man for trying," he said. A strange smile lifted his lips, and then he bit down hard. Jack heard a crunch, and Erno Tobias choked. When he opened his mouth, black blood poured from his throat.

"No!" Jack cried.

His body jerking spasmodically, the Albino's eyes rolled up in his head, then he fell forward, hanging loosely from the chair. Jack felt for a pulse, but found nothing. He yanked back the man's head, reached into his mouth to find the poison capsule. Jack was stunned.

How did I miss it? How? I searched him . . .

Jack quickly discovered that the toxic chemical had been stored inside a hollow tooth. The second the poison hit the man's system, he was dead.

Jack stumbled back, dropped into a leather chair. He still needed more information, but now at least he had a name.

Soren Ungar.

Jack rose and crossed to Erno Tobias's computer. He'd already forwarded the information stored there to Morris O'Brian. Now he began searching the files himself, looking for some clue to what was really happening, *something* that would lead him to an endgame . . .

12:59:50 A.M. EDT
Security Station Two
CTU Headquarters, NYC

After entering the security code that allowed him access to cache twenty-two, Peter Randall opened the file Tony Almeida had forwarded to CTU. It contained three digital images, which needed little enhancement. Two of the pictures clearly showed Ibrahim Noor's secret bio-weapons laboratory. The black Hummer rolling into the garage obscured much of the scene in the third picture.

Not good, Randall thought. He called up several older files from the CTU database, searching for photos that would make a good match. He selected three pictures of a Cleveland methadone lab busted by the DEA in 1996.

The Ohio lab was also housed inside a brick warehouse, the surveillance photos were taken at night, and with a little Photoshop tinkering, Randall even placed the black Hummer into the third image.

The photos would not stand up to close scrutiny, but Randall gambled they wouldn't have to.

In the mess going on now, no one will pay attention to a simple meth lab, he decided.

When Randall was finished, he deleted the original photos that Foy and Almeida had taken, replacing them with the pictures he'd selected. Then he printed them out. A final check of the hard copies revealed no obvious flaws that might give his ploy away.

Ibrahim Noor owes me for this. Big time. Peter Randall's boyish face broke into a smile. *And he's going to pay . . .*

Satisfied with a job well done, Randall shut down the security console and swung around in his office chair—to find the interim director and two security men standing over him.

"D-Director Henderson, c-can I help you—"

The tranquilizer dart hit Randall in the throat, and he gagged once. The drug took immediate effect, and he slipped out of the chair and hit the floor.

"Put this son of a bitch in a detention cell and prep him for interrogation," Henderson said.

The security men each grabbed an arm and roughly hauled the unconscious man toward the elevator.

Henderson faced Morris O'Brian, who'd been lurking in the hallway.

"Good job, O'Brian," Henderson said. "But how did you know Peter Randall was a mole?"

Morris shrugged. "I was suspicious of him already, but the real trap was the cache number I gave him. Access to cache twenty-two is only permitted to personnel one level above Randall's security clearance. Randall was so overconfident, he didn't think to ask me for the password to cover his buttocks. That's when I knew something was up—that he had all of the passwords already."

Henderson offered the man a thin smile. "So what made you suspicious of him in the first place?"

"Everyone resisted us when we first got here, Agent Abernathy included. They dodged Jack Bauer's direct questions and all but refused to cooperate. Peter Randall was the exception. He was there from the start, ready to step in and do anything we asked of him."

Morris paused. "I figured the little bugger had to have something up his sleeve. No one is *that* helpful without an ulterior motive."

1 2 3 4 5 6 7 8 9
10 11 12 13 14 15 16 17
18 **19** 20 21 22 23 24

• •

THE FOLLOWING TAKES PLACE
BETWEEN THE HOURS OF
1:00 A.M. AND 2:00 A.M.
EASTERN DAYLIGHT TIME

• •

1:02:10 A.M. EDT
Conference Room
CTU Headquarters, NYC

Jack Bauer was the last participant to appear on the
videoconferencing screen. He sat in a Danish modern
living room. Behind him, a sliding glass door framed the
night sky above Central Park's treetops. A few feet away,
on a chair of cream-colored leather, a pale form sat limply,
bound by electrical cords. Blood pooled on the polished
hardwood floor at the corpse's feet.

Christ, what a mess, thought Christopher Henderson,
sitting up in his chair. *Bauer better have something.*

Jack peered into the computer camera, then his hand disappeared from view while he adjusted the volume. "Can you hear me?" he asked.

"We hear you, Jack." Henderson tossed his pen onto the tabletop. "We can see you, too. And I know you can't see us from your location, so I'll make the introductions. Richard Walsh is on the line from Los Angeles. Hershel Berkovic, Director of CTU's Economic Warfare Division, is conferencing in from Langley, and Dr. Guilling from the Satellite Surveillance Division is here with me in New York."

"What's the current status on the trucks from Kurmastan?" Jack asked.

Sitting across the table from Henderson, the portly man with the brown comb-over and horn-rimmed glasses said, "Ted Guilling here. The trucks in Carlisle and Atlantic City were intercepted and neutralized. Another truck detonated its explosives at the General Aviation plant in Rutland, with many casualties."

Wheezing, Guilling paused to suck on an asthma atomizer. "But there's good news, too. Fifteen minutes ago, U.S. Navy military police intercepted two trucks outside the Bethesda Naval Station. Our forces suffered some casualties, but the terrorists were stopped and their bombs failed to detonate—"

"What about the trucks heading for Boston?" Jack interrupted.

"We think that intelligence *may* be bogus," Guilling replied.

"What do you mean *may*," Jack quietly challenged.

Crap, here it comes . . . Henderson glared a warning at Guilling to be careful. It was Jack who'd brought in that information, and they really didn't need Bauer blowing his top with Walsh *and* Langley on the line.

Guilling took another hit on his asthma atomizer, then earnestly explained, "We've combed all the routes from New Jersey to Boston with satellites, surveillance cameras, state and local police, and we haven't located a single truck, let alone two."

Jack didn't blink. "Maybe they stopped somewhere." He leaned closer to the camera. "Maybe the trucks are *hidden*."

Guilling's head bobbed. "It's possible."

"Walsh here, Jack."

Henderson rubbed his bloodshot eyes, relieved to hear Walsh speak up. The big man with the walrus mustache was CTU's Administrative Director, and the most senior person on this call. Henderson also knew that Jack Bauer respected few men in the CIA's bureaucracy more than Richard Walsh.

"I think we're all in agreement that we need to keep our eyes open," Walsh continued. "We should keep sweeping the Boston routes, but not at the exclusion of other possibilities if additional leads come in. Now . . . as I understand the situation, Jack, counting the truck you personally stopped outside the Lincoln Tunnel, half of the twelve trucks have been located and neutralized, one way or another. Which means, according to Brice Holman's intelligence, there are still six more trucks to find."

"Right," Jack said. "And what about the leaks at CTU

New York? Christopher? Have they been plugged?"

Henderson tensed. He hadn't expected to discuss that particular matter on this call, and he didn't appreciate Bauer's bluntness. But he was careful to answer with smoothness and control.

"We think so, Jack. Rachel Delgado, New York's deputy head of Security, has been cross-identified as a former member of Newark's Thirteen Gang. I haven't interrogated Peter Randall yet, but—"

"Randall?" Jack frowned. "I thought Layla Abernathy—"

"She's been cleared," Henderson broke in. "Randall set her up, even planted incriminating information in Agent Abernathy's personal computer, knowing we'd find it. Thanks to O'Brian, we know the truth now. Agent Abernathy is innocent. She's recovering in the infirmary—"

"Release her," Jack demanded. "I need her in the field—"

"Listen, Jack . . ." Henderson paused. "She's had a rough time. A very rough time—"

"This isn't a request, Christopher. I need Agent Abernathy to successfully complete this mission."

Henderson fell silent. He didn't like the idea of putting the woman back on line, but he could hear the steel in Jack's voice, and bickering with Bauer in front of the other men would sound childish at best.

What the hell, if Bauer wants her . . .

"All right," he finally relented. "She'll be ready for action by the time you get back."

"Listen," Jack continued, "I've been looking over the contents of Erno Tobias's computer. The Albino has been tracking currency futures. Foreign banks, financial institutions in Europe, the Middle East, Asia—they're all lining up to dump U.S. currency. Billions of dollars."

"Agent Bauer is correct," said Hershel Berkovic. Close to sixty and bald, with close-set eyes and a slight facial twitch, the man spoke on the screen out of CIA's headquarters in Langley, Virginia. "The EWD has analyzed the data coming in, including the contents of Mr. Tobias's computer, and the threat you described is very real—and very dangerous—"

"Excuse me?" Jack interrupted. "Would the man speaking please identify himself."

"This is Hershel Berkovic, Agent Bauer. I'm the director of CTU's Economic Warfare Division, and there is no reason for these monetary speculators to dump the dollar. Inflation is low, productivity high. Our American economy is sound, the stock market stable—"

"What about the terror attacks?" Richard Walsh interrupted from Los Angeles. "Don't you think they'll put a dent in our stock market come morning?"

"Yes, you are correct, Director Walsh," Berkovic replied, "except for one thing. Only the attack in Atlantic City has been reported as a terrorist incident, and the press and public believe it was an isolated event. Thanks to damage control from several government agencies, the Carlisle attack, the wreck outside the Lincoln Tunnel, even the blast in Rutland are perceived to be tragic *accidents*. The truth might eventually come out, but it hasn't. Not yet."

Henderson grabbed up his pen, impatiently tapped the table. "Your point?"

"The people poised to sell dollars must have inside information," said Berkovic. "They know about the terrorist threat to our country and are set to trade accordingly."

"There's another possibility," said Jack. "An endgame."

At CTU New York, Henderson and Guilling glanced at each other across the table. In Los Angles, Walsh leaned closer to the camera. "Go on," he commanded.

Jack nodded. "These currency trades appear to be coming from many sources, but Tobias's secure files indicate that the bulk of the trades are coming through one financial institution—Ungar, Geneva, LLC."

"My analysts detected that pattern, too, Agent Bauer, but"—Hershel Berkovic shook his head dismissively—"you must remember: Ungar, Geneva, is one of the largest currency trading businesses in Europe—"

"No," Richard Walsh interrupted. "I think Jack's on to something. There could me more going on here than some fanatical religious assault. Someone could have an ulterior motive. Someone could be pulling the strings."

"We need to look at Soren Ungar," Jack advised. "The CEO of Ungar, Geneva, LLC. He also owns Rogan Pharmaceuticals and who knows what else. Tobias gave up his name, right before the Albino took his own life."

"Excuse me, Agent Bauer?" said Hershel Berkovic, raising an eyebrow. "That man behind you in the chair? He took his own life?"

"Suicide capsule," Jack replied flatly. "An autopsy will show poisoning as the cause of death."

Suppressing a smile, Henderson tapped the keys on his laptop, pulled up CTU's file on Soren Ungar, and scanned it. "Ungar sounds like our man, all right. He's rabidly anti-American. He's been talking down the dollar for at least two years now. He funds the Foundation for a Greater Europe, a kind of crackpot Eurocentric think-tank."

"Hersh," Richard Walsh commanded from L.A., "I want you to take a hard look at all of Soren Ungar's recent and future activities."

On the screen from Langley, the bald man nodded.

"Ted," Walsh continued, "I want you to locate the other six trucks, pronto."

"I'm on it," Dr. Guilling replied at the table across from Henderson.

"What about me?" Jack asked.

Henderson jumped in before Walsh could—after all, Jack was now under *his* direct command. "Come back to New York's Operations Center," he ordered. "We'll coordinate our next move from here."

Jack looked around the apartment. "First I'm going to search this place a little while longer, see what turns up. I should be back by two-thirty."

"Okay. See you then," Henderson said, sitting back in his chair.

Jack's attitude could be grating at times, but Henderson wasn't about to hold it against him. Seminars in "managing up" were for pukes and analysts anyway. Bauer was a field man, the best Henderson had ever seen. Judging from the leads he'd uncovered already, Henderson could see nothing but an upside to letting Jack Bauer do what Jack Bauer did best.

Dubic closed the phone and tucked it into his black leather sport coat. Blond and of Eastern European descent, he was easily the palest man in the brightly lit basement. Across the room, the tangle of brown-skinned men were all focused on one individual—Ibrahim Noor.

The cult leader had traded his holy man's robes for urban street clothes. With his muscular arms laid bare, prison tattoos and scars visible, Noor's physical presence was even more intimidating. Worse still, the man's mood was foul. He'd been closely monitoring the progress of his Warriors. After some initial successes, things were suddenly going awry.

Teams had failed to take out several critical targets, and the loss of the Hawk and his crew was a particularly harsh blow. Even worse, this all came on the heels of an equipment failure that threatened to halt the final, devastating strike before it was even launched.

I lost men today, too, Dubic thought bitterly. *Two who died on the World Trade Center were comrades in arms. You don't see me getting worked up about it. The business we've chosen is fraught with peril.*

Dubic sighed, ran a hand over the rough yellow stubble on his jawline. *At least I have good news to deliver.*

Squaring his narrow shoulders, Dubic crossed the basement, careful to avoid the fresh blood that stained the concrete floor. Noor was looming over Dr. Kabbibi, arguing about a damaged aerosol dispenser.

"I can install the dispenser myself," Kabbibi argued. "It is unwise to bring a stranger into the plan this late in the game."

"I have no choice," Noor replied, his deep voice booming in the cavernous space. "Someone must operate the device, too."

Kabbibi had no reply to that.

Dubic said nothing, either. He wasn't one of Noor's addled followers, and he wasn't going to be anywhere near that dispenser when the device did its work.

Once a Serbian Black Dog, Dubic was now a gun for hire, the key word being *hire*. The Albino had been the one to contact him, employing Dubic to assemble a strike team.

Dubic cared little about the politics involved in this operation. He was in it for the money. Lots and lots of money. Bringing down the holier-than-thou Americans was merely a happy by-product.

Just then, Noor spied Dubic. "You have news?"

"Good news," Dubic said. "Our operative is on the way to Newark International in a chartered plane—with the device. I'm going to the airport now to pick them up."

"Why the delay?" Noor demanded.

"Ungar told me the part came from NATO military stores. Difficult to replace, though he managed to do it."

"Take the Hummer," said Noor. "I'll send someone with you."

Dubic nodded. "How about Tanner?" He looked around for the muscular, charismatic black man with the shaved head, but failed to see him.

"Tanner's not here," said Noor. "I sent him to Manhattan to pick up your friend, the Albino."

Dubic glanced around the basement for a second choice, but Montel Tanner was about the only man he'd ever liked in this group. The remaining pool consisted of twitchy felons and adolescent gang members—sociopathic personalities all.

"I'll go myself," he said. "It's better that way."

Dubic snatched the Hummer's keys from one of Noor's wild-eyed lieutenants. He could feel the crazy cultist staring daggers in his back as he walked to the hole cut into the basement wall, and entered the dimly lit sewer. The tunnel was dark and damp and nearly a block long.

The stench was overpowering, and though Dubic was not particularly tall, he had to crouch to prevent brushing his blond crew cut against the filth-covered ceiling. Water trickled along the floor. In the shadows, Dubic could hear rats scurrying.

Relieved to be out of the horrid pit, Dubic emerged in another brightly lit basement a few moments later. More of Noor's brown-skinned followers clustered around a moderately sized tanker truck that was parked in the back of the interior space, away from the makeshift laboratory.

Dubic thought about the vehicle's deadly contents and shuddered.

He climbed into the shiny black Hummer and gunned the engine. He drove up the ramp, and the door opened automatically. As he swerved off Crampton Street toward Howard Boulevard, Dubic pulled the cell phone out of his pocket and tossed it onto the dash.

When he reached the highway, he'd contact the Albino. But first he had to get this monster American vehicle through these littered ghetto streets.

1:35:21 A.M. EDT
Peralta Storage
One block south of 1313 Crampton Street
Newark, New Jersey

Tony checked his watch, reached for his cell phone, and hit speed dial.

"O'Brian here."

"It's Almeida." Tony was sitting in the shadows, his back against a run-down brick row house across the street from the abandoned warehouse, just a block away from the Thirteen Gang's reputed headquarters. "That black Hummer I told you about eighty minutes ago. It just departed the location, heading east."

"You sure it was the same one?" Morris recited the license plate.

"Yeah," said Tony. "Same one. I got a look at the driver this time through the windshield. Caucasian, male, blond crew cut, black leather jacket."

"Okay . . ." On the other end of the line, computer keys tapped. "I've logged it," said Morris. "Any other activity?"

"Nothing," said Tony, glancing up and down the block. "It's as dead as a morgue around here."

"Deputy Director Foy still with you?"

"Yeah."

Tony glanced at the slight woman slumped at his side. Ten minutes into their stakeout, she'd nodded off, her red-haired head hitting his shoulder. After everything she'd been through, he figured she could use the rest and didn't bother waking her.

Morris spent a minute updating Tony on things at his end. Finally, they ended the call, and Judith Foy stirred.

"What's happening?" she said through a yawn.

"I checked in with Morris O'Brian. The black Hummer just left. And according to O'Brian, CTU New York dug up another mole—Peter Randall."

"Oh god."

"Morris is going to contact Jack, let him know what we've observed. He might even ask us to infiltrate. How are you feeling? Are you up to this?"

Judith sat up straight, rubbed the sleep from her eyes. "My ribs are still a little sore, but I'm good to go."

"You sure?"

"Listen, Almeida. These scumbags killed Brice. They tried to kill me. If you and Jack come up with a plan that'll take these people out for good, believe me, I'm up for it."

1:45:03 A.M. EDT
The Beresfield Apartments
Central Park West
New York, New York

Jack Bauer had given Erno Tobias's residence a thoroughly professional toss. He'd upended furniture, yanked the pillows off couches and chairs, and gashed the upholstery to check the stuffing.

Jack had moved from room to room systematically, pulling out drawers, peeking behind pictures, checking behind curtains and under throw rugs. In the bathroom, Jack had found a miniature pharmacy composed of exotic drugs and elixirs.

Jack had wanted to search the balcony, but the sliding glass door was locked, and he hadn't yet located the keys, so he'd headed for the bedroom next.

He'd searched the dead man's dresser, his walk-in closet, his nightstand. He'd even stripped the bed and turned over the mattress.

Jack's biggest discovery, however, had been hidden inside the Albino's ornate armoire. The arsenal included a Remington M870 shotgun, an M9 Beretta with a Knight Armament sound suppressor, two Glocks, and a G36 Commando short carbine.

"Considering New York City's tough gun laws, I'd say Tobias was in violation," Jack muttered.

Along with plenty of ammunition, Jack found a long length of nylon rope, a pair of Gerber Guardian double-edged knives, and an M9 bayonet. He tucked the three knives into the Hawk's utility vest, which he still wore. Jack was considering taking the Beretta and silencer attachment, too, when the phone on the nightstand rang.

Jack froze for a moment, startled into a single second of paralysis. By the second ring, however, he'd already made the decision to answer. "Hello," he said, imitating the Albino's dry rasp.

"*It's nama, Dubic,*" a man said in Serbian.

"*Jest, Dubic,*" Jack replied.

"We are back on track," Dubic continued, still speaking Serbian. "Ungar has secured a second dispensing unit from the NATO arsenal, along with an expert to install the device. I'm on my way to Newark Airport to bring them both back to the lab."

"*Vrlo dobar,*" Jack rasped.

"I understand that Montel Tanner is on his way to you. He's going to pick you up and bring you back to Newark personally."

"*Da.* I will be ready," said Jack.

"Be careful. The mood is ugly with these men. When Dr. Kabbibi discovered the engineers had installed the first dispenser improperly, and damaged it beyond repair, the two men responsible were beheaded. I saw the whole thing. These cultists are savage animals. Worse than the Bosnians."

"*Da,*" Jack rasped in agreement.

Dubic sighed. "I will say goodbye now. If all goes according to plan, I'll meet you in front of the big bull tomorrow morning. Good luck."

"You, too," Jack rasped.

Dubic hung up, and Jack dropped the phone into its cradle. He snatched his own cell from his pocket, punched the buttons.

"O'Brian here," said Morris, at CTU's Operations Center.

"Is Tony Almeida still in Newark?"

"Hello, Jack. Yes, he is. I was just about to call you—"

"Connect me with Tony and stay on the line. I want you aware of some new intel."

Tony answered on the first ring.

Inside of ten minutes, Jack and Tony had devised a plan to intercept the "package" coming from Newark Airport and infiltrate the Thirteen Gang's Crampton Street headquarters.

1:56:59 A.M. EDT
The Beresfield Apartments
Central Park West
New York, New York

The doorman admitted the trio into the marble-appointed lobby. As they passed him, he eyed the men with curiosity.

The shortest was a good-looking African-American man with a muscular build, a shaved head, and a polished demeanor—his deep blue, tailored pinstriped suit appeared to be worth more than the doorman's monthly salary. The others were built like linebackers and looked like members of a gangsta rapper's posse.

The black man in the suit approached the desk. "Montel Tanner to see Mr. Tobias."

The desk clerk smiled. "Yes, Mr. Tobias left word that he was expecting you. Take the elevator to the eighth floor. Suite 801."

"Thank you, my man," Tanner said, gesturing to his comrades to follow.

When the elevator door closed on Tanner and his companions, the doorman spoke. "Gee, do you think they're clubbing tonight?"

The desk clerk shrugged.

Outside, three late-model Cadillac SUVs were lined up on Central Park West. The doorman scanned the cars for a glimpse of scantily clad models. But the only occupants he could see were tough-looking urban males.

"I wonder where they're going," said the doorman. "Hip-hop clubs probably. Funny, Tobias never struck me as that type."

"Mr. Tobias is rich," replied the desk clerk, "and you know the rich."

"Yeah." The doorman snorted. "They know how to have a good time."

1 2 3 4 5 6 7 8 9
10 11 12 13 14 15 16 17
18 19 **20** 21 22 23 24

· ·

THE FOLLOWING TAKES PLACE
BETWEEN THE HOURS OF
2:00 A.M. AND 3:00 A.M.
EASTERN DAYLIGHT TIME

· ·

2:02:52 A.M. EDT
Eighth Floor, Beresfield Apartments
Central Park West
New York, New York

The loud rapping on the apartment door took Jack Bauer
by surprise. He'd just finished his phone conversation
with Tony Almeida when he'd heard the knocking—loud
enough to reach the Albino's bedroom.

Jack cursed. He'd expected the desk clerk to call before
allowing visitors upstairs. The knocking came again, and
Jack crossed to the Albino's armoire. He grabbed the M9
Beretta that he'd found during his search, along with a
length of rope.

"Wake up, Tobias," someone yelled through the door. "It's Montel Tanner!"

M9 clutched in both hands, the rope looped over his shoulder, Jack approached the door, peered through the spy hole.

A thirty-something African American sporting a blue pinstriped suit and a shaved head stood in the hallway, flanked by two massive bodyguards. Jack could tell by the way the big men carried themselves that they were armed.

The black man in the pinstriped suit was pounding on the door. As Jack backed away, he heard one of Tanner's men speak.

"This ain't right. Maybe we should take down the door."

Jack moved quickly back to the living room, stood over Tobias's corpse. He unwound the rope, tied it to the thick leg of the dead man's heavy chair. Then Jack went to the computer and yanked it off the table, breaking it free of its cables.

A shoulder slammed into the front door, but the stout wood failed to give.

Jack hurled the computer through the plate glass of the locked sliding door. The glass came down in a shower of crystal shards.

The men outside obviously heard the racket because they began to shout. Jack grabbed one end of the long, nylon rope and moved through the shattered sliding door. As he crossed the flagstone balcony, he heard the door finally break open behind him.

Gripping the rope, Jack climbed over the balcony's railing and began rappelling down the terra-cotta side of the luxury building.

2:05:19 A.M. EDT
Corner of Howard and Broad Streets
Newark, New Jersey

The black Ford Explorer stopped at the corner of the run-down neighborhood, its chrome shining dully in the glow of the streetlight. The driver's window opened automatically.

"Yo, Hector," called the twenty-two-year-old African-American driver. "Over here, man . . ."

The nineteen-year-old Hispanic called Hector tucked his stash into the pocket of his baggy pants, then stepped off the curb. He approached the Ford Explorer warily.

"Leroy? Who's in there with you?" Hector demanded.

"Nobody, man, this ain't no damn ambush. I wanted you to be the first to check out my wheels."

Hector grinned, flashing gold teeth. "Sweet. Too sweet for you, *jefe*. I thought you was a customer in that chariot."

"Drivin' this, the hos can smell my money." Leroy grinned wickedly. "Yes, sir. Crack has its privileges, so long as you don't go sampling your own merchandise."

Leroy glanced at the twitchy young Hector and realized that piece of advice came too late. "So was'sup?"

Hector snorted. "Slow night. Been a lot of slow nights late—"

To Leroy, it seemed a shadow rose up from behind the car and struck Hector down. One second, the Latin King was talking, the next minute, Hector was bleeding, pistol-whipped to the ground by some yuppie-looking Latino dude.

The black youth reached for the stick shift to peel out, but the yuppie beaner was already on him, jamming the gun barrel into his temple.

"Get out or I'll shoot."

Dang, thought Leroy, *this dude ain't nothing like the Wall Street yuppies I sell to in Hoboken!*

Lifting his arms, Leroy showed his hands. He was too afraid to look the man in the eyes, so he tried to check him out in the mirror. He saw dark hair, sideburns, a soul patch.

"You gotta be a cop, right?"

"How many cops would blow your head off for this car?" said the dude. "Now get out or I *will* kill you. And leave the keys."

Keeping his eyes to the dirty pavement, Leroy stepped out of the car, gingerly avoiding the body on the ground.

"Listen, man," Leroy said, "you don't know who you're messin' with—"

The gun butt struck him on the chin. Leroy flew backward, bounced off the Explorer's door, and sank to the ground beside the other crack dealer.

Tony Almeida stepped over them and climbed behind the wheel. He honked the car's horn twice, paused, and honked again.

Hearing the signal, Judith Foy appeared a moment later.

"Two at a time. And you make it look easy," she said, stepping over the unconscious punks.

Tony glanced away. "Yeah."

The woman climbed into the passenger seat, buckled her shoulder strap. Tires squealing, the Explorer pulled away from the curb and raced down Crampton Street.

2:06:13 A.M. EDT
Eighth Floor, Beresfield Apartments
Central Park West
New York, New York

Slipping a .38 from its holster, Montel Tanner pushed through the broken door. His bodyguards followed, clutching .45s that looked tiny in their huge fists. They immediately heard the sound of something scraping across the floor.

Tanner reached the living room first—and stopped in his tracks.

He saw the wrecked chamber, the broken glass, Erno Tobias tied to a heavy leather chair. The Albino was obviously dead, but the chair was *moving*, sliding across the blood-slick floor and through the shattered sliding door.

Tanner blinked in shock. "What the f—"

The chair scraped across the balcony's flagstones, then jammed to a stop against the balcony railing, the pale corpse falling limply over the chair arm. That's when Tanner saw the nylon rope tied to the chair, the other end dangling over the edge of the balcony.

"He's climbing down the side of the building!" Tanner shouted. "Get him."

Tanner's bodyguards blundered forward, jumping through the shattered frame of the sliding door, while Tanner himself stayed in the living room and hit speed dial on his cell phone.

As the first bodyguard peered over the balcony's iron railing, Tanner heard a pop and saw the top of the man's head explode. The big bodyguard fell backward, pitching to the flagstone floor. Tanner clutched the cell to his ear.

"Pick it up, damn it."

"Yo," his driver answered at last.

"There's a guy climbing down the side of the building. I want him—*alive*."

Tanner moved to the railing, carefully looked down. Tobias's murderer was already past the Caddies parked in the street. He'd crossed all four lanes of Central Park West and was now hopping over a stone fence. A split-second later, he melted into the shadows, escaping into the wooded expanse of Manhattan's largest park.

Too late, Tanner's men tumbled out of the Caddies below.

"He's gone into the park!" Tanner shouted into the phone. "Go after him!"

The men drew their weapons and followed Tanner's orders.

2:14:26 A.M. EDT
Central Park, near Columbus Circle

Jack Bauer was outnumbered and outgunned, but that didn't bother him. During his training as a lieutenant in the Combat Applications Group—a.k.a. Delta Force— he'd learned night combat tactics from instructors of the Seventy-fifth Army Ranger Battalion, an outfit whose credo was "We own the night."

Now, Jack moved from shadow to shadow, hearing Sergeant Ryder's voice in his head. *Evade. Encircle. Move in. Take 'em down.*

Behind him, a deserted road ran through this section of Central Park. Jack could hear Montel Tanner's men blundering along it.

Untrained and undisciplined, they made every mistake in the book. They called out to one another instead of using hand gestures. They clustered under lampposts instead of sticking to the shadows. Two men carried flashlights— making them easy targets in the darkness.

Crouching between the hollow of two gnarly trees, Jack counted seven pursuers, all armed. One man had long dreadlocks streaming down his back. Another had a jewel-studded eye patch over his left eye and carried an Uzi. For a long time, Jack just watched them while they checked behind the wall he'd hopped, and the trees that clustered there.

Finally, the men fanned out, moving in a loose formation deeper into the park. Within a few minutes, they moved right past Jack's hiding place without spotting him.

Jack smiled.

As the men continued on, a straggler hung back, gripping his .45 nervously in sweating hands. When he finally passed Jack's position, Bauer rose up behind him.

One hand covering his victim's mouth, Jack slid the bayonet between his ribs and deep into the man's heart. The man bucked in Jack's arms, groaned under his hand. Then his eyes rolled up in his head and he went limp. Silently, Jack lowered the corpse to the grass, then bolted for the shadows under the next line of trees.

"Hey, over there!" someone called.

For a split second, Jack thought he'd been spotted. Then he heard the boom of a .45. In the muzzle flash Jack saw a bearded man, his toothless mouth gaping in surprise.

One gunman with a flashlight moved in, played his beam on the corpse.

"Damn it, Tyrell, you shot some bum!"

The shooter kicked the corpse. "How was I s'posed to know he was some lame-ass homeless dude?"

"The *smell*, bro."

The men snickered.

Eye Patch silenced them. "Tanner wants this guy. Keep looking," he growled, gesturing with his Uzi.

They crossed West Drive, a curved, four-lane road that was closed to traffic at this late hour. Then the group moved into a shallow valley. Here, beyond a path lined with wrought-iron benches, a baseball field was a gray patch in the moonless night. Jack continued to stalk them.

"Where's Jackson?" Eye Patch demanded when they reached the edge of the ball field.

The others shrugged. "Maybe he got lost in the dark," Dreadlocks said.

"Maybe," the leader replied.

By his tone, Jack could tell the man was wary.

"You two, circle the field and meet me at those rocks over there," the leader commanded.

The pair crossed the field until they were out of sight. The other three, including Dreadlocks, headed for a tumble of rocks overlooking the field.

Moving through the shadows like a death-dealing ghost, Jack followed the trio. When they arrived at the boulders, the men discovered a narrow passage with stone steps leading to the top of a low hill. Eye Patch climbed the stairs first, the others watching his back. Then the second man entered the narrow staircase.

Before Dreadlocks could hit the stairs, Jack struck again. Seizing the man's hair, he yanked his head back and slashed the M9 blade across his throat, cutting so deeply the vocal cords were severed along with the carotid artery. With a gurgling choke, the man pitched forward, blood spraying the rocks.

Jack hopped over the corpse and dropped to one knee. He aimed and hurled the bayonet at a second man at the top of the stairs. The blade tumbled end over end and struck his broad back, sinking to the hilt. The man went down, but not quietly.

Eye Patch heard his comrade's death howl and raced back to the stairs. He loomed over Jack, a dark silhouette against the night.

The Beretta jerked in Jack's hand; the sound suppressor

coughed. The bullet struck the leader in the forehead. The Uzi tumbled from the dead man's grip, and he rolled down the stone steps.

Jack heard a shot, and a bullet pinged off the rocks beside his head. He grunted as sharp splinters struck his face. Jack crouched low, snatched the Uzi from the ground, and bolted up the stairs.

A second shot rang out, ricocheted off the rocks.

At the top of the steps, Jack found himself at the foot of an ornate, wrought-iron bridge. He heard footsteps gaining on him.

Instead of crossing the bridge—and making himself an easy target—Jack jumped over the railing and dropped twelve feet to the riding path below.

He landed with a grunt, his knee striking a fallen branch. Still clutching the Uzi, Jack rolled onto his back. Above him, his pursuers ran to the middle of the span, their shoes clomping on the wooden surface.

Jack aimed the Uzi and opened fire.

In the hail of 9mm bullets, men jerked and sparks struck off the wrought-iron rail. With a double thump, the last of the hunting posse hit the wooden deck.

Pumped with adrenaline, Jack lay for a moment, catching his breath. Then he heard sirens, far away, but getting closer.

Time to go.

Jack cast the empty Uzi into a clump of trees and stumbled to his feet. Face bleeding, knee throbbing, he limped toward the brightly illuminated mid-rise apartment buildings along Central Park South.

A few minutes later, Jack emerged from the trees at Fifty-seventh Street. Several cabs were lined up near the posh hotels, on the opposite side of the four-lane boulevard. Gratefully, Jack hailed one.

Using the edge of the Hawk's utility vest to wipe the blood and sweat from his face, Jack climbed into the backseat and gave the Sikh driver the Hudson Street address for CTU Headquarters.

The man nodded. "Yes, sir. Right away," he said, not at all surprised to find a bleeding man, wearing a black combat vest, crawling into his cab at two fifty-one in the morning.

$$1\ 2\ 3\ 4\ 5\ 6\ 7\ 8\ 9$$
$$10\ 11\ 12\ 13\ 14\ 15\ 16\ 17$$
$$18\ 19\ 20\ \mathbf{21}\ 22\ 23\ 24$$

. . . .

THE FOLLOWING TAKES PLACE
BETWEEN THE HOURS OF
3:00 A.M. AND 4:00 A.M.
EASTERN DAYLIGHT TIME

. . . .

3:00:46 A.M. EDT
Acorn Street
Boston, Massachusetts

Claudia Wheelock was dreaming of her two young children, scampering barefoot in front of her along the sand.

The Martha's Vineyard setting was achingly familiar, a beloved island where her family had spent so many long, lazy summers. Just ahead was her father's oceanfront shingle-style cottage. She was moved to tears, seeing him there again, relaxing on the wide, wooden porch, just as he had when he was alive. And her mother was nearby, laying out a luncheon of freshly made lobster rolls and sweet lemonade.

In her early forties now, Claudia was still a strikingly beautiful woman, with a fit figure and short blond hair. Her flaxen-haired children reflected that golden beauty as they ran ahead of her, giggling as they darted in and out of the white-capped surf. Claudia laughed, feeling the joy and luster of this moment, expecting all good things to be waiting for her and her children at the end of their little stroll—

Then came the crack of thunder.

The noise was sudden, almost deafening, and it completely shattered Claudia's safe, idyllic vision. Another boom came, this one strong enough to shake the walls of her sister's Federal-style row house on Beacon Hill.

Now Claudia was fully awake. For a moment, she lay staring at the ornamental tin ceiling, wondering if she'd dreamed the noises. But she could still hear the tail end of the last report. The rumbling echoed for several seconds through the narrow cobblestone streets before dissipating completely.

Claudia rose quickly, parted the guest room's lacy curtains, and peered outside. The night sky was clear, though suffused with a strange red glow. Then Claudia heard movement in the hallway. The night had been humid and warm, and she was wearing only a flimsy tank top and underwear. She quickly threw on a short, white terry-cloth robe.

Before she opened the door, something possessed Claudia to fish in her suitcase for the item her husband had pressed upon her last year, when an unbalanced fan of her novels had begun aggressively harassing her with e-mails and phone calls. The small handgun was there, still in its case. She checked to see if it was loaded, then slipped it into the pocket of her short robe.

When Claudia opened the door, her brother-in-law was already standing in the hallway, and her sleepy-eyed sister was peeking out of their master bedroom door.

"I think I heard a bomb going off," Claudia said.

"A bomb?" Roderick practically sneered. "Don't be ridiculous, Claudia. A gas main probably ruptured or an old steam pipe cracked, nothing more than that. This is real life after all, not one of your thrillers."

Claudia was about to remind Roddy that she wrote *legal* thrillers, and the only explosions that occurred in her novels were in the courtroom. But instead she kept her mouth shut, knowing she'd be wasting her breath. As Associate Dean of Humanities at Harvard University, Roderick Cannon held all works of popular fiction beneath contempt.

Besides, thought Claudia, things were already strained between them. They'd spent much of the previous night's dinner arguing about her husband's new job as Northeast District Director for the CIA's Counter Terrorist Unit.

Roderick insisted on focusing on CTU's old directives. He kept bringing up the Unit's supposed trampling of constitutional rights, illegal wiretaps, and alleged use of torture.

Her brother-in-law refused to acknowledge that Claudia's husband was an agent of *change*, that Nathan Wheelock was working toward expurgating any CTU personnel who favored such practices. In the past year, since he'd taken the position, Nathan had abolished all racial and religious profiling within his command, made certain that his people placed wiretaps only on domestic calls to known terrorists overseas, and forbade any agent under his authority to engage in torture.

Claudia was very proud of her husband's progressive policies. She herself had been a high-profile civil rights attorney before quitting to raise her children and write best-selling legal thrillers, and she was in the perfect position to help keep her husband's career objectives on track, ensuring the civil rights of any suspect or prisoner were treated as a CTU priority.

The law was on Nathan's side, too, of course, and it helped that the current Administration was in Nathan's corner. It was only a matter of time before Claudia's husband would be elevated to a much higher position within the Agency. Then Nathan's regional policies could be implemented nationally, through every district and division of the CTU organization.

But Claudia's arguments fell on deaf ears. Roddy's mind was already made up. CTU was a useless, fascist organization that should never have been created, period.

Obviously sensing another argument in the works, Claudia's sister Gillian stepped out of the bedroom. "Since we're all awake," she chirped brightly, "I'll turn on the telly and see if we've had a minor quake."

Claudia winced at Gillian's use of British idiom. Since marrying an Englishman, she'd been suppressing her Boston accent, as well.

Downstairs, her sister put on a pot of tea while Claudia tuned into WHDH, the NBC affiliate in Boston. Her timing was perfect. After a few seconds of one of those ubiquitous *M*A*S*H* reruns, the show was interrupted by a "breaking news" interstitial, then a somber-looking announcer appeared on screen.

"We've just received word here at the studio about a massive explosion in the center of Boston. It appears the blast has collapsed a portion of Interstate 93 between Cambridge Street and Boston Harbor."

"The Big Dig," Roddy grumbled, plopping down at the kitchen table. "A monument of excess and corporate corruption—"

"I thought the Dig was a *government* project," Claudia corrected.

"In America, government and business are one and the same thing. Instruments of arrogant avarice." He imperiously waved his hand. "The superciliousness of your American officials never ceases to astound me."

"You know what, Roddy? You can always go back to England—"

"Here we are!" Gillian forcefully chirped, setting the teapot down between them. "It's chamomile. It won't keep us awake—"

Another blast, much louder than the previous one, shook the windows. Roddy jumped to his feet, sending a china cup tumbling to the floor.

"Roddy, do be careful! You've broken a piece of our good—"

Another blast shattered the kitchen window. Gillian screamed. Claudia pushed her sister away from flying shards of glass. Other windows in the neighborhood had broken, too. They could hear cries of shock and surprise.

"I'm going to investigate," Roddy declared.

"No, wait," Claudia urged. "Stay here until we know more. This could be a terrorist event."

"Now you're being absurd," Roddy replied. "Obviously your husband's right-wing fantasies have clouded your mind."

Outside, a red glow continued to spread over the pre-dawn sky. Sirens wailed. On television, the news anchor's running commentary about the troubled history of the Big Dig was suddenly interrupted when someone off camera slipped him a sheet of paper.

"We've just received word of a second explosion. This one at Harvard Medical School—"

"My god!" Gillian cried.

Roddy stormed off before Claudia could stop him. Both women were relieved when they heard him climb the stairs, instead of going to the front door.

"We have raw video feed coming in of the initial blast at the Big Dig," the anchor said.

On screen, a massive hole in the center of town was spewing fire like a live volcano. Buildings around the site had collapsed, some of them burning. Though horrified, the sisters could not turn away from the screen.

Outside, a police car raced down narrow Acorn Street, lights flashing. They heard popping sounds, like fireworks going off. Then the sound of a car crash.

Roderick appeared in the kitchen again. He was dressed in khaki pants and a golf shirt. "Here," he said, handing a phone to Claudia. "I found your phone on the dresser. Your cell's been ringing nonstop."

Claudia took the phone. It wasn't ringing now, but she had three missed messages in just the past five minutes. She was about to call up the latest one when her cell went off in her hand.

"Where are you going, Roddy?" Gillian cried, nearly hysterical.

"Out. To see what all this ruckus is about."

"No, you can't—"

"Hello," Claudia said into her cell.

"Claudia, thank God you're safe," said her husband.

"Of course I'm safe. A little rattled, maybe—"

"*Listen*, a terror alert has just been issued for the Boston area."

"I knew it," Claudia said.

Outside, the fireworks got louder, and closer.

"We got the word in earlier this evening, from an untrustworthy source, frankly," Nathan Wheelock continued. "But it appears the agent in question was correct."

Roddy stormed out of the kitchen. Gillian wrung her hands.

On television, the announcer warned: "The Mayor has just issued a command that all citizens of the Boston area are to remain inside their homes. Let me repeat that . . ."

"Roddy!" Gillian cried, rushing to the front door.

"Truck bombs, Claudia," Nathan Wheelock said. "At least two of them, possibly as many as four—"

"We heard a number of explosions," Claudia replied. "Now it sounds like fireworks outside—"

"Those aren't fireworks," Nathan cried. "They're gunshots."

On the television, the anchor took another piece of paper and visibly paled. "We've just received another bulletin. Armed gangs are roving the streets around Boston Commons and the Beacon Hill area. All citizens in those neighborhoods are advised to lock their doors and take shelter in basements or attics—"

Claudia heard a fusillade that seemed to fire off right outside their door. She heard Gillian scream. Claudia closed the phone and bolted to the entranceway. Gillian was standing in the door, clutching her head.

Outside, someone was facedown on the pavement, blood pooling around a shattered skull. It took Claudia a moment to realize it was Roderick. Another form was crumpled on the sidewalk, a youth with long hair and a brown beard, wearing tie-dyed pajamas.

Claudia dragged her sister's arm, yanked her backward, then shut and locked the door. Another round of shots rang out, one of them puncturing the stout oak and shattering a mirror in the hallway.

On the other side of the door, they heard shouts and screams—and more shooting. Claudia dragged her sister deeper inside the house just as someone slammed a shoulder against the front door.

Frantically searching for a place to hide, Claudia opened the closet and pushed her sister inside.

"Keep quiet, no matter what you hear," Claudia commanded.

She'd just closed the door on her sister when Claudia

heard a crash, then heavy boots tramping on the polished hardwood floor. She slipped her hand into the robe's pocket, touched the butt of the small handgun—but she was afraid to pull it free. She wasn't all that sure of her aim, but mostly she didn't want to provoke the man.

A burly African American appeared in the hall. He wore dirty overalls and a skullcap. In his beefy hands, he clutched a double-barreled shotgun, which was pointed at the ceiling. His eyes appeared wild, like he was drugged.

"What do you want?" Claudia asked as gently and calmly as she could. The lawyer in her took over. *If I can just remain rational, negotiate with him, get him to talk to me, then it will be all right . . .*

"I want to help you," Claudia assured him. "What can I do to help you?"

The man blinked, his eyes beginning to focus. He looked down at Claudia's long, tanned legs. His gaze moved upward, over her trim figure, attractive face, and golden, sleep-tousled hair. Finally, he met her sky-blue eyes.

"Please, just put the gun down . . ." Claudia urged.

Claudia held her breath, feeling a moment of triumph as he did what she asked. *He's putting the gun down! He's actually leaning it against the wall!*

"Good," Claudia murmured on a released breath. "That's good."

The man stood there, unarmed now. But he still hadn't said a word.

"You don't want to hurt me, do you?" Claudia cooed.

A slow grin spread over the big man's face, the wide smile showing a single gold tooth. Then he began to move toward her, his steps deliberate, his sexual interest at last apparent to Claudia.

The lawyer's mind seized up; her jaw went slack. She couldn't think, couldn't speak. Finally registering what was about to happen to her, she simply stood frozen in place, barely able to breathe.

Her courtroom tactics were useless now; but Claudia Wheelock wasn't defenseless. Something deep inside her was taking over. Like a puppeteer, it directed her hand to take hold of the heavy item in her pocket—the gun her husband had given her. As if in a dream, Claudia felt her fingers curling around the butt.

The man reached out, still grinning, the gold tooth winking. She could read the laughter in his eyes now: *Easy prey. Arrogant. Defenseless. Stupid.*

His beefy hands tore open her robe, and Claudia's finger squeezed the trigger. The weapon bucked in her hand, the first bullet ripping through the terry cloth. She pumped four more shots into the stunned intruder before he finally went down.

3:46:14 A.M. EDT
Howard Street
Newark, New Jersey

Tony Almeida peered through the windshield of the stolen Explorer. Judith Foy sat beside him in the passenger seat. The idling Ford was tucked between two chop shop wrecks, nearly invisible to anyone cruising along Howard Street—or so Tony hoped.

"There's the Hummer," he announced, sitting up.

Agent Foy followed his gaze. "That's the one," she agreed.

Tony threw the SUV into gear. "I was getting worried. The plane must have been delayed." He glanced at his partner. "Get clear *now*."

Foy popped the door and slipped out.

Inside the Explorer, Tony waited for the black Hummer to roll toward him along Howard Street. When the vehicle was almost upon him, he gunned the engine. Tires squealed and the Explorer lurched forward.

The crash came sooner than Tony expected. The noise was deafening. The hood crumpled, flew open. Then the windshield exploded. After that, Tony was blind because the front impact air bags deployed.

The tremendous force of the crash jerked both vehicles to the side. In the middle of the cacophony, Tony heard his front tire pop. Then all was quiet, save for the hiss of steam leaking from the radiator.

Tony used a knife to deflate his air bag. With some difficulty, he forced his door open. Judith was already next to him, gun drawn. They reached the other car at the same time, both leveling their weapons.

The driver of the Hummer, a man wearing a black leather blazer, with Eastern European features, a crew cut, and an unshaven chin, was obviously dead. Tony ripped open the back door, peered inside, then cursed.

Judith pushed Tony aside and looked in the backseat. Neither the driver nor his passenger had been wearing a seatbelt. Judith Foy touched the woman's throat.

"She's dead," Foy declared.

"So is our plan," grunted Tony.

"What? You can't be serious?" Foy cried. "The device they were delivering is right there, next to the corpse."

Tony barely glanced at the large metal box, just slightly dented from the crash. "The plan was for me to pass myself off as this passenger," he said. "We didn't know she was a woman."

"Lucky you have me, then," Foy replied. "We'll just reverse roles. I'll infiltrate the Thirteen Gang's headquarters, and you'll watch my back from outside."

Tony shook his head. "I don't like it."

Judith's eyes narrowed. "You don't have to *like* it. You just have to *do* it."

Tony didn't reply. Judith grabbed his arm. "Listen, I'm a field agent, too. And I outrank you. I'm going in!"

She snatched the dead woman's purse, then fumbled through the driver's pockets until she found his ID and cell phone. Tony stood by and watched, feeling momentarily confused by Judith Foy's pulling rank on him. Up to now, he was used to her following his lead.

"Wake up, Almeida!" Judith barked like one of his old drill sergeants. "Grab that box, and let's get out of here before the police show up and arrest us."

Morris O'Brian felt a presence at his shoulder and turned away from the monitor screens.

"Jack! Good to have you back again," he said, then winced when he noticed the butterfly sutures on the man's temple, the blackened eye, the cuts on his face.

"Bloody hell," Morris said. "Look at you. If you won that fight, I'd hate to see the losers."

"The losers aren't breathing," Jack replied.

"You heard about the attacks in Boston?"

Jack nodded. "While they were patching me up in the infirmary. But I need details."

"There were three trucks. Two were bombs and detonated. A tunnel under construction collapsed, and so did the neighborhood around it. Casualty figures are not in yet. The second truck leveled Harvard Medical Center. Estimates count over a hundred dead."

"What about the third truck?"

"Apparently it disgorged a veritable army onto Boston Commons. The firefight still rages all over that part of the city."

"They should have listened to me and issued a terror warning for the Boston metro area," Jack said. "I knew my intelligence was good."

Expression grim, Jack glanced at the monitors. "What am I seeing now?"

"That wreck on the right monitor is what's left of the

truck that tried to take out CIA headquarters in Virginia. Cheeky, eh?" Morris shook his head. "Two CTU strike teams stopped the vehicle on Herndon Parkway. The terrorists were wiped out. No casualties on our side."

Jack nodded.

"The monitor on the left is showing us a truck that was stopped on the Mall in Washington, D.C., right in front of the Smithsonian. The terrorists fought to the last man. Again, no casualties on our side. Bomb squads are deactivating the explosives now."

"So there's only *one* truck still out there."

The phone chirped. Morris answered. "Yes, sir," he replied a moment later. Then he hung up and faced Jack. "Christopher Henderson would like a word with you. He's in the late Brice Holman's office."

"Find that truck," Jack called over his shoulder.

Morris sighed. "How many times have I heard *that* phrase today?"

• •

THE FOLLOWING TAKES PLACE
BETWEEN THE HOURS OF
4:00 A.M. AND 5:00 A.M.
EASTERN DAYLIGHT TIME

• •

4:01:22 A.M. EDT
District Director's Office
CTU Headquarters, NYC

"Come in, Jack. Have a seat."

Christopher Henderson sat behind Brice Holman's desk.
At the computer station, Jack saw Layla Abernathy, an un-
smiling figure in a black battle suit, Glock strapped to her
hip. Her hair was pulled back and she wore no makeup,
her sallow face expressionless.

When Jack entered the room, Layla turned her back on
him.

"I want you to listen to something Hershel Berkovic,

CTU's economic warfare guru, sent me," Henderson purred.

Jack sat down. Layla breezed past him and out the door, avoiding his gaze. Henderson activated a digital recorder on the desk. Jack heard a voice speaking Arabic, then the translator talking over him.

"America's alliance with our enemy has torn the Middle East apart," the translator said in a robotic voice. "The people of America spit in our faces every day. They must be punished for their transgressions and they soon will be. And we, the Arab peoples, can profit from America's pain."

A pause, then the Arabic voice spoke again.

"The Muslim world is ready to rise up and smite America," said the translator. "When the terrorism comes . . . America's economy will suffer enormous losses. Europe is much more stable, and so is its currency. It would be wise to switch our currency standard from dollars to euros before catastrophe strikes . . ."

The speech continued, but Henderson turned the recorder off.

"The man you heard was Abbad al Kabbibi, the finance minister for the Saudi government," he told Jack. "Minister Kabbibi made those remarks last month, in a secret meeting with key representatives of the Arab League."

"Kabbibi," Jack said. "As in Said Kabbibi?"

"Turns out our fugitive terrorist Biohazard Bob is the first cousin of the Saudi Arabian Finance Minister. What a coincidence."

Jack frowned. "And Soren Ungar?"

"Kabbibi has formed an alliance with Ungar," Henderson replied. "And Ungar, in turn, has aligned himself with French financial institutions and banks in Greece, Austria, Italy, Belgium, Germany, and Japan. As far as we can tell, Soren Ungar now controls two-thirds of the U.S. dollars on the currency market. Perhaps more."

"So he *is* engineering a currency crash," Jack said.

"That's what Berkovic thinks now, too," Henderson said with a nod. "But this goes further than that. Finance Minister Kabbibi is talking about switching the Saudi currency standard from the dollar to the euro. The harm that would do to our economy would be irreparable."

Henderson rose, placed the palms of his hands on the desk.

"Think back to what happened to Great Britain's economy when the world switched from the pound to the dollar. Their standard of living dropped and continues to fall, unemployment rose, investments fled for greener pastures. The Brits have never recovered from the blow."

"What about the currency reserve held by the Chinese?" Jack asked.

"The Chi-Coms would have no choice but to dump dollars, too, once a run starts. That, or they collapse along with us."

Jack's face flushed. His fingers tightened on the chair's armrest. "These attacks were nothing but a ploy," he said, unable to hide his outrage. "Just an excuse for Soren Ungar and the Arabs to dump our currency. The Hawk, the zealots from Kurmastan, maybe even Ibrahim Noor himself, they're nothing but pawns in the world's biggest currency scam. Collateral damage, just like their victims." Jack locked eyes with Henderson. "Will Ungar pull the trigger when the markets open in the morning?"

Henderson shook his head. "He's going to wait until the full impact of the U.S. attacks set in. He's got the perfect forum, too. In two hours and fifty minutes—two-thirty in the afternoon, Geneva time—Soren Ungar is scheduled to make his annual speech before the International Board of Currency Traders in Switzerland. That's when the little bastard is going to drop the bomb."

Jack leaned forward, his voice quiet but tight. "He has to be stopped."

"How? Assassination of a foreign national is illegal, under penalty of U.S. law. Besides . . . we don't have the assets to move that quickly."

"Yes we do." For the first time since he entered the office, Jack smiled. "I know a man stationed in Geneva right now. If anyone can pull off an assassination like this, it's Robert Ellis."

"Ellis, huh?" Henderson nodded. "Yeah, he is good . . . but it's doubtful anyone at CTU will green light the operation. Not even Richard Walsh would sign off on that— too much heat. And you can forget Nathan Wheelock. Mr. Clean would never get his hands dirty with authorizing an assassination on foreign soil; besides, the internal buzz is pretty ugly on the Northeast District Director."

"Is that so?" Jack folded his arms.

"Sure. You and I will probably be asked to testify when all of this is over, but let's face it: this mess happened in his region, under his watch, as a direct result of his managerial policies." Henderson shook his head. "If Brice Holman had been supported instead of shut down, the terrorists could have been stopped. I'd say Wheelock's career is hanging by a thread that's about to snap, which doesn't leave anyone high enough to authorize the action."

Jack's gaze narrowed. "I don't give a rat's ass about Wheelock's career. What I can't believe is you, trying to find another authority to hide behind." He rose to his feet. "*We* can take action now. *You and I.* So we face charges, go to prison? So what? It's a small price to pay to save our country."

Henderson arched an eyebrow. "Spoken like a true patriot."

Jack loomed over Henderson. "You're forgetting that Brice Holman and others have already paid the ultimate price. If we do this, they won't have died in vain. And we'll be ensuring America's security."

Henderson glanced away.

"Look," Jack said in a calmer voice, "if you want to pass the buck, then I have a name for you. Tell *him* everything you know and he'll back you. He's got the clout to bury an assassination, too. I know, because he's done it before. I haven't met him, you understand? And I can't tell you how I know, but I know . . ."

As Jack's voice trailed off, Henderson rose to his full height, finally meeting Jack's eyes. "Okay," he said. "Who is this magic man?"

"The Chairman of the Special Defense Appropriation Committee," Jack replied. "Senator David Palmer of Maryland."

4:18:16 A.M. EDT
Crampton Street
Newark, New Jersey

"Slip this into your pocket," Tony said, handing Judith Foy the dead driver's cell phone.

"What's it for?"

"Keep the line open and I can hear most of what's going on around you, though obviously you can't hear me." Tony shrugged. "It's not like wearing a wire, but it will do in a pinch."

"So if this plan all turns to crap, you'll rush in like the cavalry in a John Ford movie?" Judith said with a smile.

"Something like that," he replied. "CTU knows everything we know, and probably more. CTU knows there's a biological warfare lab in the warehouse, and they know the address of the Thirteen Gang's headquarters. Once we determine Ibrahim Noor is inside, the tactical teams will be dispatched and CTU will raid the entire block."

Tony paused, then met her gaze. "You don't have to do this, you know."

"Yes I do," Judith insisted. "Noor needs this metal box, so he or his minions will let me in. Once I'm inside, I can feed you intelligence, let you know if Noor is present. Maybe we can stop something bad before it happens this time."

"I'll be no further than across the street, even if you can't see me," Tony vowed. "Use the panic phrase if you get in trouble. I'll do what I can to get you out."

Agent Foy nodded, her face pale under the ball cap.

"Remember: *Semper fi*," Tony said.

Judith nodded. "I should have figured you for a jarhead, Almeida," she said before stepping into the shadowy urban landscape.

4:20:07 A.M. EDT
CTU Headquarters, NYC

Jack Bauer barged into Layla Abernathy's office.

"Forgot how to knock, Agent Bauer?" she asked.

He closed the door. "I need to talk to you."

"Make it quick, I'm typing my resignation—"

Jack switched off her computer. Layla threw up her arms. Jack saw needle marks in her wrists, forearms. He pointed.

"Henderson did that?"

Layla dropped her hands to her lap. "I don't want to talk about it."

"Don't resign," Jack said. "At least wait twenty-four hours. See this crisis through. Then you can quit if you still want to."

"Why?" Layla cried. "For a country that betrayed me? For an organization that had me tortured?"

"For innocent people who don't deserve what's happening to them now, or what may happen to them in the next few hours," Jack countered. "If you quit and something terrible happens, trust me, you won't be able to live with yourself—"

"CTU doesn't need me—"

"We *do* need you. And I believe you've got what it takes to be an exceptional field agent."

Layla dismissed his praise with a wave. "I don't believe you."

"Don't you think there were times when I was on the outs?" Jack pressed. "I've been painted as a dirty agent, more than once. I've had my security clearance revoked, and I've faced prosecution. No one comes away clean in this business. You have to learn to stick it out, soldier through, keep your focus on what you *know* is right. That's the way to be true to yourself and your principles. Not quitting when things get a little rough."

Layla blinked and slumped back in her chair. She was quiet for a long moment.

Jack sat down beside her. "I know what you went through was terrible. But—off the record—I sometimes think that the bad things that happen to us are a kind of punishment for the things we're forced to do to others."

"It sounds like you're talking about yourself now," Layla softly replied.

Jack met her gaze. "Let's just say that I've done things I'd never want my family to know about. I don't want my wife, my daughter, to ever think of me that way . . ."

Jack's eyes drifted, his expression haunted.

"Twenty-four hours then," Layla said. "I'll give you that, Jack Bauer. We'll see if it changes my mind."

Her phone rang and she put it on speaker. "Abernathy," she answered.

"Morris here. I need you in Station One, to help monitor a situation. I believe we've located the last truck."

4:22:21 A.M. EDT
Peralta Storage
Crampton Street
Newark, New Jersey

"I hope you can hear me, Tony, because I'm about to go in."

Judith Foy warily approached the garage door of the old warehouse. She limped a little—hoping it would add to her cover story. She shifted the heavy metal box in her hand, then knocked on the boarded-up garage.

Silence. The place seemed to be as abandoned as it looked.

Foy knocked again, harder this time. She kicked the door for good measure, though her sneakers didn't make much of a sound.

She was about to knock a third time when a spy hole opened in the middle of the big door.

"Who the hell are you?" a voice demanded.

"Klebb. Sonya Klebb," Foy replied.

She flashed the dead woman's passport, too fast for the observer to notice the crude job she'd done replacing the picture of the dead woman with her own driver's license photo.

"I am a chemical engineer with Rogan Pharmaceuticals," Foy continued. "Soren Ungar sent me."

There was a long pause. Foy was about to speak again when a different voice, deep and booming, emerged from the spy hole.

"Where is Dubic?"

It's Noor, she realized. *He's here*.

"Dead," Foy replied. "We were attacked on the road. I think a gang was trying to rob us. Our car was struck by another vehicle. I was hurt. Dubic more so. Before he died, he told me where to go, made me promise to deliver the package here, to this address."

"I see. And do you have the package?"

"I do," Foy replied, displaying it.

On the other side of the garage door, she heard activity. Then a rumbling sound as the door partially rose.

"Inside, quick," a black youth said, gesturing to her.

Beyond the door, the interior was pitch-black, and Judith could see nothing. She stepped inside anyway, heart pounding in her chest.

Another rumble of machinery, and the door closed behind her. Then brilliant spotlights ignited, blinding her. Someone snatched the package out of her hand; other hands frisked her.

They were obviously looking for a weapon. She had none, and when they found her passport and Dubic's cell phone, they ignored them. She hoped they hadn't broken the phone circuit, but she couldn't check now.

"Is that the aerosol dispenser?" Ibrahim Noor demanded.

"Yes, yes it is," an accented voice replied. "I can install it in less than an hour."

"Do it," Noor commanded.

Judith blinked against the light, strained to see through her tears.

"Why did you come here?" Noor asked. "Who sent you?"

"I told you. Dubic—"

"If Dubic told you to come here, he would have given you the remote control to open the door. All of my men have it. Dubic knows our security. Anyone stupid enough to bang on our door is either a neighborhood addict or a cop."

"No! Dubic must have forgotten. He was very injured. He could hardly speak—"

"You are a fraud. An impostor," roared Noor. "Take her."

Strong hands seized her arms. Judith struggled, then yelled out the panic phrase: "*Semper fi! Semper fi!*"

Someone punched her in the face, and the lab's bright lights faded.

4:38:43 A.M. EDT
Schenley Park
Pittsburgh, Pennsylvania

From his position among the branches of a century-old oak, Detective Mike Gorman shifted the sniper rifle in his grip, then aimed his night vision binoculars at the trailer truck three hundred feet away.

The vehicle sat in the middle of Schenley Plaza, once the grand entrance to the 456-acre conservancy, now used as a parking area for county rangers and concession employees. The truck had arrived sometime between midnight and four A.M., when a sharp-eyed Allegheny County

Parks Department ranger recognized the vehicle from a Federal government alert sent out to local authorities.

Two men slept in the cab. The driver's window was open, his arm hanging out. The guy in the passenger seat slouched so low, only the top of his New York Mets ball cap showed above the dashboard.

He's the tougher shot, and I got him, Gorman mused.

For thirty minutes, Gorman and his partner, Chuck Romeo, had observed the sleeping targets, fearing they would awaken and drive away at any moment. So far they'd been lucky, but luck never lasted long—just one lesson Gorman had taken away from the McKee's Rocks mess.

I should have fired, Gorman thought, flashing back to the hostage standoff. A young mother had been held at gunpoint by an escaped convict. *I should never have waited for authorization. If I'd have pulled the trigger, that poor woman would be alive today and her murderer dead, instead of the other way around.*

"What are we waiting for?" Gorman said into his headset.

"A biohazard team with a tent," his boss, Captain Kelly, advised. "Once it's in place, we can move."

Gorman glanced across a grassy clearing at his partner, perched in a tall maple tree. He was sure Chuck was staring back at him. Then Romeo's voice crackled in his headset.

"A biohazard team? Is there something you're not telling us, Captain?"

"Relax, boys," Kelly said. "Just do your job and the Feds will do the rest."

More baffled than alarmed, Gorman lowered his binoculars and shifted the fourteen-pound M24 sniper rifle into position. The composite stock against his armored shoulder, he peered through the infrared scope.

Placing the ball cap in the center of his crosshairs, Gorman once again adjusted the instrument for wind speed, temperature, humidity, and distance. Gorman knew he had only one shot. It had to be on the money. He wasn't going to mess up again.

Minutes passed. Then Gorman heard the sound of an engine. He watched in disbelief as two white panel trucks rolled into the plaza and halted just inside the gate.

"I thought the road had been cordoned off to traffic," Gorman hissed.

"It's the biohazard team. They'll be ready to go in two minutes."

Gorman glanced through his scope again. His target was still snoozing, but the driver had shifted position.

Had he heard the vans, too?

"I think my mark's awake," Chuck Romeo warned.

"Do not fire," Captain Kelly commanded. "I repeat. Do not fire until I give the command."

"Son of a—" Gorman stifled his curse, remembering that everything he and the others said was being taped— just like McKee's Rocks.

Unbidden, the memory returned. Two A.M., outside a strip joint on the main drag of that scummy little suburb. The drunk convict, using the dancer for a shield, gun to her head. Gorman had a clear shot, begged Captain Kelly for authorization to pull the trigger, but it never came. The only shot fired that night went into the dancer's skull. The single mother from Wheeling, West Virginia, died because he'd hesitated.

Through his scope, Gorman saw the driver wake up the man beside him. Both stared at the vans with open suspicion.

"If he starts that engine, the men who are supposed to be hiding inside that trailer will know something's up," Gorman warned.

"Do *not* fire," Captain Kelly repeated.

"You ready to shoot, Chuck?" Gorman asked.

"Ready," Romeo said after a short pause.

"Fire on three," Gorman said, aiming.

"Stand down and wait for my command," Kelly warned. "Do not fire."

"One," said Gorman.

"Stand down, I said!" Kelly cried.

"Two."

Kelly was screaming in their headsets now. "If either of you shoots I'll have your heads—"

In the truck, the driver reached for the ignition. His partner pulled a cell phone from his jacket.

"Three."

Two holes appeared in the windshield simultaneously. Inside the cab, two heads exploded. The men flopped forward, dead. The driver slumped over the steering wheel; the man in the passenger seat dropped to the floor.

"Got them," Gorman whispered. "They're down. I repeat. The targets are dead."

"So are your careers," Kelly growled, his voice icy with rage.

Obviously the Feds had been monitoring the conversation. As soon as Gorman announced the kills, the doors on both vans burst open. Five men in plastic biohazard suits rushed to the truck, dragging what looked like a huge cellophane blanket.

Gorman was impressed by the speed and efficiency with which the men tossed the massive tarp over the vehicle, then sealed the edges of the covering to the pavement with some sort of instant adhesive pumped out of a glue gun.

Inside of a minute they were finished, and a third white van raced into the plaza. This one contained a huge vacuum pump that was immediately attached to the tarp.

Before Gorman and Romeo climbed down from their respective trees, the pump was sucking the air out of the bag, hermetically sealing the vehicle and all its contents.

When they were on the ground, a man in a black jumpsuit approached them. Gorman thought it was a Pittsburgh policeman, but revised his opinion when the man got close enough for Gorman to see the CTU crest on the uniform.

"You're the Feds?" Gorman asked, fully expecting to be arrested.

"Special Agent Clark Goodson, CTU Biological Terrorism Specialist, Midwest Division."

Still juiced with a killer's high, Gorman's adrenaline was pumping and his hands trembled. He fumbled for a reply.

Suddenly the man slapped him on the back. "Exceptional work," Goodson said. "If you'd waited, it would have been too late."

"Tell that to our boss," Romeo replied.

"Oh, I will." Goodson nodded. "And if that a-hole Kelly *does* take your heads, I'll find you both jobs on a CTU tac team. In fact, I hear L.A. is looking for a few good men."

1 2 3 4 5 6 7 8 9
10 11 12 13 14 15 16 17
18 19 20 21 22 **23** 24

. . . .

THE FOLLOWING TAKES PLACE
BETWEEN THE HOURS OF
5:00 A.M. AND 6:00 A.M.
EASTERN DAYLIGHT TIME

. . . .

5:07:07 A.M. EDT
Security Station One
CTU Headquarters, NYC

The euphoria of taking out the final truck was quickly dampened, once the agent at the scene delivered his report.

"That's all we found here in Pittsburgh, Special Agent Bauer," Goodson said into the computer camera.

Behind the battle-suited speaker, a boxy, six-wheeled military vehicle was visible in the predawn light. Six men in hazard suits, helmets off, clustered around it.

"The truck was packed with conventional explosives,"

Goodson continued. "C–4 manufactured in Eastern Europe. There were also maps that indicate their target was the University of Pittsburgh's Cathedral of Learning. They were planning to destroy the skyscraper during the morning rush hour. No biological or chemical agents of any kind are present."

Jack Bauer frowned at the screen. "The bio-weapon could be small, contained in a vial, an aerosol can or even a Breathalyzer."

Goodson shook his head. "We have a rolling CTU Bio-Containment Lab on scene," he said. "Along with a Fox Nuclear Biological Chemical Reconnaissance vehicle which we borrowed from the Army. Both units have scanned the entire scene with monitors so sensitive they could locate a cold germ."

The CTU operative paused. "I'm sorry, Special Agent Bauer. We found nothing."

Jack was about to protest, when Christopher Henderson stepped in front of him. "Thanks for your help, Goodson. Nice work, all the way around."

"Thank you, Director Henderson," Goodson replied, and the screen went black.

Jack sank into a chair. "So where's the bio-weapon?"

Henderson sat and swiveled toward Bauer. "The Economic Warfare Division has suggested that Kabbibi might have been brought into this operation for his *political* connections, not his skills. The fact that he and the Saudi Finance Minister are cousins—"

Jack's withering stare silenced his boss. "They're *wrong*, Christopher. Berkovic and his accountants are ignoring

Agent Foy's surveillance photos of the lab in Newark."

Henderson shrugged. "It's possible that's a simple drug lab."

"With liquid oxygen cooling tanks?" Jack interrupted. "You don't need that kind of technology to distill meth out of cough syrup."

Henderson sighed. "We'll know soon enough. Langley has finally authorized the raid on Noor's Newark headquarters. We're there in thirty minutes, whether Noor's home or not."

Jack nodded. "I'll command the raid. Agent Abernathy will be my backup."

Layla appeared surprised. So did Henderson, but neither challenged Jack's decree.

Bauer's mind was racing so fast, he was already past that decision. He was eager to focus on his enemy. "Have we learned anything more about Ibrahim Noor?"

"A little," Morris replied, calling up the man's profile. "He was born Travis Bell, as you know. By the age of thirteen, he was running drugs. By eighteen, he'd created the Thirteen Gang, which took over the narcotics trade in that section of Newark."

Morris tapped keys. "Well, well. Here's a nugget. Congressman Larry Bell of Louisiana, the former NCAA player turned politician, is Travis Bell's uncle. But apparently there's been no contact between them for decades."

"The same can't be said for other government officials," Henderson interjected. "From Tobias's computer, we've got evidence that Congresswoman Hailey Williams and Chief Justice Mary Chestnut of the Ninth District Court in San Francisco have both taken bribes from Noor or his people. Their arrests are imminent."

"What about Dreizehn Trucking?" Jack asked.

"It doesn't exist on any corporate records, state, local, or Federal," Morris replied. "It's no more than a name painted on twelve trucks."

"But it fits Noor's profile," Layla said. "*Dreizehn* is the German word for the number thirteen. Noor seems pathologically obsessed with that number."

"Thirteen! Oh my god . . ." Jack rose to his feet. "That's where the biological weapon is hidden."

"Huh?" Henderson grunted.

"There's a thirteenth truck, Christopher. And Noor is on it!" Jack gripped Morris's shoulder. "Has Tony checked in?"

"Not since he lost contact with Agent Foy. She's inside the Thirteen Gang's headquarters, but their cell phone connection has been severed. I'm afraid Tony's a bit frantic over Agent Foy's situation."

"Call Almeida," Jack commanded. "Tell Tony to stay put. Tell him we're coming—with a strike team."

5:29:53 A.M. EDT
1313 Crampton Street
Newark, New Jersey

"Your name is Judith Foy, Deputy Director of the New York Counter Terrorist Unit," Ibrahim Noor declared, looming over her.

Shaking the icy water from her body, Judith Foy defiantly met the gang leader's gaze. Only half conscious after her violent capture, Judith Foy had been dragged through a stinking sewer, tossed into a hole blasted in the wall, and dumped on a cold concrete floor. She lay there for an indeterminate amount of time, until someone poured a bucket of ice water over her.

Gasping against the freezing torrent, she found herself in a circle of street thugs, some white, most black or Hispanic. Harsh fluorescent lights buzzed over her head. Soon she realized she wasn't in the garage anymore. There was no lab here, and the room stank of sweat and spilled blood. Judith saw two headless corpses piled in the corner.

"I ordered your death many hours ago, but my command was not obeyed," Noor continued.

Head throbbing, she studied the speaker. Noor had a body like a black bear, tattoo-etched arms thicker than her waist. His voice was deep, like Darth Vader's without the asthma. Everything she knew about this man suggested he suffered from a delusional messiah complex. But when Agent Foy locked eyes with Noor, she saw no madness there—only a fierce and terrible cunning.

"And you're Ibrahim Noor, alias Travis Bell," she replied evenly. "Counterfeit holy man, full-time felon, and total wack job."

A youth lashed out, plunged the toe of his boot into her abdomen. Judith grunted, felt the world recede again. She fought to stay conscious, and by some miracle prevailed.

"Don't be so tough on Rachel Delgado," Judith gasped, tasting bile. "Someone killed *her* first."

The punk moved to kick her again. Noor stopped him with a gesture. Foy spit on the kicker's leg.

Judith should have been afraid, but she wasn't. Instead, she was filled with an all-consuming fury, a savage hatred. She would have given her soul to kill Noor right now, tear out his throat with her teeth.

"We all thought you were a religious fanatic, but you're not, are you, Travis?" Foy challenged. "You're just a street punk with delusions of grandeur, using people like pawns because they're too stupid to know better."

Noor didn't prevent the youth from kicking her *this* time. Judith howled in agony when she felt a bruised rib snap. "Tough . . . tough guys," she gasped. "Beat up on a . . . helpless woman."

"Did CTU send you?" Noor demanded.

"Actually . . . It was the neighborhood cleanup committee," Foy replied, fighting the urge to throw up. "This place . . . is such a pigsty . . . You really should clean it up."

The youth kicked out again. This time she managed to protect her vitals with her elbows. Her left arm felt paralyzed now, but at least her bruised ribs were still intact.

"If CTU sent you, they made a tragic blunder," Noor continued. "You have delivered the one tool I need to bring America to its knees."

"A boombox blasting hip-hop?"

She waited for a fourth kick, but it never came. Instead a newcomer approached Noor. "Kabbibi is finished," he whispered.

A smile tugged at Noor's lips, then he faced the others.

"It is time for me to go, my friends. When next we meet, it will be in Paradise."

The men lined up to receive Noor's final blessings, completely ignoring the woman on the ground. Foy used the time to gather her strength, examine her environment.

She saw a red steel door at one end of the windowless room and realized she was inside 1313 Crampton Street, Noor's gang headquarters.

The sewer must connect this place with the old Peralta Storage facility at the end of the block.

Meanwhile Noor waved his men back. "Give me thirty minutes to get clear of this place. After that, you may release yourselves from this world of corruption."

"Allahu akbar! Allahu akbar!" the men chanted.

Flanked by two bodyguards, Noor walked to the hole in the concrete wall and climbed through it.

As soon as their leader was gone, the room exploded with activity. Someone produced jerricans filled with gasoline. Muttering prayers—and still ignoring Judith Foy—the men began dousing the walls, the floor, the dead men in the corner, with the flammable liquid.

5:42:13 A.M. EDT
Over Newark, New Jersey

"This is Raptor One. ETA, two minutes," Captain Fogarty said into Jack Bauer's headset.

Jack, now clad in a black CTU battle suit with Kevlar chest, shoulder, and spine plates, faced the five assault troopers inside the helicopter's bay. He spoke into the headset in his helmet.

"As soon as we fast-rope down to the street, I want you to hit the warehouse. Blow the garage door and we'll move in," he said.

"The team in Raptor Two will hit 1313 Crampton on the opposite end of the block," Jack continued. "Agent Abernathy's team in Raptor Three will remain airborne, ready to provide backup if needed. Any questions?"

Grim-faced, the men shook their heads.

"Move fast and hit hard," Jack advised. "We may be dealing with a biological or chemical weapon, so capture and containment is key."

"One minute," Fogarty warned.

Jack lowered his visor and shouldered a UMP .45-caliber submachine gun. "Hit the ropes!" he shouted.

The men rose and moved to the chopper's open doors.

5:44:08 A.M. EDT
1313 Crampton Street

The stench of gasoline was suffocating. Judith Foy battled the urge to empty her stomach. Though her head was spinning, she kept her focus on a stocky Hispanic teenager with shoulder-length black hair and a Browning Hi-Power handgun tucked casually in his belt.

The youth had come down from an upper floor, empty jerrican in hand. He tossed the container into the pile of empties and crossed the room to the stack of full cans.

He was four feet from Judith when she stumbled to her feet and lurched into his path.

"I need a bathroom," she rasped. "I'm going to be sick."

The punk snarled something in Spanish and thrust her aside, eyes on the gas. Foy pretended to waver, but as he stepped around her, she yanked the gun out of his belt, threw the safety, and shot him in the base of the spine.

The youth howled and hit the floor. Five heads turned, mouths gaping in shock. Judith was a marksman and she hit her marks—first one man, then another.

Before she dropped the third man, he drew his own weapon and squeezed off a shot. The bullet struck sparks off the steel door. Judith lurched sideways and fired again, hitting the shooter in the forehead.

Two men remained standing. One clutched a can of gasoline like a shield; the other was reaching for his weapon.

Firing too quickly for accuracy, even at point-blank range, Judith hit the wrong man. The bullet penetrated the jerrican, and it exploded in an orange ball of fire.

Immediately, the pair was engulfed in flames that quickly spread. Fire scorched Judith, too, setting her hair and jumpsuit ablaze. Bolting across the basement, she dived through the hole and into the tunnel.

Judith landed in a shallow pool of fetid sewer water, dousing her burning clothes and singed hair. Choking, eyes burning, Judith crawled to her feet and raced through the dripping tunnel in a desperate bid to outpace the roaring conflagration at her back.

5:45:34 A.M. EDT
Crampton Street

As soon as Jack's combat boots struck pavement, he moved away from the fast-rope so the man behind him had a clear space to land.

Jack felt a hand grip his armored shoulder, turned, weapon ready. Tony Almeida was there, blinking against the prop wash.

"We've got to get inside," Tony shouted over the hovering chopper's engine. "Agent Foy's in the sh—"

"Fire! Fire!" someone bellowed in Jack's headset.

He glanced at the warehouse, then the gang headquarters at the other end of the block.

Smoke poured out of the roof above 1313 Crampton Street. Flickering flames reflected off Raptor Two's aluminum belly.

5:46:00 A.M. EDT
Peralta Storage

Judith burst out of the tunnel, into a cavernous basement. The space was lit by banks of halogen lights. The garage door dominated one wall, the makeshift biological weapons lab the other. There were no vehicles present—Noor was already gone.

Others were there, however. Two men in white lab coats were burning papers in a steel barrel in the center of the room. Smoke wafted up to the high ceiling. A third man sat at a small table, where he tapped the keys of a laptop computer.

A man at the barrel cried out. Judith shot him in the face, and he pitched forward, into the flames. She fired at the other man and missed.

The third man snatched the laptop off the table and ran toward the barrel, ready to toss the device into the flames. Judith shot him in the legs, and he hit the floor. The computer slid across the concrete, stopping at her feet.

The man she missed rushed her. Judith pulled the trigger. The Hi-Power clicked on an empty chamber.

The man slammed into her, and they both went down. As they struggled, the garage door blew apart with a deafening report, and men streamed through the shattered entrance.

Despite her ringing ears, Foy heard a shot. The man on top of her jerked, then fell limp. Almost immediately, someone flipped the corpse aside.

Judith blinked up at Tony Almeida, who lifted her off the floor with one hand.

"The cavalry has arrived," he said, grinning. "Not that you needed us."

"Believe me, I needed you. Grab that computer and let's get out of here! This whole place is ready to blow!" she yelled, loud enough for everyone to hear.

Just then, a rolling ball of fire roared out of the tunnel.

"Out! Everybody out!" Bauer shouted, gesturing wildly.

Tony grabbed the computer. And Jack rushed up to Foy.

"Where's Noor?" he cried as they ran.

"Gone. Ten, maybe fifteen minutes ago."

Jack cursed. "And the truck?"

Judith blinked. "What truck?"

1 2 3 4 5 6 7 8 9
10 11 12 13 14 15 16 17
18 19 20 21 22 23 **24**

....

THE FOLLOWING TAKES PLACE
BETWEEN THE HOURS OF
6:00 A.M. AND 7:00 A.M.
EASTERN DAYLIGHT TIME

....

2:00:02 P.M. CEST
Ungar Financial Building
Geneva, Switzerland

Robert Ellis avoided the crowd at the front of the auditorium, got in line at an entrance marked "Press" in six languages. A pair of security guards checked off every name on the list as the reporters arrived.

"Ellis, Robert, Theological News Service, New York," he said, handing over his identification. The guard checked his name against the roster and returned his ID.

"Through the metal detector and straight ahead, Mr. Ellis," the guard told him.

After he passed through the X-ray machine, a slight, effeminate man swathed in Armani stepped out of the shadows to greet him. His English was slightly fractured, but Ellis had to admit the man's pronunciation was excellent.

"Mr. Ellis! How good of you to come, sir. Archbishop Holzer had many good things to say about you. When His Excellency called with this last-minute request for an invitation, I could not refuse him."

Ellis smiled. "I appreciate your hospitality, Mr.—"

"Jorg Schactenberg," he said, extending his hand. "I am Soren Ungar's amanuensis."

The man's handshake had all the warmth and life of a dead fish.

"I understand you attended this event last year," Schactenberg purred.

"Two years ago," Ellis corrected. "Last year I was away from Geneva on urgent business."

"Ah, yes," the other man replied. "Always with the business. His Excellency, the Archbishop, told me you have kept him up late many times, with talking about the philosophy and the religion—and your many amazing adventures. You have a seminary background?"

"A bachelor's degree in theology, from Fordham University in New York," Ellis replied. "And I might add that Archbishop Holzer possesses an amazing mind. I have often been a guest in his home, and it was always most stimulating."

Everything Ellis told Schactenberg was true, though if today's bit of wet work ever came to light, Ellis doubted he would ever be welcome in the Archbishop's residence again.

"I'm sure Herr Ungar's speech will be quite enlightening," Ellis added graciously.

Schactenberg offered Ellis a thin smile. "As an American, I'm sure you will hear something that interests you."

The man led Ellis behind the massive stage, to a room packed with members of the international press.

"I have reserved a place for you in the reception line, Mr. Ellis. I do believe Herr Ungar will greet all the members of the media before he delivers his address."

Ellis smiled. "I'm counting on it."

6:09:32 A.M. EDT
Aboard Raptor Three

In the light of a blazing dawn, Jack Bauer, Layla Abernathy, and Tony Almeida watched the Peralta Storage facility collapse in on itself from the air. Burning cinders rose into the smoky sky. Howard and Crampton Streets were packed with emergency vehicles, lights flashing.

"There's nothing more to see here," Jack declared, directing the pilot to return to Manhattan.

Before they lifted off, Jack used a mobile Wi-Fi broadband communications system to forward the contents of the enemy's computer to experts at Langley.

Agent Foy was aboard Raptor One, on her way to CTU's infirmary, where her injuries would be treated. Jack kept the laptop at his side once he realized it belonged to Said Kabbibi or one of his technicians.

"Morris, can you hear me?" Jack said into his headset.

"Loud and clear, Jack."

"Any sign of the missing truck?"

There was a long sigh. "Jack, you're asking for the impossible now. We've established the garage under the warehouse was too small to hold a large trailer truck like the other twelve vehicles, so we really don't know what type of truck we're looking for."

"There must be something—"

"Peek out your window," Morris interrupted. "There are quite literally thousands of trucks on the road right now. It would be easier to find a needle in a haystack while blindfolded."

Jack bit back a curse. "Anything from Langley yet?"

"The bio-weapons experts are still reviewing the contents of the computer. Director Henderson urges patience."

"Patience is no virtue when you're running out of time," Jack shot back.

"Pithy, and well said," Morris replied. "I'm going to remember that one."

Layla Abernathy rested her hand on Jack's arm. "Langley will come through," she said. "They understand how urgent the situation is."

Jack nodded, took a swig of water from a plastic bottle. Across the bay from the pair, Tony slouched in a seat. Like Jack, he wore new scars from this day, and it wasn't over yet.

Morris's voice suddenly came on in Jack's headset. "I have the Director of CTU's Biological and Chemical Warfare Unit on line now," he said. "I'll put him through."

As the connection was made, Tony sat up, adjusting his own headset. Layla tapped her foot nervously.

"Dr. Vogel here," the Director began.

"What are we dealing with?" Jack asked without preamble. "Is it a biological or a chemical agent?"

"Both," Vogel replied with equal bluntness. "The agent is called Zahhak, after a demonic snake of Persian mythology, sometimes depicted with two heads. The name is apt because this substance brings death in two ways."

"Explain," Jack ordered.

"At first we thought we were dealing with a simple sarin compound," Vogel replied. "Sarin, or O-Isopropyl methylphosphonofluoridate, is a clear, colorless, and odorless nerve agent classified by the United Nations as a weapon of mass destruction. Sarin is nothing new, of course. It was developed in the late 1930s by German researchers looking for a better pesticide. What they created instead is one of the deadliest compounds on earth. Sarin has been used—"

"Zahhak is not sarin, then?" Jack interrupted.

"Not precisely," Vogel said. "Like sarin, Zahhak is very unstable. It can break down in days, which is why Kabbibi needed a lab here in America to produce the weapon. Various substances have been tried to make the agent more stable and increase its shelf life. A stabilizer chemical called tributylamine has been used in the past, with mixed results. Dr. Said Kabbibi tried something different, something revolutionary, and it worked."

Jack's impatience with the technician threatened to boil over. He opened his mouth to speak; Layla restrained him with a gesture.

"Layla Abernathy here," she interrupted. "You said this was both a chemical and a biological weapon?"

"I was getting to that," Vogel said testily. "Kabbibi initially tried to bond various bacteria with the sarin substance, hoping to make the chemical more stable. He tried many organics without success, until he stumbled upon bacteria called *Clostridium perfringens*. The result was a two-pronged weapon of mass destruction more deadly than anything previously encountered."

"Two-prong?" Jack cut in.

"Let me explain," Vogel said with a sigh. "A terrorist attack in the Middle East often involves two sets of explosive devices. After the initial blast and resulting casualties, emergency workers stream to the scene of the attack. That's when the terrorists unleash a second string of blasts, to kill those rushing to aid the victims."

Jack frowned, recalling accounts he'd read of such diabolical attacks.

"When Zahhak is unleashed, the sarin compound immediately attacks the nervous system of its victims," Vogel continued. "Symptoms present in minutes include runny nose, tightness in the chest, constriction of the pupils, nausea, drooling. Difficulty in breathing increases as the victims lose control of their bodily functions. They urinate. Defecate. Vomit. Bleed from the nose and mouth. Death soon follows—but Zahhak's threat doesn't end there."

"Explain," Jack said tightly.

"The biological agent—*Clostridium perfringens*—is introduced into the victim's body along with the gas, causing an outbreak of *necrotizing fasciitis*."

"Of what?" Abernathy asked.

"A condition commonly known as 'flesh-eating bacteria' occurs. The bacteria work too slowly to affect the initial victims of the gas, but their bodies and their bodily fluids are immediately contaminated with the bacteria. *Clostridium perfringens* is highly contagious. Exposure from a single touch, or even breathing the weaponized bacteria, can cause infection and a slow and agonizing death. There is no cure."

"This is monstrous," Layla whispered. "Emergency workers and hospital personnel would end up becoming the ones infected—emergency response would be taken out first."

"It gets worse," Vogel informed them. "Within minutes of dispersal through an aerosol dispenser, Zahhak forms a solid. In that state, the effects of the sarin are neutralized, but the malignant bacteria live on. In fact, it is virtually indestructible at this point. And the solid particles are microscopic in size, so they become airborne, spreading the contagion across hundreds of miles."

"Dr. Vogel, is there a vaccine or countermeasure to combat Zahhak?" Jack asked.

"Countermeasure?" Vogel replied, his tone bitter. "My colleagues and I are not precisely sure how this substance *works*. A countermeasure or vaccine may be years away—or a pipe dream. Once Zahhak is unleashed, it is like a genie that can never be returned to its bottle."

"What can we do?" rasped Jack.

"Stop it before it's released," Vogel replied. "In its liquid or gaseous state, Zahhak is very sensitive to moisture and heat, which is why Kabbibi needed liquid oxygen to keep the substance cool. Zahhak can be destroyed by heating it to a temperature above 160 degrees centigrade. It is also completely soluble in water—steam would be ideal to render the agent inert, but only in its liquid or gaseous state. Once it becomes a solid, there is nothing that can be done to contain its deadly effects."

Vogel ended the call at that point, informing Jack he was scheduled to brief the President. Christopher Henderson came on line.

"Any thoughts, Jack?"

Bauer's mind raced. "When I was talking to Dubic, and he believed he was talking to the Albino, Dubic said something about a rendezvous at the bull this morning. Is that a section of New York? A building, plaza, or park?"

Layla blinked. "You're kidding, right? Wait. I forgot you're from Los Angeles."

"Cut to the chase," Tony growled.

"There *is* a bull," Layla told them. "The Wall Street Bull, a two-and-a-half-ton bronze sculpture of a charging bull. It sits in Bowling Green Park. The statue was erected after the 1987 stock market crash, and it's become the symbol of the Financial District."

"That's it, then!" Jack said. "Noor's heading for Wall Street, and we're going to be there to meet him."

6:49:13 A.M. EDT
Broadway
Lower Manhattan

Ibrahim Noor steered the truck onto Broadway, joined the flow of traffic heading downtown. Though it was early, rush hour was already in full swing in the Financial District. The morning sun was bright, heralding a warm day.

In the passenger seat, Said Kabbibi twitched nervously. He was about to speak when the traffic light turned red, forcing Noor to brake. Cross traffic from Cedar Street quickly crammed the intersection.

Kabbibi groaned, tugged on the collar of his utility worker's uniform. "I fear we will not make it to the park in time. Unfortunately I cannot stop the timer now. The aerosol device will release the toxin at precisely seven-thirty."

"Relax," Noor said. "We're only a few blocks away."

"Good," Kabbibi replied, moping his brow with a handkerchief. "I do not want to be anywhere near this place when the Zahhak is released."

The light turned green, but so many cars blocked the intersection that they couldn't make it through. Kabbibi became even more agitated.

"I told you to relax," Noor rumbled. "By nine o'clock, we'll be on a private jet to Geneva, and America will be on its knees."

6:50:11 A.M. EDT
The Bartleby
Broadway
Lower Manhattan

The roof of the mid-rise Bartleby Tower, right across the street from the Cunard Building, provided a perfect perch to observe traffic rolling down Broadway.

Jack Bauer was there, along with Tony Almeida, Layla

Abernathy, and Director Christopher Henderson. Three telescopes had been set up, each focused on downtown traffic.

"I'm checking the truck that just turned onto Broadway from Exchange Street," Jack said, peering through the lens. "The logo says Carvel Ice Cream."

He zoomed in, spied a bored Asian man behind the steering wheel. "Looks like a negative," Jack said.

His headset crackled. "This is Bio-Monitor One. That truck is clean."

Jack exhaled.

"Are you sure the explosive charge is powerful enough?" Bauer asked for the third time.

"The demolition boys know how to do their jobs, Jack," Henderson replied, his expression unreadable behind mirrored sunglasses.

Jack spoke into his headset. "Morris? How about the traffic lights? We need to isolate the vehicle as soon as it's spotted."

"I'm in control of the lights along Broadway, Jack," Morris said from Security Station One. "Give me the word and I'll put in the fix. Frankly, I wish I had this kind of control in Los Angeles."

Jack tensed. "Check the Consolidated Edison truck at the Pine Street intersection. Noor's used that trick before."

All three telescopes focused on the blue and white Con Edison van, and the two men inside the cab.

"That's Noor, behind the wheel," Jack hissed, clutching the telescope reflexively.

"And Kabbibi is beside him," Layla cried.

"I see some kind of nozzle sticking out of the top of the truck," Tony warned.

"This is Bio-Monitor One. Our meters are off the chart. That truck is dirty."

"I've got the vehicle on my monitor," Morris declared. "Facial recognition software has confirmed Noor's and Kabbibi's identities on this end."

"Okay," Jack declared. "This is it."

On Broadway at Bowling Green Park, the uptown lights suddenly turned red. Cars braked abruptly. It was obvious to the drivers that something was wrong with the signals, but before anyone could jump the light, an FDNY ladder truck rolled into the middle of the intersection, blocking all traffic.

"Uptown traffic flow has been cut off," Morris declared. "Downtown traffic is next. I'll have that vehicle isolated in less than a minute."

Henderson touched the detonator in his hand. "This is your plan and your show, Bauer. Give the word and I'll set off the fireworks."

6:51:29 A.M. EDT
Intersection of Exchange Street and Broadway

At the head of the pack, Ibrahim Noor was the first driver through the intersection when the light turned green. He was also the only vehicle to make the light, which immediately turned red again, stopping all traffic behind him.

With two blocks of Broadway wide open, Noor picked up speed. But halfway down the block he slowed again, glanced into his rearview mirror.

"A fire truck has blocked traffic behind us," he announced.

"There's one ahead of us, too," Kabbibi cried, pointing to the red vehicle two blocks away.

"Something's wrong," whispered Noor.

The big man checked his right. The uptown lane was empty, too. Noor frowned when he realized the Con Edison truck was the only vehicle on the block. Bowling Green Park was directly ahead of them, and Kabbibi urged Noor to speed up.

Noor slowed the van instead, eyes scanning Broadway like a hunted animal.

6:52:37 A.M. EDT
The Bartleby

"The truck's slowing down," Layla warned.

Jack Bauer stared through the telescope. "Don't worry. He's almost reached the mark."

Through the scope, Jack watched the vehicle approach a freshly painted yellow cross on the pavement, right in the middle of the downtown lane.

When the van reached the symbol. Jack faced Henderson.

"Now," he rasped.

Henderson pressed the detonator . . .

6:53:01 A.M. EDT
Broadway

Kabbibi cried out when a powerful jolt rocked the van. Before either man could react, the pavement opened up under their wheels.

The Con Ed van plunged six feet, landing atop a massive steam pipe—part of the Financial District's underground infrastructure.

Noor cursed.

"Let me out!" Kabbibi howled, fumbling with the handle.

"Too late," Noor whispered.

At that moment, a second blast shattered the pipe beneath them.

Instantly, the vehicle was engulfed in sizzling steam. In under a second, the temperature inside the truck soared to a thousand degrees.

As he howled, Noor's scalded flesh blistered, then began to slough off his bones like chicken in a soup pot. Kabbibi's eyes popped from the searing heat, and he clutched his face with fleshless fingers.

Behind them, in the cargo bay, the aluminum tank containing the Zahhak burst with a muffled thump.

A fountain of white steam erupted from the pit, filling the near-empty street. Millions of gallons of boiling water gushed out. Then the flow turned dark brown, as rocks and soil spewed out of the seething pit. Hot mud splattered buildings. Windows broke as high as the eighth floor.

Like a raging volcano, the lavalike mixture continued to stream up from around the ruptured pipe.

2:56:24 P.M. CEST
Ungar Financial Building
Geneva, Switzerland

Robert Ellis was the fifth man in the reception line. He waited patiently, watching Soren Ungar greet each member of the press with a handshake, smile plastered across his rigid face.

Jorg Schactenberg stood at Ungar's shoulder, making introductions as his boss moved down the line.

"This is Robert Ellis of the Theological News Service in New York," Schactenberg said.

Under thick glasses, Soren Ungar's expressionless eyes regarded him. Stiffly, the financial leader extended his hand.

Ellis twisted the faux Fordham University ring on his left hand with his thumb, enfolded Ungar's pale hand with his right.

"A pleasure, Herr Ellis," Ungar said formally.

Still clutching Ungar's hand in his right, Ellis covered it with his left. He felt the tiny needle plunge into Soren Ungar's pale flesh.

"Greetings from the U. S. of A.," Ellis hissed. Then he released the man.

Ungar stepped back, obviously surprised, though his face registered no expression. The currency trader turned to speak with the sixth man in line, and suddenly his knees buckled.

"Herr Ungar," Schactenberg said. "What is wrong?"

"Nothing," Ungar replied, waving him off. "I . . ."

Suddenly white foam flecked the corner of Soren Ungar's thin lips, then a gush of dark red blood stained his chin. A stain appeared in the front of Ungar's London tailored pants, too, as his bladder released its contents.

"*Mein Gott*," Schactenberg cried in German. "Someone call an ambulance."

Soren Ungar reeled, then pitched to the floor. Almost immediately, violent convulsions wrenched the man's body, twisting his limbs unnaturally as he writhed on the thick carpet.

Reporters instinctively rushed forward. Cameras appeared and flashbulbs flashed as Jorg Schactenberg tried to wave them back.

Robert Ellis slipped out of the press room, moved toward the exit. Security guards and paramedics rushed past him, heading in the opposite direction.

Too late, boys, Ellis mused.

The poison was a clone of something the Soviets had concocted back in the Cold War era. There was no cure for the toxin, which killed its victims after about five minutes of excruciating pain.

As Robert Ellis left the auditorium, an out-of-breath businessman called to him. "Am I too late to hear Soren Ungar's address?"

"Mr. Ungar's speech has just been canceled," Robert Ellis said, and kept walking.

6:59:06 A.M. EDT
The Bartleby

Jack Bauer stood with his team at the edge of the roof, watching the steaming volcano on the street far below.

A voice spoke in his headset. "This is Bio-Monitor One. We're detecting water vapor, iron oxides, asbestos, rubber, granite, and particulate matter. No chemical or biological agents, however. The area around the blast is clean. Repeat, the area is clean."

Jack exhaled, yanked away the headset, and dropped it on the tarred roof. Christopher Henderson slapped his back.

"Good job, Jack."

Jack nodded, still numb.

Tony called out to Jack. "Morris is on the line."

Jack waved him off. "Take a message."

Tony listened for a moment, one hand on his ear. "It's the latest casualty report, Jack. Eleven hundred and fifty-eight, so far. Those figures are expected to rise."

Jack groaned, turned away.

Layla moved, too, far away from the others. In the center of the roof, she oriented herself, then faced Mecca. She threw up her hands, then folded them across her breast as she began to mutter a prayer.

Henderson tugged off his sunglasses, stared. "What's she saying?" he whispered.

"The *Salat al-Janazah*," Jack replied. "The Muslim prayer for the dead."

Henderson blinked. "I didn't know Agent Abernathy was one of the Faithful, did you?"

Jack smiled. "Yeah. I did." He faced his boss. "You'd be wise to appoint Judith Foy the new Director of CTU New York. And I'd recommend Layla for the number two spot. She's young, but—"

Henderson silenced Jack with a raised hand. "There isn't going to be a CTU New York, Jack. Not after this mess."

"You can't be serious?"

"The orders have been issued from on high," Henderson informed him. "Walsh and the President are in agreement on this."

"But what happened here *proves* the need for a CTU presence."

"Security was compromised from the start," Henderson replied. "The division was infiltrated before it even opened. The political meltdown over this hasn't even begun yet."

Henderson shook his head. "CTU will continue to guard the rest of the country. But from now on, New York City is on its own."

The man curled his long arm around Jack's shoulder. "Don't worry, Jack, you have enough on your plate with Los Angeles."

Jack stepped away, processing everything Henderson had said. With the mention of L.A., he suddenly remembered his wife and daughter, realizing in a rush how much he missed them. He pulled out his personal cell phone, noticed a text message from Teri. A reminder.

Coldplay poster. MTV store.
Don't disappoint your daughter.

He smiled.

"How about breakfast?" Henderson called to him. "On me. I'll bet you haven't eaten in a day."

Jack glanced at his watch. "Fine, Christopher, but after that I'm heading uptown."

Henderson looked at him askance. "Sightseeing?"

Bauer shook his head. "Just keeping a promise."

HE SAVED THE WORLD.
WE SAVED THE BEST FOR DVD.

24 SEASON 6 ON DVD
DECEMBER 4TH

Includes The Complete Sixth Season – Plus Deleted Scenes, Commentaries, Featurettes, Season Seven Preview & More

TWF 0108